De

**Paul Vincent Lee**

Virgin Publishing Ltd

This novel is a work of fiction. Any references to real people, living or dead, real events, businesses, organizations and localities are intended only to give the fiction a sense of reality and authenticity. All names, characters, places and incidents are either the product of the author's imagination or are used fictitiously, and their resemblance, if any, to real life counterparts is entirely coincidental.

Virgin Publishing Ltd
Thistle House
14 Stewartfield Gdns
East Kilbride
G74 4GN
virginpublishingltd.org

First published in Great Britain by Virgin Publishing Ltd 2012

Copyright © Paul Vincent Lee 2010
www.paulvincentlee.com

Paul Vincent Lee asserts the moral right to be identified as the author of this work.
Song lyrics by and © Lori McTear reproduced by permission of songwriter and available on soundcloud.com; Amazon and I Tunes.

A catalogue record for this book is available from the British Library.

ISBN:978-0-9572399-0-6

Printed and bound in Great Britain by Lightning Source UK.

*For Ryan....my joy,
Upon whose smile and wellbeing my own happiness depends.*
[Albert Einstein – paraphrased]

&

*In memory of my late father, John. I never really knew you and I know I disappointed you, but at the end you tried to understand me and for that I love and miss you.*

&

*Especially for you Tunstall; you know who you are.*

# Prologue

1960's Glasgow

We were kids. We had slipped through the hedge of "The Witch's" cottage and were lifting as many apples as we could stuff down our jumpers before she set her dog, or black cat, on us. I was terrified, Joe was laughing. We turned to see our escape blocked by Mrs Perducci. She was dressed in black and her long grey hair lay lifeless, covering her shoulders. She wasn't wearing a peaked hat.

'You're stealing, that's a matter for the police,' she croaked.

My fear intensified, Joe kept laughing.

'Technically we're not stealing. The apples were on the ground so legally anyone can lift them,' I said. I had no idea where the words had come from. I wasn't even sure it was me who said them. The crone examined me.

'You planning on being a lawyer Mr Ford?' she whispered. My fears compounded that she knew my name.

'No, a footballer,' I replied.

She turned her gaze on Joe.

'And what about you young man, what are your plans?'

'Getting to fuck out of here,' Joe shouted as he darted past the old woman leaving me stranded.

'He's not a bad person Mrs Perducci,' I said 'his family don't have much money and the apples are a treat for them. His mum makes pies from them.'

'You seem like a good friend to him Mr Ford; I hope you don't live to regret it.'

1970's Glasgow

'Who the fuck are you looking at?' Joe shouted.

The four guys on the other side of the street, who I hadn't seen doing anything other than walk along talking and laughing, stopped in their tracks.

'What the fuck are you doing Joe,' I whispered 'there's four of them for fuck's sake.'

'Good, two each.'

'We know who you are Turner, you're a prick. Piss off before we come over there and do you' one of the group shouted over. 'Yeah, we'd do it now but we're gonna meet our burds, not that you'd know anything about that ya ugly cunt.'

'For Christ sake Joe let's go,' I whispered again, pushing Joe along. I turned to the group across the road 'he didnae mean anything, too much of the singin ginger.'

'I fucking hate that tall one,' Joe mumbled. Two nights later Joe stabbed him. Two months later I stood in the witness box and failed miserably to defend his actions. He was sentenced to three years in prison.

I wouldn't have to defend Joe again for another 30 years.

## Chapter 1

I don't know for sure when I first realised that my friend was a killer. I've known him since we were wee boys running around the streets and he had had a rage towards nothing in particular and everything in general even then. But this was different. Much different.

When we were kids, Joe Turner and I had lived a few yards, yet worlds, apart. Joe was brought up in a council house by working, or mostly drinking, class parents. His was a staunch Protestant household without the inconvenience of actually having to go to church. I was born into a Catholic, middle class family with a father who was convinced that the way to show his love to his son was to have him privately educated at a Jesuit run school. He saw attending church at every opportunity as no inconvenience at all, and, most importantly, he taught me not to mix with anyone who wasn't "like us." Somehow though, as a youngster, I had managed to form some friendships with local kids. Joe was one of them. We kicked a few balls together, kicked a few rivals and kissed a few girls but as our childhood years passed into teen years the differences in our circumstances inevitably meant that our lives went in separate directions. I somehow got through my education and became a lawyer. Joe received a different sort of education when he was sent to prison for three years for stabbing a rival gang member. But as the years past, Joe got it together and ended up making a good life for himself in Spain, after turning a summer job into a career.

Often years passed without contact other than a belated Christmas card, but Joe came back to Glasgow from time to time to see his parents or to see his favourite football team and we were able to take up seamlessly from where we had left off. But now I had no option but to condemn him. I knew he had killed two people. Good people, loving people, one of whom had loved him. I had no real qualms about turning him in, I believed in the law after all. I just didn't want him to know I had betrayed him. I just wanted the killing to stop.

My name is Ray Ford and I am writing my story in the hope of forgiveness.

***

Saturday morning and two women are walking through Glasgow city centre. One apprehensive about her immediate future, the other joyous in anticipation of hers. They are walking separately, both oblivious to the existence of the other. Soon their lives would be irrevocably entwined.

It was a Glasgow holiday weekend and the city was doing what it does every holiday week-end, pouring with rain; no early morning mist gently masking the promise of glorious sunshine here. Glasgow liked to wait till its subdued inhabitants were back at work before it mockingly greeted in the balmy days of summer. Unlike many women, Detective Inspector Susan Dornan wasn't obsessed by clothes and appearance but on this particular day, this special occasion, she felt extra effort was appropriate. She had watched two episodes of "Sex in the City" the night before, chosen and discarded four "unsuitable" outfits finally opting for something chic but practical, professional but with a hint of glamour. In a "slimming" black. She had also gone to an up - market hairdressers the day before where Raul, from Pollock, had informed her that her Mary Quant bob was back in fashion. She had never been aware that it had been out of fashion. She had also bought a bottle green, silk blouse but passed on new shoes. A manicure was a definite non-starter. Two weeks previously her then boyfriend Tom had not-so-subtly hinted that she could perhaps make "a little more effort in the glamour stakes" when they had met up to go to the movies one evening. His new status as an ex-boyfriend being another reason for celebration. She was in some ways elated to be taking on her new role at Strathclyde Police's Pitt Street Headquarters but now that the day had arrived she was overcome with apprehension. Dornan parked her silver Audi TT in the reserved space befitting her new status and did a final facial assessment in the rear view mirror. 'Old, haggard, out of her depth' was her considered opinion. She grabbed her mobile phone from the facia and noticed her heirloom St Christopher medal that somehow managed to find its way from car to car, although she herself was a confirmed "don't know." She'd heard a stand – up comedian joking one night that "all religions are the same. Religion is basically guilt, with different holidays." She'd liked that. 'Don't worry Chris, we'll all be redundant one day' she ventured. Chris was strangely non-committal.

  By the time she reached the sliding glass doors of Police Headquarters she was in complete police mode. She strode across the foyer, taking just three steps to clear the Strathclyde Police crest embedded in the marble tiled floor. She stood waiting for the lift to take her to the second floor, and her new domain, and acknowledged to herself that up until now she'd loved her job. She prayed that feeling would last. She paused before the half glass, half aluminium door to the CID room. The plaque on the door merely stated "Room 112". The squad was made up of mainly experienced officers and one possible "plant" from the Chief Inspector. One of the experienced officers would be Matt Healy. She had already met, broken the ice, and built up an initial rapport with all the detectives except Healy. He had always either been on leave or "tied up" whenever a meeting had been suggested. She understood his position. Healy had been demoted several months before and there was a rumour that the Force wanted him out altogether. Dornan took a deep breath, pushed her shoulders back, turned the door handle and walked confidently into the room, frantically trying to remember if her desk was on the right or the left.

'Morning everyone.'

'Morning ma'am,' nearly everyone replied.

Newly demoted Detective Sergeant Matt Healy sat at his desk surrounded by the rest of the squad. Dornan was surprised when she actually saw him in the flesh. Although a "twenty year in" officer he was actually a lot younger than she expected, nearly her own age in fact. Although she would never admit it, especially not to Healy himself, she was desperate for him to stay no matter the personal issues. Healy had somehow acquired a "Mad Max" persona over the years but a few officers who had worked with him previously had told her this was just a bit of a front, and exaggerated at that. It was true that he was the kind of "un–PC", old school policeman that Strathclyde's Police Forces' new Code of Practice was specifically aimed at but he knew murder, especially Glasgow murder, like no other. Dornan wanted him at her side, but only if he was "on board".

\*\*\*

Glasgow is not considered by many to be a romantic city, but Kate Turner thought it was. Especially now. It was Kate's adopted home town. She visited regularly either with her husband, Joe, when he took trips home, or to see her own mother who still lived there after she retired from a teaching post she had taken up in the city many years previously. It was, therefore, an ideal cover for their first illicit rendezvous. Her boyfriend couldn't see it. He had suggested somewhere like Paris or Rome but Kate had convinced him that Glasgow made the "cover" she needed so much easier. He had picked the hotel from the Internet, The Cathedral House Hotel, central enough but not stuck in the middle of Glasgow's night scene. Kate had never heard of it but when they booked in she felt it was just right. She never checked if he had booked in as Mr & Mrs but smiled wistfully for a moment at the thought of it. Two intimate restaurants illuminated by candle light, narrow winding stone staircases leading to the bedrooms adding to the romance of the moment, even if it was overlooked by one of Glasgow's ancient Necropolis. "Her man" as Kate rejoiced in calling him also approved of the setting he had painstakingly chosen. The appropriateness of the huge ornate angels silhouetted against the east end sky, their unblinking gaze watching him with approval and their bedroom subtly lit by the periphery of the floodlights shining on Glasgow's Protestant cathedral nearby a perfect combination in his mind.

Although the longing was there in Kate, at his insistence, they were going to do the whole tourist thing before the whole duvet thing. "Christ, does the sun ever shine here for more than five minutes? Told you we should have gone somewhere else" he said as they walked hand in hand through some square surrounded by monoliths of empire builders; they, and their empires, long gone.

'Glasgow prefers crisp to sunshine,' she replied.

'Yeah, family size bags by the size of some of the arses.'

'We can't all be perfect like you.'

They were headed for The Gallery of Modern Art that was just off the square they were walking through. A number of people were gathered at the entrance, some just sheltering from the travails of the weather, others admiring the Grecian colonnades unaware that the building was originally the private house of a wealthy Glasgow slave trader, which decency should have demolished many moons ago. Inside the gallery Howson originals sat side by side with total bollocks originals. The irony of a black and white photo exhibit portraying African slaves working in present day diamond mines lost on most.

'Life's so unfair. Nothing really seems to change does it?' said Kate.

'It appears that way,' her boyfriend replied. 'Anyway let's go and get something to eat.'

'OK. Oh, by the way, I've arranged to meet Mum tomorrow afternoon and, early evening, around six, Pete for a quick drink.....wife troubles!' she added quickly.

'Don't know about the Pete thing, you might run off together, might never see you again.'

Kate knew her husband, Joe Turner, was never pleased about the "Pete" arrangements either but he had had to accept that he couldn't do much about it. He had told her that he "supposed" he didn't think there was anything going on between them other than friendship, but Pete Harris had been her "first love" after all and so it was obvious that he would wonder if they ever revived the old days.

'Don't be stupid, you know I've got to do all the usual trip home things, keep things as normal looking as possible. I'll meet up with you in The Counting House about nine, half past OK?'

'Here, in case you forget me,' he said.

He handed over an intricate gold necklace; the name "Tunstall" hanging from a delicate gold chain.

She loved it; loved it even more when he explained its meaning. And, she was beginning to think, she loved him.

*** 

Susan Dornan knew her priority was to get Matt Healy into her office and hopefully get any awkwardness out of the way. She wandered out of her office into "the body of the kirk" but instead of calling Healy over she decided to listen into his well trumpeted theory on murder which he was regaling the squad with, in a way that was most certainly non - PC like.

'Somebody you know dun it. Fucking family member, so called fucking friend, pissed –off lover, arse hole colleague, doesn't matter... they fucking knew you before they fucking killed you. Bastards might even like you. Take that case through in Auld Reekie last month. The happy couple sitting in the hot tub in the garden, her 23 him 42, lucky bastard, or so he thinks. Guy strolls into the garden, bosh bosh, thank you very much, game over. Who was it? Ex fucking husband, that's who.'

'He not like Jacuzzis then boss?' ventured DC John Frame.

Everyone, including Healy and Dornan smiled, black humour being the release valve in all police squads.

'Well what about serial killers? They don't know their victims.' suggested one of the new members of the squad, Detective Constable Jill French, a psychology graduate and "accelerated promotion" entrant.

'Serial killers? Do me a favour. Listen, more chance of being fucked by lightning on the same day you win a fucking Lottery Rollover than being fucked by a fucking serial killer".

'Do all your sentences require at least three fucks?' Jill French rather bravely replied.

'Look, just cause you went to Uni to avoid working for four years and know what a fucking noun is, don't come in here and give us of your shit.'

'I'm just saying....,' said French.

'Well don't. How many murder cases you been on Detective?'

'None.'

'Exactly. Twenty three I've done and every one committed by someone the fucking victim knew. What you got to say about that then?'

Fuck?'

'Good.'

At least she's got a sense of humour. She'll need it in this job, this city, thought Dornan.

'DS Healy, perhaps we can have a chat in my office. Now would be a good time'. Susan Dornan turned and headed for her office. Healy followed just behind. Both had faint smiles on their faces. Susan Dornan was pleased that her office was located in a completely different part of the Police Headquarters from Healy's old one. Sitting on the other side of your old desk would have been a bit much for anyone to take, never mind Healy. The paperless office was a concept with no future in police work as far as Dornan was concerned and both sides of her desk were covered in files and memos, first day or not. Healy had been demoted despite his success after his last two 'stick on' cases had been thrown out by the Procurator Fiscal due to, in one case, an illegal search and in the other a "dubious" witness statement, both failures attributed to Healy's management style.

'Nice theory about serial killers Matt, not sure about the delivery though,' said Susan Dornan.

'They've got to live in the real world ma'am, especially these fast trackers,' Healy replied.

'Maybe so Matt but there are ways and means and that example out there isn't one of them. I agree that a lot of this PC crap is over the top but only idiots or people wanting a quick passport out flaunt their disapproval. I know you're not an idiot, so do you want out?'

'No ma'am.'

'Good, then let's get on with catching the bad guys, and it's Susan when we're alone.'

Healy had studied people closely during his career and prided himself in knowing genuine when he saw it. He looked at Dornan. He had been pleasantly surprised at the "it's Susan" remark and inwardly he knew that it wasn't her fault she had been put in this position.

'I want you on board Matt but only if you want to be here, only if you are willing to work hand in hand with me, willing to be part of the team. Help me make a success of this squad and your contribution will not go unnoticed, I promise you that.'

Whilst not exactly wishing for another murder to happen soon, he knew that in Glasgow the next one would not be long in coming and he would wrap it up in jig time, his way, and show certain people what good police work really was. Besides, he felt there was something about Susan Dornan; he somehow wanted to make it work. He didn't give a toss about his contribution being acknowledged.

***

'*We've got to-night, who needs tomorrow,*' someone softly crooned over the Cathedral House Hotel's in-house radio.

'Think that's for us?' Kate Turner's boyfriend mused.

'Serendipity?' replied Kate.

'What do you mean?'

'You know, fate, meant to be...that sort of thing. Do you think we are meant for each other?'

'I think we are together for a reason if that's what you mean,' he replied.

Their earlier tour of the city courtesy of an open top bus, that two Inuit would have done well to survive, was over. The Chicken Korma they had shared later had brought them back to life and they were now ensconced in "Tunstall's" ideal hotel, in a room with a four poster king size bed, chilled wine & soft music, and a man she cared for very much.

Her boyfriend cared too, he cared a lot. But not for her. He had a higher calling.

She was in the bathroom. Last minute patchwork? Similar concerns as him? Horny or hesitant?

He could see her beauty reflected a thousand times on the mirrored walls of the bathroom through the crack in the bathroom door. It's not too late for you. Just say you can't, you have a husband, you had a moment of weakness.

'Why aren't you in that bed with a glass poured for me?' she called through.

'Aren't you even a little bit bothered by this?'

'No, why should I be?'

'Well, for a start, maybe because it's not right? You can walk away from this, it's not too late.'

'I don't believe in that kind of outlook. This part of my life is separate to any other part. I want you, maybe even more than that, and although things aren't perfect I'm making the most of what makes me happy.'

'What about your husband?'

'What he doesn't know can't harm him and no-one else matters. I only stay for the sake of the kids anyway, you know that.'

'The Lord matters.'

She loved that about him, his off the wall humour.

'Why are you here then Mr Holier than Thou?'

'To witness......and judge.'

Kate thought she detected a hint of a smile on his handsome face. His eyes searched Kate Turner's face for any sign of doubt, regret or remorse. He saw none. She moved towards him, allowing her negligee to slip to the floor.

'Strange way of putting it, but what's your verdict?'

The sex wasn't what she expected; intense, true passion. Nothing had prepared her for this. Not even 25 years of marriage. Especially not 25 years of marriage. It was a long time ago that she came to realise that in her marriage bedroom was an anagram for boredom.

'How are you feeling?' he asked.

'Lost,' sighed Kate from another place.

'Yes, I think you are Tunstall, I think you are.'

'What are we going to do?'

They both lay and contemplated. Although they were splayed across the bed, not even touching, Kate had never felt closer to anyone. Her fingers caressed her new necklace, his token of love.

*'I know your plans don't include me'* the voice sang quietly in the shadows of their contentment.

## Chapter 2

*Puff of smoke and a hip flask.*
*Man outside the station is clutching it to his chest.*
*What did he do; where did he go wrong?*
*Questions he asks himself but he is getting no answers.*
*Man in rags.*

*** 

Boom Boom Banks liked his name. He was christened Colin but that wasn't a name for the likes of him.

Boom Boom, that was a name.

He wasn't sure who first called him it. He only knew that that's what everyone called him now.

'What's happening tomorrow big yin?' the kids would shout.

'Boom! Boom!' his arms flowering into the ubiquitous mushroom cloud.

The kids thought he was the business, even gave him fags and the odd can.

'On yir sel Boom Boom, on yir sel.'

Boom Boom lived most places. Old warehouses. Old cars. Cardboard boxes. Shop doorways. He didn't have a mortgage on any of his places and that's the way he liked it. Mortgages, credit cards, H.P., it only ends one way...boom, boom. If he could have ever gotten his eyes to focus and his addled brain to function long enough to read a paper during these times he would have seen just how right he was. His favourite residence didn't have a roof but it had everything else. A comfortable bed, food and running water. Some people called it the Clyde Valley. Give him his carrier bags, his string, his knife, his coat and his matches and, with good luck or global warming as, unknown to Boom Boom, the papers called it these days, he could stay in his favourite spot till October. The combination of weathering on his skin, dirt and life's travails made him of indeterminate age and in truth he couldn't remember himself what age he was. He sometimes had clouded thoughts and vague images of a rather grand terraced house, a train set, a doll and an austere woman, her hair tied back in a bun and a black blouse buttoned to the neck, but he wasn't at all sure if he longed for those memories or was happy for them to remain somewhere in his subconscious. He knew he wasn't stupid, conversations with hostel wardens defined stupid for him, and he knew that he liked to read when his eye's focus, and opportunity, coincided. A rare occurrence in these days of wine; and not so many roses. He also knew he was one of God's children, blessed by being born into Holy Mother Church, the Jesuit teachers at his school had told him so, belted him with a leather belt to demonstrate His love, although on winter nights in and around Glasgow he didn't feel very blessed even when he said six Hail Marys.

Mother church, hail Mary, mother, women, whores.

***

Susan Doran had never married, had no kids and had always found it difficult to keep a boyfriend. Not because she wasn't attractive. Compared to most Glasgow women in their forties that was; most of whom had allowed life's travails, and their remedies to them; cigs, booze, maybe the odd puff of wacky or line of Charlie, to take their toll. Neither was it because she wasn't good company but mainly because she had thrown herself into her career in the police and now she was a lot of Glasgow men's biggest nightmare, intelligent and in 'the polis.' Not that every guy in Glasgow was a crook and for some the uniform was a turn on, it was just that not many fancied living with a cop. Why? She wasn't sure but had gotten used to it. Neither was it a sexual thing. More a slightly suppressed emotional need. She was glad she had joined the police and was proud of what she achieved. Proud of her new rank. Susan Dornan was a week into her new role and although things were rather slow in terms of work load for the squad as a whole, she had been busy getting the operational systems she wanted in place. She sat at her desk looking out through the glass partition which separated her office from the main squad room, weighing up her team. Nothing much was happening but everyone was managing to look busy. Except Matt Healy of course who was eating a sandwich, drinking tea, reading the Daily Record racing section and calling poor P.C. Allan something that she couldn't quite make out but was definitely non – complimentary.

  Jill French was reading a statistical report that was circulating the office. She looked over at Matt Healy. 'Sir, it says here that 60% of 16 year olds in Glasgow housing schemes are regularly incapacitated through alcohol. Terrible isn't it. What chance do they have?'

  'Yeah, terrible. Who's looking after their kids, that's what I want to know' smirked Healy.

Healy turned to DC Brown who as usual appeared to be in deep thought or asleep.

'What you up to then Rab?' asked Healy

'Oh it's the wife's birthday next week and I can't think what to get her for a present. She's worn out these days and I'd really like to get her something special, something, you know, that would light up her face.'

'How about a torch?'

Healy was in fine form. Even Jill French laughed. Partly relieved it wasn't only her that Healy ribbed.

'Bit of a male chauvinist then sir?' replied Brown.

'Only one thing worse than that Rab and that's a woman who won't do what she's told.'

Susan Dornan still didn't know what to make of Healy. Somehow all the effing and blinding and sarcastic comments seemed a put up job to her. She knew that like her he had never married and had no kids. He was certainly a bit of a dinosaur when it came to the new, sparkling white, politically correct Strathclyde Police but he got the job done and was it really necessary to call rapists, murderers and paedos "Sir". She didn't think so and Matt Healy was never going to. She got the impression Healy was scrutinising her, weighing her up, but couldn't be sure. She also felt there was more to young PC Allan than met the eye. He was young of course, but she liked him and was sure he wasn't any of things Healy delighted in calling him. The fact that he might well be gay was bye the bye.

As well as inheriting Healy, Dornan had also inherited DC John Frame who, some had warned her, had lived up to his name in the past. She had decided that everyone was starting with a clean slate, and, although it was obvious that Frame was ambitious, she didn't put any store in gossip, especially of the internal police variety, and preferred to think that fit – ups were a thing of the past in policing. Frame was similar to Healy in some ways but Dornan felt that Frame was serious when he joined in the squad banter, a kind of inner anger there, momentarily allowing itself to come out before Frame's wiser side put a check on it.

DC Rab Brown was the opposite of Frame. He was always polite, never said anything remotely offensive and still appeared to blush at some of the more outrageous comments made by the other squad members.

'Yeah and don't forget to get batteries for that torch Rab. At least batteries have a positive side and she can use them for her vibrator while you're in here,' suggested Frame.

'Very funny Frame,' responded Brown.

'Don't be offended mate, only telling you how it is. Take me for instance. I knew my marriage was on the rocks when I asked the wife one night why she never told me when she reached orgasm anymore. She told me that she didn't like phoning me at work.'

Rab Brown laughed, self-deprecating humour always something that is appreciated in the harsh reality of Glasgow life. Dornan was sure Brown was actually asleep at his desk sometimes and he did not show much drive or initiative but he was, apparently, a PC genius.

That assessment however came from Healy who "didn't believe in E mailing." He had just recently become the proud father of twins so that could also account for his zombie like appearance. Susan Dornan often wondered if she would ever experience that kind of feeling herself, wondered if she wanted to. She glanced over at DC Jill French. Could she see herself from 15 years or so ago in her? She was keen, intelligent and willing but would she be able to hack it when the first young girl's body with an Irn Bru bottle forced into her vagina and twigs rammed up her nostrils was placed in front of her? Her psychological training possibly being a bonus, or a hindrance, to the squad. The other squad member she could see was a bit of a conundrum for Dornan. Glasgow was now a "multi-cultural" city that "embraced" migrants. DC Jack T'Bhat was, as far as Dornan could make out, of so many cultures that he could be "embraced" to death. Part Iranian, part French, born in Hamilton, half Christian, half Muslim he was so diverse no-one knew what to do with him except have his picture on all the flyers and posters that Strathclyde's finest plastered over places like Sighthill and Govanhill; home to many of Glasgow's migrants. Dornan shut down her PC and tidied up her desk as best she could, do these memos never stop, before heading for an early exit. She had arranged to meet a friend for a meal later that evening and "maybe a wee bop."

Healy watched her out of the corner of his eye as she surveyed the squad room and took part in a little banter with one of the police civilian workers.

'Off out tonight ma'am?' asked Jim Rodger, a clerical worker who helped out around the station.

'You asking?' smiled Susan.

'I wish. Wife might have something to say about that!'

'You can't blame a girl for trying eh Jim. Yeah, it's Friday night and that means I'm going down to the Merchant City for a couple of drinks. Maybe end up in Arta.'

The Merchant City had been a rundown area of Glasgow city centre, housing the old fruit and cheese markets, but like many former commercial sites in cities it had been transformed in recent years to accommodate wine bars, eateries and night clubs for Glasgow's glitterati. Susan didn't quite fall into that category but a warrant card works wonders with stroppy door men and to be fair the people that went there were quite diverse.

'Glad I'm married then, I couldn't afford you, have a ball.'

She gave Healy a nod as she left for the night.

## Chapter 3

Matt Healy lived alone and had never been to the Merchant City, he preferred "traditional" bars, locals, but in truth didn't consider himself much of a drinker. Not by Glasgow standards at least. He still lived in his mum's house but she had died a few years before. He didn't particularly like the furniture, wallpaper or carpets, but couldn't be bothered changing them. When you've seen carpets, wallpaper and furniture with assorted parts of the human body splattered all over them then colours and designs aren't high on your priority list. He never had visitors anyway. He was a sociable enough guy, some of his superior officers felt too much so with his old squad, but he kept his private life just that. He liked women, had had his fair share of girl friends over the years but with his job commitments, and his mum, had never seemed to find one that he felt like settling down with. They all seemed to disappoint him in the end. He thought DI Dornan might be an exception though. She was somehow different; confident but vulnerable. Needed kept in her place certainly but definitely food for thought there.

***

Joe Turner was an ordinary guy. He knew that because his wife, Kate, told him often enough. He and Kate had met 20 odd years ago when she had turned up in Spain looking for seasonal work and he was a bar manager. Life had moved on since then. He now owned a couple of bars of his own and they had a couple of grown up kids. Although life had moved on neither Joe nor the resort had. It was still all Full English Breakfasts, chips with everything, Tetleys on draught and two euros for a litre of any of the local knock out poison. Kate may not have moved on physically but her mind had. The Costa Brava was now Costa Barasic, and she was trapped with a man she didn't love. Joe was partially aware that Kate had moved on in her ambitions and desires in life but she would never leave him 'they were solid.' Joe Turner was an ordinary guy but he wasn't sure if even he believed that so sometimes he had to "remind" her that they were never going to split. Kate had become distant. She still loved him, she told him she did "in a way", but things had changed. Bed was for sleeping in, meals were for eating in silence and Kate's job seemed to call for more overtime than before, but "things were fine."

Strangely enough the sexual rationing wasn't really an issue as he was banging one of his staff whenever he wanted and there were always plenty of holiday makers impressed enough by "the bar owner" tag to drop their knickers for an after - hours "wee drink".

Joe Turner was an ordinary guy. Wife at home, bit on the side, pissed when he wants and not slow to keep the wife in line when necessary. Besides, things would work out, just as long as you didn't talk about them. Kate had told him that she wanted to go and see her mother more often in Glasgow as 'she was getting on.' Joe understood, that's what daughters do, especially when they want to discuss womanly things, who better than your mum. The only thing he didn't like was that "that fanny" Pete Harris would be there, and although she was always open about meeting up with him when she visited Glasgow, he still didn't like it but it did let him make his own arrangements so he didn't make much of a song and dance about it. He didn't see why wives had to meet up with ex – boyfriends, especially ones who 'wanted to talk.' He had asked her once if she was honestly saying that Perfect Peter wouldn't have her knickers off in a minute if she let him. She agreed he would, 'he was a guy wasn't he', but 'he wasn't like that' and would never get the chance anyway. Joe had decided he was going to make Spag Bol when they both got back from their separate trips and go as high as eight, nine euros on a bottle of red. Everything would be fine, she'd forgive him. She might even be willing to have sex. Joe Turner was an ordinary guy.

***

Pete Harris loved Kate Turner. He'd loved her when they went dancing 30 odd years before. He was her first lover and she his first "true" love. There was an age difference but it didn't seem to matter to them back then, but Pete Harris knew it began to matter to Kate. He still loved her when she moved to Spain saying it was only for 'the season' even though he knew she wouldn't be back, not to him anyway. He still loved her when he married his first wife Ann, and his second wife, Sally. He loved her when they met up on her occasional visits back to Glasgow to see her mum. He loved her last night even if she seemed to have changed from the Kate he knew.

The evening had gone well:

'I only meet you for sedimental reasons you know Kate.'

'You mean sentimental?'

'No, I'm scrapping the bottom of the barrel.'

They had always laughed together. He had hoped she would stay longer but she seemed distracted and keen to get away. He thought it was something he'd said, he was always telling her to leave that loser Joe, slipping in that he was thinking of leaving Sally. Hope over reality.

'It's not you Pete honestly. You're a dear friend. I ignore most of the things you say anyway!' Kate laughed.

'Well there's something about you that's different. You're kind of glowing. Shit, you're not pregnant are you?' although why that notion panicked him he couldn't say.

'At 46! What you on Pete? Although I wouldn't mind if I was, I'm in love.'

Pete's mind raced between confusion, disappointment, resentment and anger.

'Thought that would be the last thing you and Joe would want.'

'It would be. It wouldn't be Joe's.'

Only anger remained in Pete Harris' head.

'You mean?'

'Yeah, I'm seeing someone. It's complicated but......'

Pete Harris erupted from his stool, his latte overturned, its contents slowly dripping from the edge of the table, the hotel restaurant's collection of gourmet sauce sachets scattering over the wooden lounge bar floor.

'Where are you going?' Kate stuttered.

'Away from you.'

'What? Why? Christ Pete, what is it?'

'Why! You know I've always been in love with you. I tell you every time we meet. You always say "Joe, the kids" and all the time you've been up for a shag with anybody. Why not me?'

Kate was flustered and confused, she hated confrontation, but she was not prepared to take this unwarranted verbal assault.

'Don't dare speak to me like that Pete. I not up for 'a shag' as you so charmingly put it with anyone. I happen to be in love, just not with you. Pete I was only a kid when we got together.'

Pete Harris was swaying where he stood, his anger refusing to subside.

'I never stopped loving you. You know that. How could you hit me with this?'

Kate had collected up her bags and was trying to put on her jacket whilst preserving some sort of dignity in front of the smattering of other diners.

'Pete I'm sorry. I never thought you would react this way. I'd better go anyway.'

'Yes you'd better, and don't keep in touch you fucking cow.'

Kate shuffled out of the restaurant into the hotel grounds by the river, her mind's turn to race from disappointment to confusion to anger. She quickly realised she had taken a wrong turn; away from the front entrance. She had only wanted to extricate herself from the situation, get away from Pete, back to "her man" but now she realised she had a bit of a dilemma. How to get from a quiet riverside hotel in the Clyde Valley to Glasgow city centre, without transport, and no signal on her mobile phone.

Several minutes later Pete Harris left the bar. He looked around frantically, he saw Kate trying to source a source a signal on her mobile.

'Get away from me Pete.'

'Kate I'm sorry, you just took me aback that's all. Let me give you a lift.'

'Not a chance Pete, I'm phoning a taxi and I don't ever want to see you again.'

Peter Harris looked at the ground 'here, let me see if I can get a signal' he moved towards her.

Kate neither saw nor felt the initial blow. All was darkness. Later, the freezing water of the river brought her back into the present as she slid down the embankment and the waters enveloped her torn dress; her violated body. She grasped at some exposed roots and pulled herself from the waters. She managed to get to her feet by balancing against a tree trunk. She saw his movement through her pain and distress. Her reaction on seeing him approaching her was one of overwhelming relief, her shock and outrage momentarily dissipated by the knowledge she was alive. A little surprised perhaps, but the last few moments had been so surreal her mind couldn't seem to process any kind of rational thought. Why had this happened, how, what had come over him?

'Thank......'

Strangely, the feeling she felt as the blade sliced into her body was one of contentment. She had never really feared death, just the pain of it, and there was no pain. Will the kids will be distraught when they hear? Mum will blame herself.

The second blow was harsher, sharper. She wondered if the dirges she was forced to listen to long ago in Sunday School might be true. She hoped so. She smiled. I'll see dad again. Has he stopped? Am I alive? Is he moving me or am I moving myself? It's such a lovely evening. Please, not the river, not the cold. My new red shoes.

Her former lover walks away and, as darkness envelopes Kate Turner forever, the heavens applaud.

\*\*\*

It was a beautiful sunny Monday morning. Even the normally sullen Glasgow commuters seemed to have a spring in their step as they headed to their various places of employment.

An angry man was checking out of The Cathedral House Hotel. He had spent the whole of Sunday drifting between rage and agitation, resentment and confusion; he had read in the hotel's In-House magazine that the city had built up an economy based on the provision of Call Centres for global organisations; Christ, ship building to bullshitting in a generation, and realised that that was exactly what Kate Turner was, a bullshiter.

The bar area in The Cathedral House Hotel doubled as the hotel's reception area but the quirkiness of the arrangement seemed to add to the hotel's appeal in his eyes, rather than take away from it.

'Something's come up and I have to book out early. Sorry,' he said to the foreign receptionist.

'This is a shem. We hope you enjoy-ed your stay,' Ivana replied.

'Everything's been fine.'

'And your lady friend, she is going from us too.'

'So it seems.'

The Polish receptionist Ivana was slightly confused by the exchange but put it down to losing something in the accent.

"Tunstall" had moved about a mile down river by then.

***

*Azrael was glad and relieved when he finally got home. Home to his music. He knew he would have to prepare for getting back to work the next day but the lyrics, his inspiration, would help with that. He loved Linda Ronstadt. She didn't necessarily write the songs she sang, something he preferred, but she sang them from the soul and, on balance, that was the most important thing. She had obviously repented. He had seen a musician being interviewed once, he couldn't remember who, he only seemed to remember the women. The guy had said that his music was a way of turning "daydreams into sound". He loved that, wished he had said it. He had never craved material things and he had sought forgiveness for what was without doubt a sin of indulgence when he spent so much on his Bang and Olufsen sound system but he consoled himself by acknowledging that if you seek perfection then you have to have the equipment to achieve it. It had been a shame how things had worked out over the week-end but he was merely the instrument, she had had the opportunity for redemption, she chose her own path, her own fate. He believed in destiny and fate. Destiny leads you to the path, it's up to you to walk down the road or not and destiny had led her to him. He was her fate. Freud wrote that although it was true that men could be envious it was mostly due to not being able to "achieve" in life whereas women's envy came solely from sexual issues so the only way to give them the chance of redemption was to allow them the opportunity to forego the sexual act. If they spurned that opportunity then so be it. Destiny. He lay down on the couch, his favourite place in his flat, and let the music and words sweep over him. Names, initials, messages swirling in his mind.*

***

Healy didn't really know why he automatically seemed to go into a gruff, aggressive mode with liberal doses of swearing, whenever he was dealing with junior colleagues. It wasn't his true persona but one that just seemed to have formed of its own volition over the years.

'What's your name again son?' said Healy.

'DC Paul Allan sir,' replied the rookie

'Well, DC Paul Allan, why CID?'

'I feel it's the sharp end of policing sir and solving murders is why I joined the force.'

'Is it? Is it really? Well would you like to know how I see you fitting in to this squad?'

'Yes sir. Definitely.'

'Right. Don't get in the fucking way, say fuck all and get me cups of tea even when I don't fucking ask for them. Got that?'

'Yes sir, but may I just ask..?'

'No you may not.'

Allan wasn't too dispirited. He'd heard all about Healy from his uncle. In fact, he'd requested this move because he wanted to learn from the best and Healy was the best. He realised he might be a bit difficult at first given the squad's new hierarchy and that he probably suspected that Healy, like Dornan, probably thought he was "a plant" but he wasn't and he'd prove his worth. Besides he kind of thought his uncle was a bit of a prat.

'Oh and one last thing, you ever come flying into the squad room and shout "Sur, there's been a murdur!" and I'll punch your lights out.' Paul Allan walked away smiling.

Matt Healy thought about Susan Dornan. She was one of the new breed, highly educated. He was never quite sure why these kind of people wanted to join the police, what their motivation was. He found it difficult to initiate small talk at the best of times, hence his outbursts, his fake persona, but there was something about Dornan, he would make a conscious effort to help her. *'Her looks aren't exactly a barrier either' b*ut in truth he didn't think that being around death and mayhem was a proper place for woman. He glanced out of the window at a passing black van with gold lettering on the side:

"Co-Op Funeral Directors" followed by a 0800 phone number. The van stopped in a queue for the traffic lights on the corner. Healy spotted the smaller writing on the van's door:

"Sponsors of Glasgow's Phoenix Choir", *'Jesus only in Glasgow'* thought Healy *'only in Glasgow.'*

\*\*\*

It was a balmy Tuesday evening on Rocca Grossa, the hill overlooking Lloret de Mar where most resident Brits had their homes. Joe Turner had woken from his "afternoon shift" with his usual hangover. He was confused at first. As the years had passed it was taking him longer and longer to pull himself together after his afternoon sessions. He knew Kate wasn't around but he wasn't entirely sure if it was that day or the next that she had been due back. He just knew he had needed to be back in Spain before her. He shuffled to the kitchen for a glass of water, tripping over a pile of unopened mail lying in the hall. He noticed from the stamps that there were a couple from the UK but knew they would be for Kate as no-one ever wrote to him. He decided to phone her mum.

'Martha it's Joe, is Kate there?'

Kate Turner's mother, Martha Reid, was the quintessential secondary school English teacher. Not quite Jean Brodie, Glasgow couldn't accommodate that, but not far off. Unlike the fictional character, Martha considered her life to be content and fulfilled. It was true that Kate's father had disappeared to Australia with a younger women many years previously, she had heard he had died a few years ago somewhere near Brisbane, but she had thrived in academia and had felt no need for a second go at the roulette wheel of marriage. She had taught in an all-girl school but time and location had dissolved all illusions of Marcia Blaine. Martha was retired now but kept active and walked every second day to her part – time job in a flower shop rather aptly named "Thanks a Bunch" in the area's Byres Road. She didn't need the money but the company was welcome and on a Friday evening she was allowed to take home a bunch of fresh flowers to adorn the teak coffee table that sat in her flat's bay window.

'Oh hello Joe. No. Isn't she home yet?'
*So it was today.*
'No, I thought she maybe decided to stay on with you for a couple of days. Maybe she's phoned, I've not been in the house much to be fair.'

'Must be something like that. Maybe the flights been delayed, you know what they're like.'

'When did she leave your house?'

'Well as you know she wasn't actually staying with me. I saw her on Fri evening, a couple of hours on Saturday afternoon was the last time, but she was staying with her friend Julie. More fun I suppose.'

'OK Martha that's fine. I'll get her to call you.'

'Do that. Bye Joe.'

Joe sat beside the phone for quite a while. He opened a bottle of Estrella to help him think. Kate had never mentioned that she wasn't actually staying with her mother and as far as he knew Kate and Julie only spoke occasionally and he was certain that Kate hadn't told him she was even meeting up with her, never mind staying with her.

Joe made a conscious decision not to panic. Nothing had changed, maybe it was even better.

\*\*\*

A few moments after Joe Turner had, unknown to me, finished his conversation with his mother in law he had picked up the phone again. My nightmare was about to begin. I had taken the day off. I wouldn't say I loved my job as a lawyer as the nature of the beast was that you did indeed have to deal with the odd beast but, in general terms, I got satisfaction from it and it did afford me a good life style. Despite being away from the office I was sitting in much coveted silence reading over some case notes. My phone rang.

'Is that you Ray?'

'Yes. Who's this?'

'It's me. Joe. You tosser.'

'Joe! How are you? It's a bad line.'

'Well OK I suppose but I'm a bit worried to tell the truth, needed someone to talk to' said Joe.

'Right, what's up? Business crap?' Joe had occasionally phoned me in the past to bemoan the fact that British tourists had moved on, both geographically and in their tastes, and I was assuming this was another call along the same lines.

'It is as it happens, but no, nothing like that. You know how things have been a bit strained between me and Kate recently?'

'Well you did say something about that, yea.' In all honesty I hadn't remembered Joe telling me anything like that but I did sometimes tend to switch off when Joe was in full rant mode so I had more than likely missed him saying anything about him and Kate.

'Right. Well she went over to Glasgow on Friday, supposedly to see her mum and she ain't come back.'

'What do you mean she hasn't come back, have you spoken to her?'

'No.'

'When was she due back?'

'Around 11.00 Spanish time this morning. She was booked on the early flight.'

I didn't quite know how to react to what I was hearing. Joe seemed to want to talk but I knew him well enough to know he wasn't telling me the whole story.

*'This isn't like the Kate I know but at the same time I knew she could be a bit off the wall at times.'*

'Have you phoned her mum?'

'Yea. Nothing. She wasn't even staying there. Staying with that cow Julie Connor apparently.'

'Have you called her then?'

'Can't, no number for her.'

'What about Martha, does she have a number for her?'

'No. Apparently the Julie one jumps about from hotel to hotel doing her relief manager, in more ways than one no doubt; fucking cow. Martha hasn't a Scooby which one she's in.'

'Right.'

I didn't really know what to say. What do you say exactly when a million thoughts are flashing through your brain and most of them you don't want to even think about never mind mention to the person you're talking to.

'Where do you start, think I should phone the police?' asked Joe.

'Was she on the plane?'

'How the fuck should I know?'

'Right. Well, maybe she went on a bender with Julie, just missed the flight'

'Or some cunt.'

'What?'

'Let's face it Ray she might be with some guy.'

'No way Joe, get that out of your head. Has Martha checked the hospitals? Bet she hasn't.'

I was trying to say all the right things but the truth was that the first thing that had come into my head was that Kate was with some guy. I was pretty certain that Kate had had affairs over the years, nothing "serious", just excitement, fun. Despite supposedly being in the entertainment business Joe wasn't exactly a major player in those departments but after 20 odd years with the one partner who was? But I did know she would not just up and away. She would never just leave the kids. Never.

'Surely Julie would have phoned if anything like that had happened?' said Joe.

'Maybe she doesn't know or doesn't have a number for you or Martha.'

'Maybe.... Ray?'

'What?'

'I think it's a guy. What will I do if she leaves me?'

'You're talking bollocks now. Calm down. Do you want me to phone Martha? See if I can hunt down Julie? It would be easier from here.'

'OK thanks Ray, you're a mate, but if there's no word by tomorrow morning it's the cops.'

'Well let's just wait and see. What's Martha's number?'

During the conversation I had started to pace the room, tension forcing me to move around my "executive" rabbit hutch in Glasgow's " much sought after" Waterfront apartments. Although these days the people doing the seeking were mostly Building Societies trying to repossess properties from up and coming young executives who had upped and gone. I sat down on the old rocking chair that sat beside the phone stand, the only memento I had from my childhood "family" home. I had a bad feeling about this. It was at times like this that I wished I was into music, meditation, anything that could help with the tension I felt when under stress but none of those had ever been my thing. I had mentioned that I was thinking of trying meditation once to a girlfriend a few years back. She had ventured back with, 'Why not, beats sitting around doing nothing'. I was never quite sure if she had been serious or not.

'Kate I hope you haven't done anything crazy.'

\*\*\*

The phone call from Joe had played on Martha Reid's mind. Joe was a decent man but not who Kate should have married. He stifled her. She was removed from him. He obviously didn't know Kate was staying with Julie. He hid his surprise, his concern, but she knew. She wasn't senile just yet. Still, they had been together for a long time, a not inconsiderable achievement in this day and age, and when their children had come along Martha had experienced a new manifestation of love, so that was something. The following morning, after spending a few moments admiring her magnolias she picked up the phone.

'Joe? It's Martha. Has Kate popped up? Full of excuses.'

'No, not a dickie bird. Getting a bit worried to be honest.'

'What? Why didn't you call me Joe? Have you called the police?'

'Bit early for that don't you think? Look I'm sure everything's fine. You know what she's like. I'll call you as soon as I hear.'

'Yes. Please do that Joe. Bye.'

Martha Reid did know her daughter and this wasn't "like her." She was calling the police, Joe or no Joe. They would be able to trace Julie. She would give Kate a piece of her mind. Martha Reid spoke slowly and distinctly, 'I'd like to report a missing person please.'

'Certainly madam and who would this person be?' the officer on the desk at Pitt Street Police Office replied.

'My daughter, Kate Turner.'

'I see and what age is your daughter?

*'Fourteen.....back by tea time'* thought the PC

'Forty six,' replied Martha, the number surprising even her.

'Her address?'

'Well she actually lives in Spain but is over here for a short visit.'

'And she was staying with you, yes?'

'Well no actually. She was staying with a girlfriend of hers, I'm not sure where; some hotel in the city. The thing is she was due home, in Spain that is, yesterday but she's not arrived. Her husband, Joe, and I are very worried.'

'I see. Has he checked with the airline?'

*'Few drinks in the Corinthian, some smooth, good looking bastard....' some hotel in the city" is probably right dear.'*

'Not as far as I know. He thinks it's too early to panic.'

'I'm sure he's right, nearly always a simple explanation for this kind of thing.'

'What airline was she flying with?'

'I'm not certain. Easyjet or Ryanair I think.'

'OK well her husband should check with the airline and take things from there. If she was on the flight then it's probably more an issue for the Spanish police. If she wasn't on the flight get back to us and we'll check hospitals, that sort of thing. I'm sure everything will be fine. That OK?'

'Oh. Well right. Yes. I suppose so. If you think that's for the best.'

'I do madam. Bye.'

Martha was not convinced by the way things had gone but that was both Joe and the police not seeming too concerned so maybe she was fussing over nothing. Still...

The desk officer logged a call from a Mrs Turner, re "missing Spanish person". He was looking forward to his long week end off, starting one hour from then.

Martha suspected there was a man involved, she knew it wouldn't be the first time. Unfortunately, Joe Turner knew that as well.

***

Boom Boom Banks liked a nice cup of warming tea in the morning, morning being when he woke up and not any arbitrary notion of time. Time for Boom Boom didn't exist, he was either awake or comatose. He dug a tea bag out of the left hand pocket of his overcoat. He was sure he had only used this one a couple of times so it would be fine. His matches, as always, were safe and dry. It had been a warm night as far as he could remember so there would be no problem lighting a fire. Boom Boom's joints groaned as he rose from the base of the tree and scuttled down to the river to fill his tin can. His fuddled mind retreated to a former place and time, his body, like now, stiff and sore but he was just a lad, his Jesuit mentor reminding him of the sanctity of the human body and the virtue of silence.

At first he wasn't quite sure what it was he was looking at. Old clothes? Flood debris? He thought there might be something worth salvaging and pulled on the sodden mass.

'Ah lassie. What have you done to yirsel?'

Boom Boom knew this was hassle and unwanted attention for him but;

*'the poor lassie, the poor, poor lassie.'*

He pulled the girl's inert body onto the bank and gently pushed the hair away from her face. The water and its various forms of life had left their mark but, returning to his former life momentarily, Professor Colin Banks could see that she had been a good looking woman, mid-forties and probably had given birth at some stage. Boom Boom wondered if she had any money, cigs or anything worth selling, after all she wouldn't need them now. Half an hour after pulling the girl from the river Boom Boom had done what he felt compelled to do and was on the move. He would report the body, he had never been devoid of compassion, but anonymously;

*'No need to get involved.'*

He saw from a gold necklace on the body that the lassie's name was Tunstall.

*'Strange name that my poor wee soul.'*

He knew he could probably have sold that necklace, but he wanted to let *'The lassie get hame to her family.'*

Besides, he would be able to sell the mobile phone to some smack heid.

*'Get a couple of tinnies as they say in Oz.'*

Boom Boom shuffled his way onto the Lanark road and found one of the rapidly disappearing red phone boxes but that still survive in some country locations. He knew he needed no money to make a 999 call.

'Is that the polis?' the phone box reeking of piss even out there, in the countryside.

'Yes sir. Your name is?'

'Never mind. There's a lassie's body on the riverbank about a mile up from Garrion Bridge. She's been murdered.'

'Oh yes, where exactly is this body sir?' weariness rather than concern the overriding tone.

'You want an Ordinance Survey reference constable? You're the police. Seek and ye shall find.'

'Sir can I......?'

The sound of rapid pips cut short the officer's next question.

Boom Boom shuffled away. He knew, even through his haze, that he was in serious trouble.

*'Why Boom Boom, why?'*

The anonymous phone call was passed onto the Police station at Hamilton as they were nearest to the alleged site. No great urgency was attached to it. There were no recent Missing Persons enquiries and the caller sounded a bit strange, well-spoken and pissed at the same time.

The banks of the River Clyde take on many shapes, sizes and even roles as they meander through the Scottish countryside, through Glasgow city centre and on to the Atlantic Ocean but not many parts are more beautiful than the stretch that P.C.'s Gardner and Wright wandered up and down chatting about nothing in particular a few hours after Boom Boom's call. After about a half hour of what under other circumstances would be considered a pleasant stroll P.C. Gardner vomited where he stood. Within another half hour D.I. Susan Dornan was looking down at the livid white mass that only a few hours previously had been a human being and D.S. Matt Healy was throwing every obscenity he could think of at the unfortunate constable. They didn't make him feel any worse though as he hadn't seen a partially decomposed body before.

'You've completely fucked up this crime scene you fucking useless cunt.' roared Healy.

'Sorry sir.'

'Sorry. Fucking sorry. You fucking kidding me. How long you been a cop?'

'A year sir.'

'A fucking year and you've never seen a dead body. Too busy shagging sheep out here in the sticks or what?'

'No sir. Sorry sir.'

'Piss off before you end up in the river.'

'Yes sir'

Healy hated the next part. Identify the body, go see the relatives.

'*Jesus, please no wee kiddies at home.*'

Dornan was doing a thorough job going over the body whilst allowing Healy to vent his frustration. She would speak to him about his "Management Technique" later, *Rome wasn't built in a day* and the young cop will have learned an important lesson he wouldn't forget in a hurry.

'No money. No cards. No Driving Licence. No mobile. Picture of two kids. No picture of man, you know, husband partner. A receipt, don't know where from. No rings on, but two in her bag. Wearing gold necklace with the name Tunstall.' Dornan had moved away from the body needing a break from the sight and smell of violent death. She also guessed that the dead woman would be roughly the same age as she was and that somehow affected her more than other bodies she had seen. At times like these she tended to ponder death; the reality of what it actually was. The certainty of it. Her own death. In the end what depressed her most was the world's indifference to it. *Tomorrow this murder will be all over the local papers, the nationals too busy reporting on who has been evicted from Big Brother to report something as mundane as another murder, but people will still put their dinner on their lap and show more interest in the "lives" of people in Albert Square and Coronation Street than the life, and death, of a young woman a few miles from their white plastic, double glazed front door. Maybe that was the real reason for double glazing, to keep the real world at bay. Big Brother not really needing to watch us anymore as we're all watching it.*

'Tunstall....think that's her name or what?' Healy's voice dragging Dornan back into the gruesome present.

'Could be I suppose but a bit unusual, and she's a bit old to be wearing that sort of thing.'

'Is it even a name? '

The Scene of Crime Team had arrived and so had the pathologist on call.

'Ignore the vomit. It belongs to that tosser over there. Right Doc, what you think?' Healy had automatically taken charge, not out of disrespect Dornan knew, just habit.

'She's dead.'

If Dornan and Healy had a quid for every time they got a sarcastic, apparently witty reply from a police pathologist they could retire.

'Yes, very good, never heard that one. Can you enlighten us to probable cause and time of death doctor?' interjected Dornan, afraid the pathologist, his apparent indifference to death probably understandable, might end up in the same place the body had obviously been should Healy get his way.

'Cause – multiple stab wounds. Time – no idea. I'll get back to you on that.'

'Please do doctor please do. Oh by the way there's a Strand Comedy Club opened up on Woodlands Road if you fancy turning professional.' said Healy to the retreating back.

The pathologist ambled away, oblivious to death and sarcasm.

'Any middle aged women reported missing recently Susan?' Healy asked on the drive back into Glasgow.

'Not that I'm aware of'.

An overturned lorry on the M8 motorway had forced Healy to take a diversion through Easterhouse, one of Glasgow's bleaker Housing Schemes, the city's new marketing logo : "Scotland with Style" understandably not too prominent there. Susan Dornan stared glumly out of the passenger window, her thoughts returning to society's indifference to life. Satellite dishes festooning every building including those that didn't even look fit for human habitation allowing the inhabitants to escape into a mist of game shows and celebrity life styles, the forlorn hope of winning one to allow them the latter somehow appearing possible in a fog of cigarette smoke, alcohol misuse and a drug induced stupor. She felt that somehow, in some way, reality had disappeared from society and been replaced by the imaginary worlds of computer games, media images and simulated events, with these bizarrely and with no apparent hint of irony being described as reality. The only shops they passed being graffiti covered fortresses whose sole purpose appeared to be to supply the very illusions of escape but that lead only to further imprisonment. They passed the spot where a local youth had been stabbed to death a fortnight before. The rusted fence where he fell festooned with King William of Orange, UDA and Rangers FC flags along with a couple of Celtic FC tops perhaps placed there by someone who felt that there had to be more to life, or should that be death, than the version they lived here. Susan had, unfortunately, seen too many of these shrines that had seemed to become a ritual in recent years whenever tragedies struck a community. Often people with no connection to the victim seemed compelled to attend and Dornan often wondered why. Perhaps their lives were so empty they needed to check they were in fact alive by being part of a public event. Maybe they had no other way to let the world know that they, at least, were still alive.

'Did you notice the tan Susan?' Healy's voice again bringing Susan Dornan back from her inner thoughts.

'Yes....significant? Half the female population of Glasgow have a tan these days.'

'I know but hers looked natural to me. What you think?'

'Could be. The post mortem will tell.'

'Bet it's the husband, or boyfriend.'

Susan Dornan smiled.

They arrived back at Pitt Street at around 18.00 hours. The Gods had apparently decided to give the city a break and a glorious summer's evening belied the horrors that had obviously taken place a mere 20 minutes' drive away. Dornan brought the rest of the team up to speed and allocated tasks whilst Matt Healy put the little information they had up on the new-fangled, see-thro Incident Boards that all the detective squads now used. Matt Healy was a bit of a Luddite but this was one innovation he approved as, he explained to Susan Dornan the previous day, 'you can see what brass is coming into the room and duck out a side door.'

At this point however it was a waiting game for the Post Mortem and to see if anybody files a Missing Persons. DC Allan had been told to call everyone in the phone book with the initial T as a first name, as there was no-one with it as a surname, and ask if their name was Tunstall. He wasn't sure why because if their name was Tunstall they were probably dead and wouldn't be answering the phone any time soon. Still, he wasn't passing his views on to Healy, not just yet.

Jill French Googled "Tunstall" but had only come up with screeds about a pop singer which she felt would hardly be relevant to a 46 year woman and she wasn't going to court Healy's derision by even mentioning it.

Martha Reid's missing persons call report was still in the Front Desk In – Tray about three inches below the latest call concerning Patch, a missing mongrel.

***

I was trying to keep my wits about me but I knew Joe would be demented over Kate's antics. I had become tied up with some issues over an up and coming case and hadn't put as much effort into Joe's worries as I'd have liked but the following day I had more time to concentrate on Kate's possible whereabouts. One thing did bother me though *'What was Kate thinking about not even calling anyone, not even her mother?'*

I picked up the number Joe had given me for Martha Reid.

'Hello Martha. It's Ray Ford here, Joe and Kate's friend.'

'Oh hello Ray. How are you?' replied Martha.

'Fine, fine. Listen Martha, I had a phone call from Joe yesterday. It seems Kate hasn't arrived home after visiting you this week-end and he's a bit worried. You know anything, they had a fall out and she's teaching him a lesson maybe?'

'Oh no Ray nothing like that. I'm very worried myself but the Police said they were sure everything would be all right and to leave it twenty four hours.'

'The police? You called the police then? Joe said you hadn't.'

'Well Joe's Joe and I'm me and I know my daughter, something's not right.'

I smiled, Martha Reid may well be what some would refer to as a genteel older lady but she had spirit and all her wits about her and would do what she thought was correct despite anything Joe said. I also felt she was right.

'Joe said Kate was staying with Julie, did you tell the police that?'

'Yes but when I didn't know exactly where that was they lost interest I think.'

'Do you have a number for Julie?'

'No.'

'Do you know what hotel group she worked for?'

'Oh yes, The Marriott but not which one.'

'Did you tell the police that?'

'No. Do you think I should phone them back and say?'

'No, I'll get the numbers from Yell and phone around. I'm sure I'll find Julie and Kate will probably be with her. Even if she's not, Julie might find it easier to speak to me if Kate is just trying to put Joe in his place or something.'

'That's very good of you Ray. Please let me know. Bye now.'

'Don't worry, I will. Bye Martha.'

I hoped and prayed Kate had actually stayed with Julie and that wasn't just a cover for something else, something that would rock Joe even more. I didn't know for certain but I was pretty sure that Joe may well have given Kate the odd slap from time to time. Violence against women was something I never understood and absolutely abhorred, especially the domestic variety, but it wasn't my place to interfere. Knowing Joe, he probably wouldn't want to know anyway.

There are three Marriott's in Glasgow but I struck lucky at the first attempt. I was put through by the hotel's well-spoken receptionist practically straight away.

'Julie? My name is Ray Ford. I'm a friend of Kate and Joe Turner's.'

'Hi. What can I do for you?'

'Just wondered if you'd seen Kate Turner recently?'

'Kate? God no, I haven't seen Kate for over a year. Why?'

'Or spoken to her?'

'No. What is this about?'

'Sorry. It's just that Kate was apparently in Glasgow for the weekend and hasn't arrived back in Spain.'

'Shit'.

'I know. Joe phoned me and I've spoken to Martha, Kate's mum, but no joy. Martha seemed to think she was staying at one of your hotels, presumably with you.'

'No, as I said I haven't seen or spoken to Kate in over a year.'

'Right it's obviously just crossed wires. I'll track her down eventually I'm sure. Sorry to bother you.'

'No it's fine. Listen get Kate to call me when you speak to her.'

'Will do. Bye Julie.'

I had to think, take stock. Hearing Julie's voice reminded me a bit of Kate's voice but didn't bring me any comfort. I knew something was very wrong. I'd have to get back to Joe and Martha eventually but I wanted time to think of what to do next, what to say even.

## Chapter 4

As expected the Post Mortem results showed that the woman on the river bank had died of multiple stab wounds caused by the same knife; one straight edge, one serrated, in what could only be described as a frenzied attack. She had injuries to the eyes, mouth, neck and body which Healy new from previous cases normally indicated murder driven by anger which, in turn, meant the victim knew the killer.

'Knew it Susan.' Healy said to Dornan as they sat in her office trying to absorb the report.

'There were no definite defensive marks either, which again indicates that the victim hadn't immediately sensed danger in the seconds before the attack. I think your theory's going to stand up Matt.' Dornan added a few moments later

Two issues did arise though that were difficult to fathom initially. Firstly, the wounds were such that death would have been instant yet the corpse had some water in her lungs. She hadn't drowned but there was water and, secondly, there were traces of two separate semen types on the body. Dornan got DC Brown to phone the pathologist for confirmation that due to the sustained nature of the attack then the perpetrator had been sexually motivated.

'That would be the first thing you would think on seeing these injuries" the pathologist agreed but could offer no light as to the two separate semen samples being present.

'You're the detectives,' his pointed response.

He did add though that the human body contains five and a half litres of blood and that this was practically all gone. Some would have seeped away in the river but the attacker's clothes would most definitely be covered in blood and he also felt that although there were no real signs of a struggle taking place the attacker would have some defensive marks on them as the attack took some time and the victim was bound to have resisted to some extent. The exact time of death was also a problem. In most cases the time can be narrowed down using the internal body temperature to within about five and a half hours but this "window" increases as time passes. He added that he was considering calling in an entomologist for his input after studying the fly and maggot activity on the body but warned Healy that even this method wouldn't get them much closer as the body had probably been submerged in the river at various times. Dornan and Healy had moved out of her office and were standing in front of the incident board. The rest of the team gathered close in a rough semicircle.

'Two different semen samples. You have got to be kidding me. She didn't look like a hooker or anything.' Healy mumbled more to himself than anything.

'What do hookers look like sir?' asked Paul Allan. Healy's return stare its own reply. Frame was trying desperately to suppress a laugh, Jill French suddenly found something of overwhelming interest around her feet, Rab Brown looked either to be concentrating on the board or was asleep with his eyes open and Jack T'Baht suggested the victim may "have been a bit of a girl".

'Right that is enough of that. I mean it. Enough.' Susan Dornan was determined she would have no trouble establishing the pecking order and up to now that had been easy as there hadn't been any pressure situations to deal with but now was the real thing and she was going to solve this case and get the squad on its way to re-establishing its reputation.

'Right then, one of the samples was post death,' Susan Dornan added.

'Jesus H Christ, post death? What the fuck are we dealing with here?' asked T'Baht

'I don't think she was a prossie ma'am,' said Brown.

'Why not?'

'Just doesn't feel right.'

'As it happens I agree with you. Our corpse was no prossie and even if she was she deserved a better end than that.'

Dornan issued a raft of orders and instructions to her squad which boiled down to one thing, find out who the victim was. It was now three or four days since the killing as the pathologist reckoned she had been killed sometime on Saturday, possibly Sunday and she knew that the possibilities of solving the crime diminished with each passing hour.

'Why has no-one reported her missing?' asked Brown.

'Why you think that is?' she asked Rab Brown.

'Lived alone, tourist, who knows.'

'OK, you and Allan check all the city centre hotels. See if they've any guests who haven't shown up or failed to check out. You know the drill.'

'Yes ma'am.'

'Any other leads?'

'We've traced the phone box the call was made from. Out Lanark way, forensics are there now.'

'Right. Good. Anything else, anything at all.'

'Sorry ma'am, nothing.'

Healy surveyed the Incident Board. At this point there was very little on it but he knew, hoped, that would soon change and once the various connections were made they would have their man.

*The husband Matt, check the husband.*

\*\*\*

Martha Reid was exasperated. She was standing at the public counter in the Police headquarters building whilst a young policewoman was looking through some paperwork on the other side of a frosted screen. The constable returned to the desk with a puzzled look on her face.

'Sorry madam, can I just confirm your name again?'

'Mrs Martha Reid, I called yesterday.'

'I'm sorry Mrs Reid we have no record of your call,' the police woman on the desk explained.

Martha had decided to travel into Pitt Street Police office from her flat in Glasgow's salubrious West End rather than phone back, and she was now glad she had.

'What was your call concerning?'

'I wished to report my daughter missing.'

WPC Yvonne Miller switched up a gear, aware that a woman's body had been found.

'What age was your daughter Mrs Reid?' for once hoping the reply would be eighteen.

'Forty six.'

'When did you last see her?'

'I met her for lunch in Byres Road on Saturday. That's handy for my flat you see, I don't need to take a bus, not like coming here. She's forty six, but doesn't really look it' a mother's pride kicking in.

'And her address?'

'Well she lives in Spain you see. She was only over her for a couple of days to visit me.'

'Oh lovely, lots of sunshine, good for the tan.'

'Yes, but you have to watch you know. I sometimes think Kate can be too brown' quickly adding

'If you know what I mean dear.'

'Sorry Mrs Reid, I should have asked already, what was, is, your daughter's name.'

'Mrs Kate Turner.'

'Can you take a seat over there Mrs Reid and I'll get someone out to speak to you, take some more details.'

Martha Reid sat surrounded by warning posters about knives, drink driving, illegal dogs and missing persons. She prayed Kate Turner's face wouldn't be joining them.

It wouldn't, it would be joining a much darker, sadder list.

***

Whilst Martha Reid was sitting on a plastic chair in a police station foyer surrounded by images of the human condition that she had always been cosseted from, Colin Boom Boom Banks was swimming. Not in the sea or a river but between the past and the present, consciousness and oblivion. He yearned for the latter but long gone were the days he controlled his thoughts. Unless obliterated his thoughts haunted him of his past; tormented his present, annihilated his future.

*Why was it his mother and his mentors wore the same clothes, black flowing robes? Why were they always angry with him? He wanted to be a good boy, tried his best every day, but he always failed, always had to be punished; always in his room alone. Why did God make women if they were so terrible? Wasn't the Virgin Mary a woman? What was a virgin? If he was so bad why was he Father Tobin's "special boy"? What had he done that was so bad that his mother and Father Morgan had to sit in her room right through the night deciding "what to do with him?*

Colin Banks floated into the present. Boom Boom didn't know what to do. He wanted to carry on as normal, as normal as he could manage anyway, but knew it would only be a matter of time before the police caught up with him. He was sure he hadn't killed the lassie, didn't remember doing it anyway, but the toilet cleaner and after shave mix he had graduated on to drinking these days did funny things to the mind. He had done the right thing afterwards, he did know that.

He had also managed to get well away from the Clyde Valley; *pity really, I liked it there.*

He had always been happy in that place and it had been good to him. He was holding an example of his good fortune in his hand at that very moment. Just as his old knife had finally given up the ghost, the handle was in that many pieces he couldn't tie it to the blade any longer, he had found this one. Not new by any means but solid, the kind fishermen use. One of them must have left it behind after a day's trout fishing.

*Too bad, finders keepers.*

His new abode wasn't bad at all. Still by a river, he wasn't really sure which one, Kelvin maybe, didn't really matter. It was quiet but within an hour's walk of some restaurants that he couldn't have afforded to frequent even in his former life but like most others they discarded perfectly good food out the back and so now he ate there almost daily. Most importantly there was also an Offie for when he had cadged money from some deluded do-gooder.

Boom Boom went over everything in what was left of his mind.

*Was the lass definitely dead when he found her? Yes, she had been for a while, days perhaps, his training told him so. He had never seen her before, though that was hard to tell given how she looked. But how did he know when he found her? So many blanks. He hadn't killed her, he hadn't. So what if he took some money, no way anyone would know. She had no use of it.*

His head started to spin. Things become blurred. He muttered about DNA and urges. He saw the blackness, and swam towards it. It was dark when he awoke. He wondered what time it was, what day it was, would there still be a shop, garage, anywhere still open that sold household cleaning fluid for people who didn't have a household.

\*\*\*

'Mrs Reid? I'm Detective Inspector Susan Dornan and this is Detective Sergeant Matt Healy. Would you like to come through?'

Martha Reid was unsure of the ranking system in the police force but both of these people appeared to be senior officers and she quietly congratulated herself for making the journey, for being persistent. She wasn't sure what Kate would make of all the fuss but Martha didn't care,

*That girl's in for a good talking to anyway.*

Martha Reid didn't watch television so was slightly taken aback by the bleakness of the interview room, not at all like the rooms she was used to.

'Would you like a cup of tea or anything?' asked the nice female officer.

Martha had seen one of those "dreadful" tea and coffee making machines in the hallway outside the room they now sat in and had also surmised that the tea would not be served in proper cups so had already prepared her answer if offered refreshment.

'No thank you.'

'I understand you're concerned about your daughter's whereabouts Mrs Reid?'

'Yes. She was just visiting for a couple of days, she lives in Spain you know, but no-one has heard from her since Saturday and she never got on her flight home apparently.'

'Lives in Spain eh? Nice. Good tan?' asked Dornan.

'Oh I'm always telling her to watch that but she seems to be used to it by now.'

Healy and Doran exchanged a quick, knowing glance.

'How do you know she didn't catch her flight or get a later one?'

'Well Joe, that's her husband, checked with the airline, Ryanair, very reasonable I understand, and she wasn't on the flight she booked and, well, she's not home yet so I don't think she caught another flight.'

'And I've been told your daughter's name is Kate, is that right? Is she known by any other name? Nick name perhaps?'

'No, not that I know of. Why?'

'No nothing, just routine.'

'Do you have a recent photo of your daughter Mrs Reid?'

'Nothing recent I'm afraid. Joe might have one though.'

'Do you have a contact number for Joe? He's in Spain at the moment right, he didn't come over with Kate?'

'No too busy with the pubs. Busy time with British tourists apparently. I think they like to visit that area for the Gaudi buildings.'

Another glance between Healy and Doran; suppressed smiles.

'Yes, more than likely.' Susan Doran said.

'Were her and her husband, Joe is it, having any problems do you know?'

'Not that I know off. No doubt they had their moments, what couples don't, but she won't just have run off if that's what you're thinking.'

'Mrs Reid it's useful to us in this kind of investigation to have a sample of the missing person's DNA. Can we visit your house and see if we can get anything? Hair from a hairbrush, an old toothbrush, her clothes, anything.'

'Well she wasn't actually staying with me. She was staying at a hotel in the City Centre. I don't know which one. Sorry. Joe didn't know about that, he was quite angry when he found out I think although he tried not to show it.'

Healy and Dornan glanced at each other for a third time; this time there was no need to suppress smiles.

'Did you say hair just then?' said Martha.

'What?'

'Hair. Did you say you'd like some of Kate's hair. It's just that I've got a lock of her hair, you know these things parents do, sticking locks of hair into books every ten minutes after a child is born. Would you like it?'

'Yes. I'll get an officer to drive you home and collect it if that's all right.'

'Oh yes. Lovely.'

*The curtains will be all a quiver on Hyndland Road when they see me coming home in a police car. How exciting. I'll tell them it was shop lifting!*

She was confident her visit had sorted everything out, Kate would soon be found *but I won't tell her I gave out her lock of hair, she could be quite childish at times.*

\*\*\*

Pete Harris was in turmoil. Kate, his love, his life. What had he done? He was sitting in the living room of his semi in Uddingston, just outside Glasgow, not sure if things were real or he just needed to waken up. He knew that this was not the stuff of dreams or nightmares. You wake up eventually from even the worst of nightmares. Over the last few months he had been thinking of starting his own business. He had gone to a seminar on business start – up, "Dream to Reality" was the slogan, Christ how he wished he could hide away from this reality.

*Run or stay?*

*Hand himself in or try and sit tight?*

*What would happen to his wife and kids?*

*What would happen to him? What had possessed him?*

*He loved her, would never harm her. Why did he do it?*

*But why had she not come to him for love? Once she finally realised that Joe Turner was not right for her why had she not come back to him? She knew he was waiting, she knew.*

He looked back on the good times with Kate. It was one of the better things that had come out of tracing his estranged kids by Ann, his first wife; although his son had never forgiven him for putting them up for adoption, even changed his name.

*I was only 22 at the time, two babies, for Christ's sake, how could he be expected to cope with that? Fuck him.*

His daughter had at least kept in some kind of touch, and it was through her that he had met Kate, *wonderful, vibrant Kate.*

*Besides it wasn't his fault their mother, the booze bag, had fallen down the stairs. He had hardly touched her.*

"Paralysis by analysis" was part of the management speak they'd used at the seminar. He now knew what it really meant. He couldn't make a rational choice, found it hard to even physically move. He hadn't been to work this week. Sally, his second wife, knew there was something wrong but put it down to disillusionment with his job.

*What kind of job was Male Nurse anyway? They didn't say Female Nurse so why Male Nurse?*

He felt it was because normal men wouldn't even consider it as a job, it was women's work, like shopping, cleaning and watching kids.

*Christ, his kids.*

Peter Harris wished he believed in God, Divine Intervention. His parents had sent him to Sunday School but like most people in Scotland he had drifted away from churches and prayer in his teens. Christenings, weddings and funerals were the only times they saw the inside of a church or even heard prayers, never mind said any.

*Strange for a country blighted by sectarianism.*

When Kate had gotten into the car she looked beautiful...and sexy. On the way out to the bar in the Clyde Valley she had squeezed his knee a couple of times, even leaned over and kissed his cheek once. She was hyper about something, tactile, familiar, said she wanted to talk to him, tell him something. She was sending out all the signals he'd longed for. He knew her better than anyone, especially that pillock husband of hers. She did love him. He was sure. She'd just realised, that's what she wanted to tell him. He had been certain. Why then did she come out with the shit she did? She couldn't have meant it. Didn't know what she was saying. He was the one for her, not this guy she'd just met.

Pete Harris was able to sit and cry openly. His wife was at Asda with the children.

***

The Incident Room was buzzing. The whole squad was in, all the lights were on despite the bright morning and the coffee machine was on its second fill. Photos of what was left of Kate Turner adorned the see - through screen at the front of the room. D.S. Matt Healy was in deep discussion with Dornan in front of the screen and Detective Chief Inspector McFarlane was overseeing operations. In his own mind anyway. As far as the squad were concerned he was an irrelevance. Susan Dornan was eager to get things moving and to show McFarlane that she could lead her first murder enquiry without any input from him.

'Right you lot, we all know the score, why we're here. OK facts.'

The press were pushing for information but Kate Turner's family hadn't been informed yet. The pleasure of calling on Martha Reid was yet to be allocated. Matt Healy knew he would do it. He always felt the family should be able to put a face on the guy who was going to nail the bastard who was putting them through this.

'We're pretty sure the dead woman is Kate Turner nee Reid. Originally from Oxford but now, or should I say up to now, resident in Spain. Married to Joe Turner, who is originally from Glasgow, but who hasn't lived here for thirty-odd years. Two grown up kids. Back for long week-end ostensibly to see her mother, Mrs Martha Reid, 48 Hyndland Road out in the West End, but did not actually stay with her. Apparently staying with a pal, Julie Connor, in a city centre hotel. Paul Allen has traced her to the Marriott and Matt Healy and I are going to interview her now. Her husband by all accounts didn't come over with her but we'll need to check on that, might have to involve Spanish police with that. The victim died due to multiple stab wounds, no weapon found at the scene, but was still alive when she went into the river, small amount of water in lungs. Traces of semen from two different males found on the body. We're waiting for DNA on these. As you can see, body badly decomposed and subject to attention from wildlife. Estimated that she died and went into the water late Saturday early Sunday. Signs of possible forced intercourse. Any questions up to now?

She had a gold necklace with the name Tunstall. Any ideas anyone?'

'Kids name? Nickname?'

'OK we'll ask the husband. He'll have to come over here anyway to identify the body, can't ask her mum to face that. Right, get moving.'

'You happy to deal with the media sir?' Dornan enquired of the Chief once the room was cleared.

'Yes, yes leave that to me. I'll take that worry off your hands,' the Chief replied.

Somehow Dornan was expecting that answer.

'Thank fuck for that Susan' Healy said to Dornan on their way to the squad car 'double result, fucking leeches and vultures of the fourth estate out the fucking road and McFarlane as well, result.'

Neither Healy nor Dornan spoke again on the way to Hyndland Road. They broke the news to Martha Reid as gently as they could and then moved on to The Marriott Hotel to speak to Julie Connor.

'Julie when was the last time you spoke to Kate Turner?' Susan Dornan asked.

'Don't know exactly, over a year ago. We used to speak every two or three weeks but the gaps just got bigger over time. She was in another country, married with two kids, I'm more of a career woman.' Julie's last words were said with a hint of sarcasm as she looked round her tiny office and a hint of regret that Dornan silently acknowledged.

'So you were unaware she was even in Glasgow last week-end?'

'Not a clue.'

'Julie, over the years did Kate have any affairs?'

'God, what a thing to ask.'

'It could be important.'

'You think she knew her killer? Was meeting him?'

'It's possible, probable even' said Dornan, deferring to Matt Healy's theory.

'Shit. Kate may have had the odd fling, I don't know, 30 years is a long time with the one man, especially Joe but...' Julie's reply tapered off.

'You don't like Joe then?'

'No it's not that, he's a nice enough bloke just, well, thick.'

'Not enough for Kate.... intellectually.'

'Exactly, never really understood what she saw in him to be honest.'

'Money?'

'Money?' Julie was laughing. 'Are you kidding? British bars on the Costa Brava are a waste of time.'

'So they had money problems?'

'Not problems, Kate earned reasonable money, but they weren't flush.'

'Julie, Kate was staying in Glasgow for a few days. She didn't stay with her mum or you, any idea where she would have stayed and why?'

'No, not really.'

Dornan handed Julie her card.

'OK Julie we'll be in touch if there's anything else. Call me anytime if you remember anything. You be in this hotel for the next wee while?'

'Yes, unfortunately.'

'Why you say that, looks like a nice place?'

'The job isn't what it used to be. Take this hotel for example. Three quarters of the staff are foreigners and I'm no racist but it makes the job incredibly difficult, too many different cultures, different standards.........mind you their English is better than the locals.'

All three smiled but Susan Dornan remembered reading a few days ago that there were thirty thousand Poles alone living in Glasgow and wondering what the outcome of that kind of trend would mean for the city.

Julie Connor was wondering if she was doing the right thing, agonising over whether to tell the police everything she knew about Kate's life.

\*\*\*

At first I couldn't make out who was on the phone or what they were attempting to say.

'Goony Ray.' the voice wailed

'What'

'Goony. Topped'.

I realised it was Joe.

*Sounds bloody pissed.*

'Joe, what is it, what are you saying? You pissed?'

'Kate Ray, they've found her body, she's dead Ray, dead.'

I felt paralysed.

'What are you saying? Who told you this?'

'Martha phoned. Police have found a body. They're pretty sure it's Kate. I've to go over for formal ID.'

My head was spinning, the room reeling.

'Must be a mistake Joe, must be.'

'No Ray, it's her, I know it's her.'

'Joe.'

'Will you meet me Ray? Tomorrow. I need someone there apart from Martha. Will you Ray?'

'Sure Joe sure. What time are you flying in?'

'Land about two. Police said they'd meet me. I need you there mate.'

'Did the police say anything else Joe. What happened? Was it an accident? Any witnesses, suspects?'

'Martha never said. Dare say we'll find out tomorrow.'

'Right. Don't drink anymore Joe, try and get some sleep. I'll see you tomorrow.'

I hung up and threw up at roughly the same time. This wasn't happening. I had to call Martha.

'Martha it's Ray Ford again. Joe just called. Is it true, surely it's a mistake?'

Martha Reid was dignity and calmness personified. I had only met her once or twice but she was old school, stiff upper lip etc.

'I wish it were Ray but there's no mistake. It's very good of you to call.'

'Are you OK...well.....Christ Martha.....I don't know what to say.'

'It's alright Ray, I'm fine. Kate had a brother you know?'

'No I didn't know that. She never mentioned him to me anyway.'

'He died. Twenty odd years ago now. Car crash. Do you know something Ray, what the real sorrow surrounding death is? Of course you are devastated at the time but the real sorrow, the real pain, is realising that you keep on living. Josh, that was his name, he was gone but I had to exist, function, communicate...live, but one of my reasons for living was gone. That is the real sorrow Ray.'

'You still had Kate,' I replied, instantly regretting my stupidity.

'Yes, that was certainly true then.'

I wanted to move on but to where, what, there was only one topic of conversation.

'What did the police say apart from......' my question tapering off into the ether.

'Well one thing Ray, the hotel Kate was staying at, did you find Julie?'

My mind was racing, frantically trying to weigh up what to reply.

'I did Martha but the thing is Kate didn't actually stay with Julie. In fact, they haven't spoken in over a year.'

'Stupid girl.'

It took me a moment to realise Martha wasn't talking about Julie Connor.

'Oh my, I just can't make head nor tail of this Ray. What was my poor Kate up to?'

'I'm sure she wasn't up to anything Martha. She wasn't like that. It's no secret she and Joe had their problems, maybe she just wanted to get off the treadmill for a while. We've all felt that way at some point Martha.'

'Well she's off it now that's for sure Ray.'

In another context Martha's reply may have sounded comical but the heartache travelled down the line and entered my heart as sure as if it had been placed there by hand.

'I'll see you soon Martha. Joe asked me to meet him when he comes to Glasgow, for support.'

'As I said Ray, you are very kind.'

I sat down. My thoughts suddenly, strangely coherent. Joe's temper. Kate's flirtatiousness. Shit.

*What am I doing? He wasn't even in Scotland for Christ's sake.*

I forced my mind back to the present. I would have to get organised at work. Thankfully I didn't have any court appearances to make over the next two or three days so I would be able to organise everything else so I could help Joe out with all the things that would hit him over here. I looked down, *I'll need to clean up my vomit or the carpet will smell.*

***

The following day, Dornan, Healy and Joe Turner were standing outside Glasgow City mortuary, a nondescript red brick building wedged in between the new and old Glasgow High Court buildings. Joe Turner didn't smoke but had a Benson and Hedges he mooched off a morgue attendant lit and stuck between his lips.

'Joe, that building there is Glasgow's High Court and I swear I'll have whoever did this to Kate standing shitting themselves in there as soon as is humanly possible.' said Healy. The added m*aybe you* featuring only in his mind.

The identification was mercifully brief. Joe had been warned that Kate was not as he remembered her. He looked at her legs and body, avoided her face and said it was her. The sheet went back over her and she was gone from his life forever.

'Joe,' it was Susan Dornan speaking 'we'll go back to the station now. We need to ask you one or two things OK?'

'Will she want buried here or in Spain do you think?' Joe ventured to no-one in particular.

'Plenty of time for that Joe, I'm afraid it might be some time before the body can be released.' said Susan Dornan in the background.

'Right, right' muttered Joe.

Matt Healy and Susan Dornan sat opposite Joe Turner in the same room Joe's mother in law had sat in. He had no thoughts on the decor.

'Joe, I know this is difficult but we need to ask you some things. OK?'

'Right.' Joe appeared almost as if he were in a trance.

'You alright Joe?'

'Terrific.'

Healy was neither surprised nor fazed by the reply.

*How would any human being react to what this guy had gone through in the last twenty four hours...still.*

'How were things between you and Kate, Joe?'

'We'd been married 20 odd years, how do you think they were. Hard sometimes, mostly good. I loved her.'

'Why did you not come over with her?'

'Too busy. You ever been to the Costa Brava in the summer? Blackpool with the sun and just as shit.'

'Did she ask you to come?'

'No.'

'That normal? You both taking separate breaks.'

'We go on family holidays together when we can, you know during the close season, but I go on breaks with the lads sometimes, you know, golf maybe over here for a Scotland match and she comes here to see her mum.'

'Told you she was staying at her mums then?'

'Yeah.'

'But she wasn't.'

'So?'

'So does she normally lie to you?'

'She didn't lie I just don't listen half the time.'

'Where do you think she was staying then?'

'She has a pal here, Julie, she was staying with her apparently. Her mum told me.'

'She wasn't staying with Julie either.'

'Eh?'

'We spoke to Julie, she never even knew Kate was in Glasgow.'

Joe sat, his body rigid. He couldn't quite take it in but he knew, he knew.

'Where you think she did stay then Joe?'

'No idea.'

'Did Kate wear a wedding ring, engagement ring Joe?'

'Yeah, of course.'

'She wasn't wearing any when we found her.'

'Bastard who did this stole them then.'

'We found them in her bag. Why would a married woman take off her rings do you think Joe?'

Joe Turner's eyes seemed to glaze over. Somehow the thought of her cheating was worse than her death. He lent forward, put his head on the table, wrapped his arms around his head and wept.

\*\*\*

DC Brown entered his sixth hotel of the afternoon, The Cathedral House Hotel. The hotel was next to Glasgow Cathedral, The Royal infirmary and the Eastern Necropolis Graveyard. Brown smiled to himself,

*Best name link choice from those three possibilities methinks.*

'Afternoon. DC Brown, Strathclyde Police. We're trying to trace the hotel where a woman may have stayed over the last few days. Well I say stayed, we think she may have booked in for three or four nights but only stayed for two. Didn't come back to check out.'

'Not the woman who was found murdered is it?' replied Yvonne, the receptionist.

It never ceased to amaze him how quickly bad news circulated in a city of over half a million people.

'Sorry can't say.'

'Don't think so. Do you have a photo?'

'Not at the moment, no. So no-one has failed to return to book out as far as you know.'

'No but that is not as unusual as you might think. Some people are even happy to leave a few things behind.'

'Did that happen here over the last few days?' he asked.

'Not that I know of but I wasn't on duty over the week-end, it was a girl called Ivana and she's actually left now to go to another job.'

'Right. Thanks.'

Brown had only walked ten yards from the hotel when he turned back.

'You said people don't come back and that they sometimes leave things behind.'

'Sometimes.'

'Definitely nothing left behind by a non-returner in the last few days?'

'No. Anything that's found in a room is stuffed under reception here. Sometimes people come back weeks later.'

'Right. Thanks.'

Brown handed the girl his card and cursed all the way back to his car. He'd have to go back to the other five hotels and ask about articles left in rooms.

*Fucking hell.*

Ivana Jakonowski had gotten a much better job. She enjoyed the variety in the Cathedral House, bar, reception, chambermaid but the chicken factory was nearer her Red Road flat and her wages had gone up to £4.25 per hour. She hadn't forgotten about the nice red suitcase she had found behind the bathroom door in Room 6 after the room's guest had checked out. She knew she should have left it at reception and not on a shelf in the cleaning cupboard, but she had done her 12 hours and just wanted to get home. Someone would find it.

\*\*\*

Matt Healy had never dated another cop but Susan Dornan could be the exception. She was smart, good looking and, most important of all, he liked her. He hadn't ever had problems with woman in the past exactly it was just that he never felt entirely relaxed in partnerships but he was at ease with Susan. He was sure she was interested in him.

'Fancy a drink Susan?'

'When? Tonight?' Dornan replied. She hoped not, she was planning a night on the razz with the girls. To celebrate life.

'Yeah, if that's OK?'

'Sure.' The girls could wait. Healy must have something in his head concerning the case, something bothering him maybe.

'Fine, The Horse Shoe at eight? Maybe get something to eat, plenty of Chinkies about?'

'Fine.' Susan noticed that Healy was as P C as ever but at least he wasn't swearing. Paul Allan came back into the office to write up his notes.

'Allan you fucking skiver where have you been?'

'Sir, I've been trying to trace the hotel Kate Turner was staying in. Like you ordered, sir.'

'And did you?'

'No sir.'

'Fucking useless you are Allan. Tea, no sugars, on a diet.' Gently tapping his belly.

'How do you know she was staying in a hotel sir?'

'I don't but where else you going to stay in a city you don't live in if not your maw's or pals.'

'I was thinking sir...'

'Who told you to think? In the job ten minutes and you're fucking Colombo.'

'It's just that, well, rings not on her fingers, what about a boyfriend? Or ex-boyfriend?'

Healy smiled to himself. He and Dornan and had already put the boyfriend thought in the mix back at the crime scene but the ex-bit had possibilities. At least the lad was thinking.

'You got any ex-girlfriends Allan?'

'Yes sir.'

'Only surprise there was you having a girlfriend in the first place. And would any of your many ex loves want to meet up with you again in the future for passionate sex?'

'Don't know sir. I didn't necessarily sleep with all of them.'

Healy didn't know if the lad was winding him up or not but he was beginning to take a shine to him.

'Wee prick in more ways than one then? OK Go speak to Martha Reid, ask her about Kate's old boyfriends. Use your obvious charm with the ladies and see if a current boyfriend was a possibility.'

'Right sir.'

DC Allan was just leaving the squad room when Healy called him back.

'Allan, two more things. Check with Martha Reid about Kate's girlfriends, could have been a lesbo, or bi, and watch Martha doesn't try and bed you, you being so irresistible and all.'

The few squad officers in the room laughed, Susan Dornan knew she should be squirming, regretting agreeing to a drink, but she wasn't regretting it. Despite herself she quite liked Matt Healy, not in a romantic way, more a respectful way, his uncompromising manner.

***

Joe Turner could have stayed at Martha Reid's, she offered, or with me but he felt it would be best if he had somewhere he could retreat to. To be alone. I respected him for that even if I was a little surprised at him admitting to an emotional side. He opted instead for a B & B close to Martha but, more importantly, close to the numerous pubs in Partick and Byres Road. The police knew where Joe would be "should they need him." We were sitting in a bar trying to make sense of the last few days. Joe was still reeling from his grilling from Healy and Dornan.

'The wankers think I did it Ray. Killed my own wife. How can they think that Ray?'

'They don't Joe. They just have to cover every angle that's all. Trust me, I know how these things work. They just needed to eliminate you so they could concentrate on looking elsewhere. They have to think of the husband first on these kind of occasions Joe and to be honest, they're usually right. It usually is the husband.'

'I was in Spain for God's sake!'

'Once they establish that then you'll be fine....well, not fine but you know what I mean.'

Joe Turner's head was bowed over the table, his eyes fixed on the top of a pint of lager.

'Yeah, well slight problem there.'

'What? Why?'

'Yes...No. Well yeah... I was.... it's just that I wasn't there all the time.'

'What are you talking about Joe?'

I thought I was going to faint, last night's thoughts roaring through my brain.

'You know how things were with Kate and me Ray, a man has his needs.'

'What? You were with another woman?'
'Yeah.'
'Well as long as she confirms that then you're fine. The police aren't here to judge your morals Joe.'

Joe still looked peevish. Another thought came to me.

'Christ, you were in Spain weren't you?' I was indignant, I didn't quite know why.

'Yeah.'

'Well then. You'll have to get a hold of the woman. Get her to back your story up.'

'Well that's the thing, she's married. Spanish...catholic....no chance...wouldn't even ask.'

'Fuck that Joe. This is lying to the police in a murder enquiry, Kate's murder in case you've forgotten, you got to get her to back you up.'

'No.'

'No?'

'No.'

'What then?'

'Well I was wondering if you would cover for me.'

All my fears over everything surrounding the last few days swamped my brain. I couldn't really fathom what Joe was saying, asking.

'What? How? Joe are you off your fucking head. I'm a lawyer for Christ's sake. '

'All to the good. Say you were over on holiday. We went up the mountains camping.'

'You ever been camping in Spain? Or anywhere else for that bloody matter.'

'No'

I couldn't believe I was actually having this conversation but more importantly I wanted to know why Joe was having it.

'And what about my passport? The fact that I was in my office, my legal practice that is Joe, every day. You've lost it Joe.'

'Is it any wonder?'

I looked across at him. My anger dissipating slightly as I studied his apparently broken frame but there was still something Joe wasn't telling me.

'Where were you doing this shagging, maybe the hotel staff would remember you.'

'Edinburgh.'

'What! You telling me you were only 30 bloody miles away from where Kate was murdered?'

'Seems so, yeah.'

'Sweet mother of God Joe. You've got to tell the police Joe, you've got to.'

'I'm going to risk it. My staff are all half pissed or worse most of the time. Don't know if it's New Year or New York. They'll probably just say I was there or they can't remember. I think I'll be OK'

'Suit yourself Joe but you're being stupid, really stupid. And you can leave me out of it.'

An uneasy silence fell between us. I felt I was going to throw up again. I couldn't fathom out what Joe was thinking. Wasn't sure I wanted to.

'Listen Joe I've got to get back to work tomorrow. It's really busy at the moment and I've already had a couple of days off this month.'

'No problem Ray, I know, you've been a mate. I'll call you. Let you know what's happening.'

I could sense Joe was glad. He realised as soon as he said it that he shouldn't have told me about Edinburgh, friend or not. In fact, I was even more relieved than Joe was. I just had to get away from him. Get space to think. To think what to do. We walked back to Joe's B & B trying to make small talk on the way but Joe telling me he was only 30 miles away from the scene of Kate's killing had never left my thoughts. I stood by the window watching out for the taxi I had phoned as he stomped around the room getting ready to go to his bed. I couldn't really understand his reaction to Kate's murder. Sure, he was distraught, apparently, at first but now he was quite happy to go out drinking with me and if I didn't know what had just happened I wouldn't have seen much of a difference from the "normal" Joe. In fact earlier in the day he had been bent double with laughter when we had overheard some ladies, apparently from Glasgow's more up-market West End, who had gotten into conversation with some guys standing beside them and when one of the guys had replied, when asked what he did for a living, that he was a painter; the woman had said:

'Oh really, landscapes and things.'

The guy had replied:

'No, fire escapes and things.'

My mind raced. I knew Joe was involved somehow.

*Could he have paid someone to do it? Christ Ray, get a grip, it's not a movie.*

I knew I would have to let the police know, betray my friend. I stood there wondering how I could do it without any direct involvement. It was the police's job to put the whole thing together but they needed all the pieces and if those pieces showed Joe was not involved then no-one would be happier than me. Joe sat on the edge of his bed, emptying the contents of his pockets on the small pine table beside his bed. Joe got up and went into the toilet. My taxi blasted its horn impatiently in the street below.

'Night Joe' I shouted as I passed the bedside table to get to the room door. My glance at the detritus from Joe's pockets convincing me both of his guilt and of how I could guide the police to him.

\*\*\*

Matt Healy was early. He had planned on getting a couple of halves in before Susan turned up but as he wasn't a big drinker he had decided to bin that idea, nerves or no nerves, he'd be fine. He knew he wasn't being professional in fact he didn't know why he was behaving like this at all other than that he liked her.

Dornan walked into the Horse Shoe dead on eight o'clock, Matt liked that and thought she looked great. He wished he knew what she thought.

'What you fancy Susan?' asked Healy, an infantile memory hoping she would say "you".

*God what age am I?*

'G and T thanks, loads of ice,' replied Susan.

'Thought you were going to say Magners there. Every female you see these days is drinking it.'

Susan looked around the bar, no-one was drinking Magners, and he hadn't used the F word. *Someone's nervous. Christ he can't be thinking......*

'Grab that booth in the corner, I'll bring them over.' Matt Healy ordered a half of lager.

'What's the latest with the case Matt, I've been in court all afternoon.' Healy knew that, he always knew where she was. 'Bloody waste of time that was too. Sat about all day then the case gets adjourned for God knows what. That's the third time. Had a laugh though, listen to this. You know that snooty young defence lawyer, Price I think his name is, who thinks he's the new Beltrami. He's questioning a wee arse from Drumchapel in Court 3 apparently and he says to the guy:

'You say you went to your friend's house that night for a tap. Is that correct?'
'Aye.'
'Are you a plumber?'
'Naw.'
'Ah, so to use the vernacular, you went to borrow money?'
'Naw.'
'No, well what kind of tap are you referring to?'
'A Selic tap.'
The judge had to adjourn the case for ten minutes.'

'Welcome to the world of Glasgow Courts counsellor' smirked Healy. He looked at his drink for a moment and continued. 'Kate Turner, she wasn't killed where we found her but we kind of guessed that. About a mile, mile and a half tops up river according to the local gillie, river man or whatever the fuck you call them. Sorry...thought I was talking to Allan for a moment. I've organised a search from about a mile and half up river to where the body was found for tomorrow morning. Hope that's OK with you. See if we can find the actual kill site.' Matt Healy was blushing. Susan Dornan blushed as well. She thought it was sweet he was making such an effort but he surely doesn't think...*oh shit.*

'Right.'

'Forensics got loads of stuff from the phone box and crime scene, well from where she was found, trying to match it up as we speak. Maybe the killer had a conscience, doubt it though. Where do we go from here do you think?'

'Well I think all we can do is speak to Joe Turner and Martha Reid again, and Julie Connor, see if we can get anywhere. Any luck with where she might have been staying?'

'Naw, needle in a haystack stuff. I don't think she wanted anyone to be able to find out where she was staying. For her own reasons obviously.'

'Man?'

'Man.'

They had another couple of drinks and chatted pretty aimlessly. Susan thought Matt Healy was lonely, which was a shame, but she couldn't help him there. Definitely no way. Healy appeared to have forgotten that he had suggested a Chinese meal and didn't react when Dornan said she was moving on to a club to meet up with some friends, relieved she had only altered her previous arrangements and not cancelled them.

Healy went home feeling the evening had gone well. *Very well indeed.*

**Chapter 5**

Jill French had been put in charge of supervising the river bank search. It had proved to be a pretty futile exercise as nowhere on the mile and a half stretch of both sides of the river had thrown up any connection to either the victim or any signs of a violent incident having taken place. Except one unusual find which Jill French was showing to Dornan and Healy back at H.Q. It was a business card.

"Azrael. Retribution & Vengeance."

'Where was this found?' asked Dornan.

'It was on a tree by the river. Quite close to The Four Pillars as it happens. A police constable saw it by chance really.' replied French.

'What do you think it means?'

'No idea ma'am. Maybe an ad for a heavy metal band or something. Nothing probably.'

'OK. Have it sent to the lab anyway.'

'Yes ma'am.'

'And Jill. Well done.'

***

Joe Turner, my friend and now client, and I were sitting in a bright but nevertheless bleak, interview room in Pitt Street Police Headquarters. I couldn't say whether Joe's head was spinning or he was feeling under any sort of pressure. I only knew that I was. I was also aware of how attractive D.I. Susan Dornan was. The introductions were made, the tape machine switched on and the roll call of those present made 'for the benefit of the tape.'

'Right Joe, how you coping?' asked Matt Healy.

'Alright,' replied a bedraggled Joe.

'We need to go over one or two things. Anything you want to tell us first?'

'No.'

'OK. Joe we've spoken to a couple of members of your staff in The Star and Garter and they said that you told them you were going to be away on business the week-end Kate was killed, for four days to be exact.'

'No, they're pissheads, that was the week-end before.'

'Right. Where were you away to on business?'

'Madrid.'

'How did you get there?'

'Drove.'

'Long way.'

'Yeah.'

'OK so you were in the Costa Brava last week-end?'

'Yeah.'

My quandary was complete. I knew then that I should have dismissed myself from representing him but Joe wasn't stupid. He had thought over things and when we had met up outside the station he had told me that he had only been kidding about being in Edinburgh 'winding you up mate.' I had to defend my client's position even if I didn't believe what he was saying for one minute; or at least say nothing.

'How come none of your staff in The George saw you either then?'

'Cause they're all arseholes as well.'

'Need to do better than that Joe. Somebody has to have seen you.'

'Loads of people, yeah.'

'Fine. Names?'

'God I don't know...loads. Juan.'
'Juan who?'
'Don't know his second name.'

Healy lent forward on the desk, stared into Joe Turner's eyes.

'Why do you think Kate had her wedding rings off Joe?'

'Told you already...don't know.'
'You carry a photo of Kate, Joe?'
'Yeah, so?'
'She doesn't carry one of you.'
'So?'
'So why you think that is Joe? Didn't she love you Joe? Thinking of leaving you was she Joe?'

'Better ask her.' Joe regretted it as soon as he said it.

'Not very nice thing to say Joe. You glad she's dead Joe?'

'Don't talk bollocks. I loved her.'

'But did she love you Joe? Scorned partners do crazy things sometimes. Did you do something crazy Joe?'

Joe Turner jumped to his feet, slammed his fist on the table and leaned forward. Matt Healy never flinched.

'This is shit. Fuck this.'

'Joe, sit down. The sooner we get this over with the better.' Susan Dornan was the Good Cop.

'Joe, do you think Kate may have been meeting someone in Glasgow? A man.'

Joe slumped back into his chair, his anger dissipated along with his spirit.

'Who knows.'
'But it's possible?'
'Suppose.'

'Does the name Tunstall mean anything to you?'

'No, where is it?'

*'Cool Joe, cool'* thought Healy.

'You've never seen Kate wearing a gold necklace with the name Tunstall on it?'

'Told you, no, Tunstall?'

'If Kate was meeting a man can you think who it might be?

'No idea, honest. I still can't get my head around the whole thing.'

'Did she have any men friends in Glasgow, pals from the old days that sort of thing.'

Joe looked up, he seemed to be almost pleased.

'There was one guy she used to meet with when she was in Glasgow, ex-boyfriend but lot older than her, but she told me all about him, married, kids, bit of a sado according to Kate.'

'What's his name?'

'Pete something. Hold on ....Old Grey Whistle Test, I called him........Harris, that's it, Peter Harris'.

'Did she tell you she was going to meet him on this trip?'

'Yeah, no, shit I don't know.'

'You going to be in Glasgow a few more days? '

'Yeah, a few more days.'

'We'll need a sample of your DNA Joe, for elimination purposes. OK.'

Joe looked at me. I nodded.

'Fine.'

'You still staying in the B&B in Partick?'

'Yeah, it's close to Martha but not too close if you know what I mean. Might move though, think the manager, cleaner or whoever have helped themselves to a couple of things. Not certain though, might just have lost them, been drinking a lot.'

'How do you get on with Martha anyway Joe?'

'OK I suppose. I always felt she thought Kate could have made more of herself if she hadn't hooked up with me. Maybe she was right. Doesn't really matter now though, does it?'

'You ever hit Kate Joe?' Healy asked quietly.

'Go to hell.'

I interrupted.

'I think we should leave it at that if you don't mind.'

Joe Turner knew he was smirking, knew he shouldn't be, but he hated cops especially the arrogant ones *like this tosser Healy.*

*Anyway, the odd slap is not hitting, not really.*

As we all left the interview room we all knew that Joe's DNA was not for elimination purposes.

***

Boom Boom was relatively sober. As sober as someone who had drunk what he had drunk over the last ten years can be.

He was sitting in his new home by the river and had all his possessions beside him. It was always a source of amazement to him but no matter what seemed to happen in his life and for no matter how long he spent in his "other place", his possessions were always there by his side.

Since discovering the girl's body he had managed to pretty much eliminate her from his thoughts, one way or the other. It was his dinner time. He didn't know what time it was for other people but that was the time it was for him. He sat scooping tuna out of a tin with his new knife. He couldn't quite recall now where he had gotten it but was grateful for it none the less.

He had thought about moving on, right on, England maybe because, although he didn't remember exactly why, he knew he was in trouble. He knew that he had encountered death many times, touched it, sometimes loved it but he had never caused it, never delivered it.

*What about this time? So many blanks, so many questions, so many doubts. Father Tobin should have lived, why did God do that to one of his servants? His bare arms enveloping him, his soothing words whispered from behind, their gentle secret.*

He knew the main thing was his mother not finding out what he'd done, whatever it was. He hated the never ending hours alone in his room and his mother's shrill voice repeating over and over that *Colin was such a naughty boy.*

*Well he had a tin of tea now, he couldn't have been too bad, couldn't have done it.*

Professor Colin Banks' mother had been dead for 15 years.

***

*A picture of Kate Turner and the necklace, Tunstall, had appeared in the Evening Times and on Reporting Scotland a couple of evenings before and that had worried him a bit but coverage was brief and patchy. The fact that Tunstall was "foreign" and that one person a week is stabbed to death in Scotland added to the apathy. Azrael's only concern was the hotel. He'd paid cash and the receptionist was foreign and couldn't even talk properly but he harboured a nagging doubt. He had thought for a moment of going to the hotel to check on her, maybe pass her on the pavement, see if she recognised him, but decided not to. The Lord would guide him.*

***

Dornan had gone to the machine for a coffee after letting Joe Turner go and was walking back to her office when she caught up with Matt Healy talking to John Frame. Frame had just taken a call from the finger print people saying that two sets of prints from the call box in the Clyde Valley had been matched with records. They belonged to a Peter Harris and a Colin Banks

'Did you say fucking Peter Harris?' asked Matt Healy.

'Yes sir and a Colin Banks,' replied DC Allan.

'What's Harris on record for?'

'That's the thing Matt. Harris was questioned over the suspicious death of his first wife but nothing ever stuck. His prints are on record though for giving his second wife a slap. He was charged but his wife didn't want to pursue it. Banks is just a couple of vagrancy related things.'

Frame handed Dornan Harris's address.

'Get two uniforms to meet me and D.S. Healy outside in no more than five minutes' said Susan Dornan.

'Yes ma'am. What about me ma'am?' replied Frame.

'You found out where Kate Turner was staying yet?'

'No ma'am.'

'Well that's what to concentrate on then. Oh and Banks. Where does he live?'

'No fixed abode ma'am.'

'Right. Check with hostels etc but where she stayed is the priority.'

Matt Healy was pensive in the car on the way to Uddingston to question Peter Harris. He knew from experience that murder enquiries are either wrapped up within weeks or not at all. The fact that Peter Harris was an ex - boyfriend, albeit a long time ago, of Kate Turner also fitted in nicely with his oft trumpeted notion of victims already knowing their killers. However he still harboured a deep suspicion over Joe Turner's part in all this.

'What you thinking Matt?' Susan Dornan enquired.

'Not sure,' replied Healy. 'If this guy's semen is a match with one of the samples then it's looking good but I still have a stone in my shoe over Joe Turner.'

'A stone in your shoe?'

'Yeah, you never seen The Godfather then?'

'You think he did it? Flew over, murdered his cheating wife and then flew back again all within forty eight hours.'

'Why not?'

'Just doesn't seem feasible to me. Sorry.'

'We'll see. I've got French checking passenger lists.'

The two police cars arrived outside Peter Harris' house. Healy and Dornan went to the door, white plastic with matching window frames, the two constables waited around the back just in case Harris decided to run. Healy pressed the doorbell.

'Mr Peter Harris?' it was Dornan who asked. Softly, softly at this stage.

'Yes.'

Both Healy and Dornan noticed that Harris looked as if he hadn't slept in a week.

'We'd like to ask you some questions concerning the death of Kate Turner. We understand you knew her.'

Peter Harris had read of Kate's murder in the Evening Times. He didn't know what mode he was now in; denial, panic, distraught, defensive.

'Yes, yes I did. My wife and children will be back soon, can we do this at the station?'

That was a new one on Dornan. Usually the last place a suspect wanted to go was away from familiar surroundings, but all to the good. Peter Harris got his coat and the entourage entered the Pitt Street office car park half an hour later. The interview room used this time was not the same one Joe Turner and Martha Reid had been in, but it was equally pleasant to the eye.

'Will I need a lawyer?' Peter Harris asked quietly.

'Don't know...will you?' it was Matt Healy asking the questions now.

'No.'

'Good, let's get started then.'

'Tell us about your relationship with Kate, Peter.'

'We've been friends for years.....childhood sweethearts.'

'Well her childhood at least,' Dornan suggested trying to illicit a reaction.

'Not in the way you're implying' countered Harris.

'What about recent times?'

'What about them?'

'Well, when was the last time you saw her for instance.'

'OK I know I should have come forward sooner but I have a wife...you understand.'

'You didn't come forward at all Peter, we came looking for you.'

'Oh I knew you would. It was no secret that Kate and I met up occasionally when she was back in Glasgow.'

'So did you meet up this time?'

'Yes.'

'When? Where?'

'We met up for a quick drink and chat early on the Saturday evening.'

'The Saturday evening?'

'Of the weekend she apparently went missing.'

'You're telling us you met up with a woman who ends up murdered a couple of hours later and it didn't cross your mind we might want to speak to you? Where did you meet, go?'

'I picked her up from outside the Superstore at Celtic Park. That idiot of a husband of hers is football mad. She was buying some stuff, posters that kind of thing for his pubs.'

'You know Joe Turner?'

'No.'

'Pretty strong opinion of him though.'

'Kate told me.'

'What, Kate told you her husband was an idiot?'

'No not exactly but over the years they've grown apart. She was always too good for him.'

Dornan noticed that Peter Harris now looked quite relaxed, pleased to talk about Kate.

'Where did you go after you picked her up?'

'The Four Pillars, out the Clyde Valley.'

'Long way to go for a quick chat and drink wouldn't you say.'

'It's one of the places we used to go to when we were courting.'

'Nice. Romantic?'

'I think so.'

'And were you trying to be romantic Peter?'

'No, not in the way you're meaning anyway.'

'What way's that?'

'Sexual. There was nothing sexual involved. Just nostalgia.'

'Nothing sexual?'

'No.'

'Kate had sexual encounters with at least two different men over that 48 hour period Peter. Anything to say about that?'

Peter Harris looked straight into the eyes of Susan Dornan. She could not determine if there was fear, disbelieve or defiance there but she could tell that Peter Harris' world had changed forever.

\*\*\*

John Frame and Paul Allan were now working on two main aspects of the case; where Kate Turner stayed on the Friday night and tracing Colin Banks. The problem was the hotel, or wherever, was a dead end. If the thinking was that she was kipping up with some guy then her name wouldn't be shown anywhere anyway and there are literally thousands of people passing through Glasgow every week-end. If a photo in the paper and her picture on the telly hadn't generated any leads, and with not even her mum or husband coming up with any suggestions about where she might have stayed, then what chance did they have. Paul Allan decided to concentrate on Colin Banks. The link to the murder was more tenuous than the hotel but he might get a result and then go back to the hotel thing on a high. He had dug out the file on Colin Banks and it was startling to say the least. He might be a down and out alky now but at one time he was anything but. Professor Colin Banks was at one time a respected surgeon at Glasgow's Ross Hall Hospital. It didn't say in his file but Allan felt that surely something catastrophic must have happened about fifteen or so years ago to cause this scale of fall from grace. Allan had checked all the hostels and spoken to some of the down and outs who lived under the arches and derelict sites around Glasgow but nothing came up. He decided to talk to the hospital. It was a long shot but he might get some useful back ground information. He phoned the hospital and, after a slight delay while the receptionist enquired who would be the best person for him to speak to, he was slightly surprised to be put through to Mary Stringer, one of the hospitals Clinical Psychologists. Allan explained why he was calling.

'You'd better come in and see me officer. I certainly can't discuss this over the phone.'

Allan had really only been going to try and find out where Banks lived but something told him there was more. Paul Allan had never been more right.

***

After giving a DNA sample Peter Harris had been released. Dornan and Healy both knew they could have pressed him further but felt they wanted the DNA result before they really put the pressure on. They were both confident Harris wouldn't try to run. Dornan had also sent a couple of officers to pick up Joe Turner and bring him in for "an update"; and to allow Healy to follow – up on his conviction that Joe Turner was somehow involved in the murder.

'Where's boy wonder?' Healy asked no-one in particular.

'Out all day sir. Trying to locate that Colin Banks guy I think,' DC Jack T'Baht replied.

'Think John Frame left something on your desk though sir' DC Jill French added.

He looked at the note on his desk and was, for a short while, glad Dornan had let Harris go and was bringing Joe Turner back in. He showed the note to Susan Dornan and smiled.

'What am I always telling you?'

Dornan just shook her head.

***

When Joe called me to say the police wanted to speak to him again I wasn't surprised. I had resolved that when Joe's inevitable call came I was going to tell him that I couldn't represent him. I would make up some legal explanation but Joe would know the truth. But when it came to the crunch I felt I couldn't let a life - long friend down. Also, he was entitled to representation, a defence, and I did not actually know that he had done anything wrong at all. I therefore found myself sitting in the same interview room as I had a couple of days previously, an unidentifiable liquid from the coffee machine in the hall in a paper cup in front of me.

'Afternoon Joe. How you bearing up?'

'Just great,' Joe replied.

'How's Edinburgh these days?'

Joe sat and stared. He knew he was in trouble but his spirit had been slowly ebbing away over the last few days anyway and he actually felt a sense of relief that he could just be straight now.

*Straight-ish.*

'Look OK I lied. I was with someone....a woman...while my wife was being murdered. Would you broadcast that?'

'I would if it eliminated me from being a suspect.'

'What? Are you serious? You think I killed Kate?'

'You've lied already and told us things weren't great between you and agreed Kate could have been meeting a man here so ....'

'I loved her. I....,' Joe was wilting fast, the full realisation of his stupid plan enveloping him.

'What is the woman's name Joe? The one you say you were with.'

'Look she's married I don't want...oh Jesus.' Joe's head was in his hands, his tears glistening through his fingers.

'So let me get this right. You are seeing a woman and you want to keep that fact from your wife. She's flying off to her mum thousands of miles away and so, out of all the places in the world you could take your lady friend, you practically follow behind your wife ?'

'She's cultured, wanted to see the castle, all that shit.'

'Understand what she sees in you then' Dornan said. I could have objected to that comment but in all honesty I could see her point. I also found her manner very attractive.

Joe Turner just stared.

Over the next half hour Joe gave the woman's name and how she could be contacted. He begged Healy to make sure the Spanish police were discrete when they went to question her. He also swore he never came through to Glasgow. We left the police office and parted on the street outside. I told Joe I had to get back to the office. In truth I was going for a drink. I just didn't want him with me. I had to think.

***

Dornan and Healy sat in Susan Dornan's room. Dornan didn't like Joe Turner but believed him. Healy didn't like him much either and definitely didn't believe him.

'It was the husband. No doubt.'

'No Harris is our man.'

'Weekend in Marbella says it's Turner.'

'Deal.'

The word had come out of Dornan's mouth before she had really thought about what the bet actually was. Healy left her office with more than a hint of a smile, Dornan followed, a look of bewilderment on her face.

The DNA results from the semen samples would be available in the next couple of days. Dornan and Healy were both confident things would be clearer then.

'Susan, fancy a quick drink tonight?'

Susan felt awkward. She might be reading Matt Healy all wrong but woman's intuition and all that.

*It was only one drink.*

'OK, fine.'

'Maybe catch a bite to eat,' said Healy, 'hear Dan's Diner is not bad.'

***

'Colin Banks was a very good surgeon officer. Some would say a little bit strange, distant, childlike, odd even but it was when his mother died he completely retreated into his own world.' explained Mary Stringer to Paul Allan as they sat in her office in Ross Hall hospital.

'In what way?' asked Paul Allan.

'You have to understand the background officer. It's not an excuse for what Colin became; merely a partial explanation.'

'Can you tell me...this is a murder investigation.'

'Colin Banks lived with his mother right up until her death about fifteen years ago. She was the real monster in my opinion; a domineering, frightful woman. A staunch catholic in the very worst sense, she brought up Colin alone after her husband ran off with another woman when Colin was only one or two. Guilt and punishment were the order of the day and an almost pathological hatred of women, "fallen, all of them, sluts". Colin never stood a chance.'

'Yet he became surgeon.'

'Oh yes he was extremely intelligent but the pull of Oedipus is strong officer, too strong for many to resist.'

Paul Allan wasn't exactly sure what that statement meant but he had a very uncomfortable feeling about it.

'Please go on.' he urged.

'As I said Colin was always a little bit odd but after his mother's death things started to be noticed here and eventually a Funeral Home Director contacted us to question if it wouldn't be more appropriate if our research were carried out at the hospital.'

'What kind of research?'

'That's just it we didn't know what he was talking about.'

'So Banks was carrying out research on his own?'

'I wish that were the case officer. I do so wish that. To cut a long and complex story short Colin Harris had been removing tissue from dead patients, females only. He didn't have access to enough dead bodies here in the hospital and so he had approached some Undertakers with a complex story about vital research, saying he only needed a short period of access to the bodies. Paid them of course, no questions asked. It was later found out he was removing tissue from the bodies.'

'What was he doing with the tissue?'

Mary Stringer shrugged.

'That's not all I'm afraid.'

'Oh.'

'It was noticed that a certain substance appeared on the bodies or the coffin or sometimes here on the sheets of a dead patient's bed.'

'Certain substance?'

'Semen.'

Paul Allan thought he might well throw up.

'You mean...?'

'Strictly no, not necrophilia, penetration never took place. Colin Banks masturbated over the bodies. You know officer a man is far more likely to turn into the thing he hates than kill that thing.'

'Meaning?'

'He became a hater of women.'

Paul Allan thanked Mary Stringer and left her office as quickly as possible, more for fresh air than a desire to get back to the station. He was glad it was now his week-end off, he needed a drink and to take his mind off what he had just heard.

Like any major city Glasgow has a wide cross section of the human condition, and an ample number of night clubs to cater for all tastes. At any given moment in time there are "in" places, "so yesterday" places, and places that trendy footballers and policemen are never seen. These clubs are otherwise known as gay clubs.

Paul Allan was always discreet and he was sure that no-one on the force knew about his private life. He wasn't entirely sure why it was that he felt he had to keep his sexuality private, he just knew that it would be better all round.

He was standing at the bar in Bennets, Glasgow's foremost gay club. He was relaxed enough and was receiving admiring glances but despite downing a couple of JD's and cranberry he couldn't get Colin Banks' past proclivities out of his head.

*And they call us queer. Jesus Christ.*

## Chapter 6

A fortnight had now passed since the killing of Kate Turner. Pressure had been put on the Forensics labs to produce the results for the DNA samples that had been sent but sheer volumes of work meant that no specific times could be guaranteed. However Dornan had received a call the previous evening to say that the results would be known in the morning. Dornan had called Healy and they had agreed to meet up at 7.00am. Healy still had a good feeling about the way their drinks night had gone. Susan Dornan spent the drive into work wondering how to deal with what she felt was becoming an awkward situation. Maybe she should be flattered but for reasons too numerous to count there was no chance of a romantic relationship with Matt Healy forming. *No way.* She would have to let him know, but how to do it without causing a rift between them or, even worse, having to request a move for Healy, further damaging his career and self-esteem. She would mention in general conversation that she had a date the following night and that would maybe ease the situation. In truth she had been quite surprised when she had gotten the call from Tom Barbour, a man she had met a few nights previously in the Merchant City, but he *seemed nice* and he had booked "Rococco" for a meal so he was no meanie. U*nless he expected her to go Dutch of course.*

They had both grabbed for what passed as coffee and were sitting in Dornan's room along with DC Paul Allan. The rest of the squad hadn't arrived yet.

'Jesus fucking Christ.' but for once Matt Healy wasn't shouting at Allan who had just recounted his conversation with Mary Stringer.

The DNA results from the two sets of semen found on Kate Turner's body had come in that morning as promised. One didn't throw up any matches but it had been confirmed that one of them belonged to Peter Harris.

'Right let's think this through. We've got that bastard Harris but that still leaves one sample of semen unaccounted for,' stated Susan Dornan.

'What if Banks....you know.' Allan glanced at Dornan as he spoke.

'We don't even know Banks was anywhere near the body. We've got to find him though. Absolute fucking must' said Healy.

'The other semen sample could be the mystery boyfriend's since we know for sure it's not Joe Turner's' Allan was enjoying his input.

It had been confirmed at the same time Harris was put in the frame that Joe Turner was out the immediate picture for now. Dornan was somehow pleased about that, she felt Joe Turner was a bit of an arse but he'd been through a lot, and Healy could maintain his theory on murder still stood; Kate obviously knew Harris. But in some ways the results didn't change a thing for Healy.

'We don't know for sure there is a boyfriend Susan. But yeah let's assume there is. It still doesn't prove that Turner didn't kill his wife. Jesus this is a right fucking mess but well done Paul '

'OK Paul you concentrate on finding that weirdo Banks. Matt you and I will pick up Harris. I'll get the rest to keep trying on the hotel thing although I think that's a waste of time. And see when this is over I want that hospital investigated. ' Dornan said.

Paul Allan left the room with only one thought in his head, Matt Healy had just called him Paul.

*Cause for celebration or what?*

'I've organised a couple of back-up Susan but hopefully this will be same as last time. Unless his wife kicks off of course, hope the kids are at school.'

When they reached his house Peter Harris was not at home. His wife Sally opened the door. Dishevelled and strained looking. She also had bruising clearly visible around her left eye and she had obviously been crying.

'Are you Mrs Harris?' asked Dornan.

'Yes.'

'Is your husband at home? Are you OK?'

'No, no he's not. Come in.'

Dornan and Healy were shown into the living room. It was neat and tidy; perhaps surprisingly so given that two children also lived here. Sally Harris sensed their reactions.

'Peter insists on the house being tidy.'

'Really. Where is he at the moment?'

'I don't know. Honestly.'

'Is there anything you want to tell us Sally?'

Sally Harris slumped rather than sat down onto the couch. Susan Dornan sat down beside her. Healy sat on the edge of the coffee table.

'I'm leaving him.'

'Why? Because he hits you?'

'No. Because he killed that woman.'
'What woman?'
'Kate Turner.'
'How do you know?'
'On the night she died, he phoned me from a call box. Said he had a burst tyre somewhere out Lanark way. When he got in he had dirt all over him and blood on his hands. Some on his T shirt. I asked what had happened. He said the jack was useless and had slipped a couple of times and caught his fingers, that the dirt was from changing the tyre and wiping his hands and stuff.'
'Did you believe him?'
'No reason not to at the time.'
'When did you start to think something was wrong?'
'Last night. I was cleaning in here and found an old copy of the Times down the back of the couch. When I read the story about the dead woman being from Spain, her name, I put two and two together.'
'What did you do?'
'I confronted him.'
'What did he say?'
'He laughed. Shouted at me. "Killed her? Why would I do that? I loved her." God how I hate him.'
'What are you going to do?'
'Collect the kids from school. Go down to my mother's in England. Stay there till I pull my thoughts together.'
'Write down the address and phone number Sally. We'll need to talk to you again.'
'It won't be the first time you know.'
'What won't?'

'That he's killed someone.'
'What do you mean?'
'Ann, his first wife. He killed her. He told me. Some sort of row over the kids. I thought he was just trying to scare me. Not now.'

\*\*\*

The owner of Mario's Restaurant, not far from Boom Boom's spot, was getting a bit hacked off. He complied every time with Council regulations about putting waste food out and nearly every time the next morning the refuse bags were open. Sometimes it was probably the foxes he saw quite regularly in the area, other times he knew it was the bloody tramp who was always hanging around. He had complained to the police but that had been a waste of time. This time though wasn't going to be because the tramp was still there, sleeping beside the discarded food.

'Sir, sir wake up please sir,' said Constable Toal as he shook the tramp.

The tramp came round. He was stinking but seemed sober enough. Normally Toal would have told him to shove off somewhere else but he remembered word was out that the murder squad guys were looking for a "no fixed abode".

'What's your name sir?' Toal asked.

'Professor Colin Banks at your service constable.'

Constable Toal radioed in and quickly received word to bring Banks in immediately. *Gold Star for me then.*

\*\*\*

Frame and Allan conducted the interview.

'Where are you living these days Colin?' John Frame asked.

'Everywhere my good man. No fixed abode as they say.'

'Lived out the Clyde Valley recently?'

'Quite possibly, memory not all that it was I'm afraid. A virus I suspect.'

'Booze I suspect.'

'Yes I like a small libation I admit, good for the heart, keeps out the cold.'

'What's your favourite tipple then Colin?'

'Anything I can afford young man, even brake fluid if necessary.'

'Jesus.'

'It's OK, I can stop anytime. Get it? Chic Murray would appreciate that one don't you think?' Boom Boom added with droll comic timing.

Frame suppressed a smile, Allan was too intense to even notice.

'That was a nice knife we found in your pocket Colin?'

'Yes, fine workmanship.'

'Where you get it?'

'Seek and ye shall find.'

'Where?'

'By a river, dammed if I can remember which one though old chap.'

'Would that be the river next to the phone box you were in the other week. The time you found the dead girl and graciously phoned the police to let us know.'

'Ah. Quite possibly.'

'You don't seem too bothered by these questions Mr Banks, sorry Professor Colin

Banks once of Ross Hall Hospital and various Undertakers of these parts.'

'Ah.'

'Ah. That all you have to say?' it was Paul Allan who asked.

'Long time ago dear boy besides nothing ever proved. I've moved on to another life now.'

'Yes you have Colin, problem is your old ways seemed to have gone with you.'

'Ah.'

'The name 'Tunstall' mean anything to you Colin?'

'Hand maiden to the Greek goddess Aphrodite?'

'Eh?'

'Only teasing. No, nothing.'

'You kill the woman Colin?'

'Certainly not. I am a doctor, I have taken the Hippocratic oath sir. I found the body, poor lass, phoned you lot and moved on. I have committed no crime.'

'Wanking over a dead body, stealing a mobile phone and money, disturbing a crime scene, I'd say there's a crime or two there Colin.'

Frame was guessing but he was pretty sure.

'You have no evidence I stole anything. As for the rest, my lawyer will challenge your assertions that an actual crime was committed in a court of law.'

Frame noticed he hadn't denied his first point.

'Lock him up, take DNA sample, get him overalls, send what passes for clothes to the lab.'

Frame and Allan were leaving the Interview Room.

'Officers, I'll be entitled to three meals a day I assume.'

Frame nodded.

'Thank you,' replied Professor Colin Boom Boom Banks.

Frame and Allan walked back towards the squad room not quite sure what to make of Colin Banks.

'Well Paul you've got a dilemma.'

'What's that?'

'Whether to charge our Professor friend with interfering with a crime scene, or interfering with himself.'

\*\*\*

Dornan and Healy had arrived back from Harris's house. Healy was busy arranging an arrest warrant for Harris. The phone went on Susan Dornan's desk.

'Dornan.'

'Yes, hello, it's Julie Connor.'

'Sorry I .....'

'From The Marriott Hotel.....Kate Turner's friend.'

'Oh yes, hello Julie. Sorry, There's a lot happening.'

'I understand, it's just that I think I should speak to you.'

'OK, what about?'

'Joe.'

'Joe Turner? What about him?'

'Kate was leaving him, she'd met someone.'

Susan Dornan reflected immediately on Matt Healy's conviction that Joe Turner might well be the killer. She waved him over. Julie Connor agreed to come into the station immediately, as being questioned in the hotel was not really an option, not with delegates from the 2014 Commonwealth Games Committee swanking around the foyer. Julie Connor had a haunted look as she sat in, the deliberately bleak, Interview Room 2. She told Dornan and Healy that Kate had been in touch both before the fateful week-end and that she had been part of Kate's alibi should the shit hit the fan.

'What shit might that have been?' Dornan knew but sympathised with Julie's awkwardness.

'Kate had met someone, she was leaving Joe as soon as she could but the kids were the issue.'

'Who had she met?'

'I don't know, honestly I don't '

'Could it have been Peter Harris?'

Both Dornan and Healy could see the surprise in Julie Connor's eyes.

'No way.'

'You know him then?'

'Yeah, you could say that. It wasn't him. That's a definite.'

'You seem awful sure of that.'

'She would have said but no, believe me, it wasn't him.'

'Do you think the guy is from Glasgow or Spain or what?'

'I don't think Spain. Why meet him here if he is?'

'Did she even mention a first name?'

'No. Any time I asked she just laughed.'

'Was it Tunstall?'

'I don't know. Possibly. Why?"

Dornan and Healy could tell Julie Connor wasn't telling the whole story. She was fidgeting in her chair, twisting her hair around her fingers and looking generally agitated.

'What else is bothering you Julie?'

'Joe was very jealous of Kate. He knew, especially in recent years, that she had out grown him. He was terrified she would leave him and......'

'And what?'

'Well you know he was in prison, a long time ago that is, when he was a boy, for stabbing someone.'

It was Dornan and Healy's turn to look incredulous not even bothering to try to hide their surprise. Dornan thanked Julie for her help and quickly wound up the interview. A few minutes after showing Julie out Dornan sat in her office as Healy paced the room.

Depending on how long ago the conviction had been, if Joe Turner had been a juvenile at the time, a cursory check would not have come up with this information. As far as Healy was concerned it was another tick in the "close relative dun it box". Harris was still very much in the picture but there was something about this Joe Turner guy that ate away at Healy. Dornan still felt Harris had raped Kate and then, perhaps in a panic, had killed her but where the knife would have come from at the critical point was something even she didn't have an answer for. On Healy's insistence the barmaid from The 4 Pillars had been brought in to ID Harris in a parade. He knew that an I.D from a photo was no good. Some smart – arse defence lawyer could always raise doubt by going on about the angle of the picture, the age the defendant was at the time, anything to plant the germ of "a reasonable doubt." She confirmed Harris was the man in the bar with Kate and that they'd obviously had a row but had also stated that there was no way Harris could have gone into the kitchens unnoticed and lifted a knife. A search of the kitchen had also confirmed that they didn't have any knives similar to the one used in the murder. As Julie Connor left the station, a strange feeling of guilt and relief enveloped her. Healy had resolved to have another crack at Joe Turner the next day.

The following morning CID were sharing a laugh over an article in the day's Daily Record, or Daily Retard as the officers called it, as Susan Dornan entered the room. Two groups of youths, one that had been breaking into garden sheds and another that had been breaking into cars, had been jailed the day before after being arrested the previous January through in Edinburgh after the police had followed their footsteps in the snow straight back to their front doors.

'Surprised Lothian Division could even manage that,' quipped Healy on hearing the story

'Maybe brought in Rebus' suggested Frame.

Dornan indicated for Allan to go through to her office.

'What's the latest on Colin Banks?'

'Definite fruitcake but I just don't see him for the murder ma'am.'

Although "Of No Fixed Abode", no previous record of violence and the fact that he had phoned in the whereabouts of the body, had allowed him to be released on bail that morning. He had also agreed to phone some solicitor, a friend from Jesuit boot camp days, who to

Dornan's admiration appeared to have stuck by his friend despite his fall from respectability, every few days to see if the police wanted to speak to him. She considered that he was still very much in the frame for some sort of criminal charge. She just wasn't entirely sure which one.

Allan had looked further into Banks' past and had established that although he had never actually been convicted of any serious offence it was generally accepted that Colin Banks was a deeply troubled individual that the medical authorities had been right to quietly remove from the profession and that no purpose would have been served by calling in the police. Although Allan hadn't been sure about that, he did agree that an actual conviction would have been difficult. His eyes were further opened by the fact that doctors removing tissue and parts from bodies was not as isolated an occurrence as people may think. There was an apparently lucrative market involving doctors removing body parts, including bones, without patient or relative consent, and selling them on to legitimate "Biomedical Services" who in turn sell them on to other doctors for transplant purposes. Allan couldn't decide if what Banks was doing was worse or better than that. When he had asked if relatives hadn't noticed missing bones from arms or legs at funerals he had been told that the bones had been replaced by PVC piping. Allan's innocent acceptance of the medical profession had been destroyed forever.

Healy had felt that the fact that Banks' erratic behaviour had seemed to intensify when his mother had died warranted the exhumation of her body. If a post mortem established that she had in fact been murdered then a precedent of his ability to be a killer was there and Banks would have to be considered in a new light. Dornan felt that in reality Banks was just a sad weirdo, perhaps a victim of an overbearing mother but she could see Healy's reasoning.

***

Joe Turner was not a happy man. He had tried to book a flight back to Gerona but Celtic were playing Barcelona in a Champions League tie in Barcelona and Ryanair had hiked the fares up knowing fans would be travelling en masse and he wasn't prepared to pay the inflated prices. He knew if he waited another day the flights would be at least half. Now though he was sitting in the police station waiting to speak to the police again ruefully regretting his decision. The good looking female cop appeared at a door just to the right of the foyer desk and summoned him in. They walked in silence down to the interview room he had already been in before.

'How's things Joe?' Matt Healy asked.

'Shit. That it? Can I go now?' Joe replied.

'You got a problem Joe?'

'No, no. My wife's just been murdered by a guy I told her to stay away from, my business is going to fuck and I'm sitting here again. Why would I have a problem?'

'You seem very aggressive Joe.'

'You think this is aggressive? '

'Kate was leaving you Joe. You know it and now we know it.'

'Shit.'

'She'd found someone new Joe. Loved him by all accounts. You were history.'

'Who told you that?'
'Couple of people actually.'
'Shit.'
'You knew, didn't you?'
'Shit.'
'Ever stabbed anyone Joe?'

Joe's mind was racing. He knew that the police obviously knew about his past, and about Kate, he knew he would have to tread carefully.

'That was thirty-odd years ago for Christ's sake and Kate was not leaving me.'

'She was. You know it and I know it. Kate's PM showed that she had old bruises as well as new bruises Joe. You hit her?'

'No.'

'Don't believe you.'

'Tough shit for you then. Prove it.'

Matt Healy and Susan Dornan watched Joe Turner walk away from the station. They had batted another couple of questions and loaded statements between them but they had nothing concrete to hold Joe Turner with.

'It was him.' Matt Healy said.

'I don't know. I still think it was Harris.'

Healy turned to Dornan and smiled 'Fancy discussing it over a meal?'

Susan Dornan was torn. She liked Matt Healy, perhaps more than she should, but there were just too many obstacles to it being a smart move. The date with Tom Barbour had gone well. He seemed like a decent enough guy but somehow that vital spark wasn't there for her. She felt that he would probably call her again and that maybe she should persevere, but wondered at the same time that if you had to try hard to really like someone then perhaps that person wasn't right for you in the first place. She had had a couple of dates in the last few months or so that were similar scenarios and she sometimes pondered that it was her who was too fussy but, on the other hand, maybe some fairy tales did come true.

She looked at Healy.

'OK.'

'Great. Lauders at eight?'

'Fine.'

Susan Dornan realised assertiveness was not her strong point when it came to male relationships.

***

Joe Turner had phoned me on my mobile. I felt an underlying sense of uneasiness that he was now in touch with me so often. It seemed more than friendship or just keeping me informed.

'Have you been speaking to the police?'

'No. Why would I? Have you?'

I was telling the truth. Despite my concerns I just had not been able to contact the police, to betray my friend.

'Yes. They questioned me again this morning.'

'Why didn't you call me?'

'Don't know. Anyway, I can handle it. Sorry mate. It's just that someone has been speaking to them. Know all about me, even stuff from 30 years ago. They know Kate was going to leave me.'

'No. They're just saying that to rattle you Joe. Ignore them. Besides I didn't know Kate was leaving you. You never told me that.'

'No. It's true, she was. She told me.'

'What? What did you do, say?'

'I scudded her.'

I couldn't take it in. All the doubts, fears, thoughts came flooding back. I was torn between my long term friend; what I knew of his temper and the information I felt he was now drip-feeding me, probing, gauging my reactions, my response.

'You hit her?'

'Not much, a bit.'

'For fuck's sake Joe. Do the police know?'

'No, but you know who I think has been talking?'

'Who?'

'Julie Connor.'

'Talking about what? Did she know?'

'Christ knows but Kate was obviously keeping her in the loop. I'm going to see the fucking bitch.'

'Don't be so stupid Joe. If she is speaking to the police then she'll contact them straight away if you go near her.'

'Not if she can't fucking talk she won't.'

'Don't be such a prick Joe. Are you off your head? Leave it. Go back to Spain.'

'We'll see, got to go. I'll call you.'

My mind was in a fog unsure if I had even just had the conversation. Things were getting out of hand, Joe was out of control. Even so I felt I could not just phone the police directly and betray my friend.

*What, exactly, would I say anyway? You don't know me but my best friend has maybe killed his wife and is maybe going to do the same again. Name?...Sorry I don't want to give my name....get real Ray.*

But I knew I had to do something. If Julie Connor had the courage to go to the police then I had to have the courage of my convictions too.

## Chapter 7

Dornan had called a Case Review meeting. Healy sat in the office with Susan Dornan before going out to address the squad. He really felt things were moving on in his relationship with her. Their meal the other evening had gone well and although "nothing had happened" she had given him a peck on the cheek at the end of the night. Susan Dornan was thinking about their evening as well but in a different light. She couldn't quite understand her own actions when it came to Matt Healy. The evening had been pleasant but not romantic yet she had wanted to kiss him at the end of the night; not passionately, but a kiss none the less. She saw nothing but problems in continuing down this road with one of her own officers but there was something there that made her want it to continue. Perhaps her view, held since childhood, that she would know when "the one" came into her life had been her downfall in the past. Perfectly decent guys had been cast by the wayside because they hadn't lit her fire but maybe a slow build up, mutual respect, solid reliability is what she should be seeking. Dornan turned to the assembled squad. The group looked their usual, tousled, tired and disinterested selves but she knew that was just an image, a front, they were ready.

Susan Dornan spent the next hour outlining the facts and her interpretation of what the situation was now regarding the murder of Kate Turner.

Colin Banks had been found with the murder weapon on him. The knife had only two samples of DNA on it; Banks and Kate Turner's. It had also now been confirmed that Banks' semen had been found on the body. Banks had been in the vicinity of the crime scene at the time of the murder. Kate Turner's DNA had been found on his clothing. Playing Devil's Advocate, but in this case believing her agenda, Dornan outlined reasons for doubting Banks was the killer. Banks was obviously a confused individual with scrambled eggs for brains. His clothes had no traces of Kate Turner's blood on them, DNA yes, but not blood despite the "frenzied" attack. What would Banks' motive have been? Purely sex? Possibly robbery, but unlikely. Kate Turner had definitely been raped but not by Banks; by Harris. So how soon after this had Banks' come along and killed her; and why?

Next issue up was the husband. Dornan let Healy take the floor. Joe Turner was a jealous, violent man. He knew his wife was going to leave him. He was sleeping with another woman; more than likely his wife had a boyfriend. Did he know about the boyfriend? He had lied about being in Scotland at the time of the murder. However, none of the two semen samples found on the body were his. His DNA was not on the knife and he had no blood on his clothing although he could have easily disposed of any stained clothing before the police caught up with him. Healy didn't hide the fact that he rated Turner as his Prime Suspect.

Dornan then moved on to Peter Harris, the favourite of the squad bookie Frame. His semen was present and he had all but admitted to rape. The victim's DNA had been found on his clothing. Her blood had also been found on his clothing but not in amounts consistent with multiple stabbing. His DNA had been found on the inside of the victims thighs, on her underwear and under her finger nails. Harris had basically admitted to everything, with the rape sure to be proved, but consistently denied the murder. Why, to lessen his sentence? The small amount of water in Kate's lungs also backed up the story that Harris left her alive in the water whereas the pathologist said the knife attack meant instant death.

The questions for the squad therefore were; did Harris return, possibly in panic over what he'd done, and kill Kate? Did Banks come along after Harris had left and kill her? Was Joe Turner somehow at the scene and killed her? Did a fourth, as yet unidentified person, kill her?

The briefing split up for lunch and Dornan was sitting in her office with the Procurator Fiscal and Healy. The PF explained that although they had a strong case against Harris, they could only charge him with rape at this point. The defence would also highlight the fact that Kate Turner was almost certainly in Glasgow to see an as yet untraced lover who had disappeared without even reporting her missing. Despite Healy's protestations, the PF also felt that they had no case against Joe Turner so no charges were to be brought against him. Banks was to be charged, in time, with interfering with the scene of a crime but that there was no urgency required for that.

***

Joe Turner was booked on a flight back to Spain for that night and he'd *never be back*. He had decided Kate would be buried in Spain despite Martha's feelings and that bitch cop Dornan could think again if she thought he would fly back to speak to her whenever she fancied; *fuck her and that prick that's always with her.*

Outwardly he was calm but inside his anger was simmering. He stood at the reception of The Marriott in Argyle Street waiting for Julie Connor to appear. The girl on reception had told him that Ms Connor would be right down. He saw her approaching from the corridor in front of the lifts. She was smiling, but nervously. She was slightly surprised that Joe Turner had called in to see her but glad of the diversion. It had given her an excuse to get away from the sad old git who laughingly referred to himself as her father and who had turned up distraught and unannounced at the hotel a half hour previously looking for "sympathy and understanding".

'Where were you all my life when I needed you?' she had shouted at him.

'I was always thinking of you Julie; show some compassion' he replied between his sobs.

'Too little too late. Compassion? For you?' Julie was laughing now.

'I've got to go. Someone's in reception who deserves compassion. Don't be here when I get back.'

She walked out of her office without a backward glance, oblivious to the rage in her visitor's eyes. She saw Joe standing in the foyer, close to the sliding glass entrance.

*He looks like shit. No wonder though.*

'Joe, I'm so sorry about Kate.'

'Sure. Thanks. Fancy going for a coffee or something?'

'I'll order something here.'

'I'd prefer somewhere less plush. What about the pub on the corner?' Joe said sheepishly.

*Never did have much taste, except for Kate. Jesus, what did she ever see in him?*

'Fine let's go.' Julie let the receptionist know she'd be back in an hour.

Neither Joe Turner nor Julie Connor noticed the man watching as they kissed in the hotel foyer, Julie rub his arm familiarly. He watched as she said something to the receptionist and walked out of the hotel, taking Joe Turner's arm as she went.

*Bitch.*

He too left the hotel soon afterwards.

Julie and Joe sat in a booth at the far end of the Public Bar.

*Christ, not even the lounge. Real class Joe, real class.*

The man from the hotel watched their reflection on the large mirror behind the bar from his stool in the deserted Lounge bar. From what he knew of Joe Turner's temper he estimated that it would hold for ten minutes before he confronted her. He was two minutes out, probably because Joe Turner wanted some information from Julie Connor before he hit her.

'Kate was going to leave me.' It was a statement, not a question.

'Look, Joe'

Turner raised his hand to silence her.

'Who was the guy Julie?'

'Joe, I don't want to ....' again the raised hand.

'Was it Harris?'

'No'

'No, then who?'

'I don't....'

The blow from the outside of Turner's right hand took her completely by surprise. A couple of Argyle Street veterans, perched at the bar, didn't bother to look over; they'd seen it all before.

'You bastard.' More a whimper than a shout.

Julie Connor rushed to the door of the Ladies screaming, 'no wonder Kate was leaving you, you fucking arsehole'

The man watched, considered intervening but waited. Intrigued as to what Joe would do now. Turner sat in the booth unsure himself what to do. He rose to head for the door, turned, walked to the Ladies and went in.

Julie was bent over a grubby hand basin, dabbing the side of her face with a damp paper towel.

'I loved Kate, Julie.'

'Well she didn't love you. I wonder why, eh Joe.'

Neither Joe nor Julie would ever be fully aware of what happened in the next few seconds. Blows rained down on Julie, Joe thought of Kate with another man, semen stains, leaving him. When he looked down Julie was sitting in the corner, her face bloodied and tearful, shock and fear in equal measure in her eyes. Joe turned and walked out of the door, crossed the sparse bar area and out into the dull Glasgow afternoon.

The man entered the toilet corridor from the lounge area, unseen.

Julie Connor heard the toilet door opening.

*Was it Turner coming back? Was it the barmaid coming to her aid?*

Her reaction on seeing him coming over to her was one of overwhelming relief, her shock and outrage momentarily dissipated.

*Why had this happened, how, what had come over him?*

Confusion and surprise swirled in her mind but at least she was safe.

The blade was cool as it sliced her neck from the base of one ear to the base of the other. The smart blue suit Julie wore to work was slowly enveloped in a dark red shroud.

The man turned in disgust from the site of the sanitary towel dispenser that Julie Connor's head rested against and left the toilet and bar the anonymous way he had entered.

\*\*\*

Jill French stood at the door of Susan Dornan's office.

'Ma'am, there's been another woman murdered, stabbed.'

'Yeah, I just heard. Welcome to the City of Culture eh.'

French was confused, she couldn't understand Dornan's reaction.

'What are you talking about?'

The tone and urgency in French's voice alerted both Dornan and Healy, something was wrong.

'What are you talking about?'

'Julie Connor, from The Marriott, it's her.'

Dornan, Healy and the rest of the team and all the backup services were at the murder scene within ten minutes. This sealed it for Healy, Joe

Turner was their killer. For a fleeting moment he thought of the weekend in Marbella. The barmaid and the couple of regulars who were in the bar reluctantly gave their statements and although it was obvious they didn't want involved their description of the man who had struck Julie Connor and then followed her into the Ladies matched Joe Turner. She also told them that the guy who had done it was carrying a suitcase. Healy signalled to Dornan to come with him. The Argyle Street pub was just at the base of a slip road onto the M8 motorway which went straight past Glasgow Airport. Healy drove and reached the airport in less than fifteen minutes. Joe Turner was sitting in one of the bars in the Departure Lounge, his bruised fingers wrapped around a pint tumbler.

'Not going to say cheerio Joe?'

Joe Turner looked up.

Dornan was sure he had been crying.

Healy was sure he was a murderer.

'Better come with us Joe.'

'Fine, but the bitch deserved it.'

Matt Healy really was thinking about Marbella now.

***

I have always considered myself to be a diligent enough worker so it was unusual for me to have "thrown a few sickies" recently and I was using up my holiday entitlement fast but how can you sit in an office when you think that someone you know has killed and may well be considering killing again. I sat in my flat, decimating the coffee jar, and trying to reconcile friendship with "the right thing to do." I wished I had one of the many so-called bad habits that other people seemed to have no worries about having; smoking, biting my nails, drugs even, anything that might help alleviate this inner turmoil. I wasn't even into music that much, so I couldn't even allow myself to become absorbed in something like that as a distraction. I kept turning over in my mind that a friend was dead and another friend may well have killed her. I hadn't spoken to Joe for a couple of days, not since he was ranting and raving about Julie Connor, and I wasn't sure that I actually wanted to speak to him, although I did think it was strange that Joe hadn't phoned me from Spain to say he'd arrived back. At that point I became aware that the phone was in fact ringing.

*Christ, this whole thing is freaking me out.*

'Is that you Ray?'

'Yes.' I recognised the voice but wasn't quite sure who it was; a woman from Personnel probably, just checking my current health "status" as they liked to call it these days.

'Hello Ray, its Martha Reid, Kate's mum.'

'Martha. God that's really weird, I was just thinking of Kate and Joe and things. How are you?'

'Well, not too good actually Ray. I have some terrible news.'

*Terrible news, what could be more terrible than what had already happened?*

'Jesus Martha, what's wrong?'

'Kate's friend, Julie Connor, has been murdered.'

All sense of reason, balance, normality left my life as if someone had just flicked a switch. I wasn't sure if I could even talk.

'What..when...how....are you sure?'

'Yes, this afternoon. But it's worse than that Ray. Joe has been arrested for it.'

'How do you know?'

'The police phoned here. I'm the only family member they knew how to contact.'

I had never felt anything like the sensation I felt then. This was my fault, I had killed Julie Connor just as surely as if I had put a gun to her head and pulled the trigger.

*Joe, you fucking, fucking bastard; I will nail you for this, I swear.*

I was breathless yet my chest was heaving at the same time. I had tears in my eyes but wasn't crying. I was angry at Joe Turner, the world, but mostly at myself. I was also resolved. I would be phoning the police as soon as I got off this call. This was the end, it was over for Joe.

'I thought I'd phone you straight away, especially since you spoke to Julie so recently.'

'Yes sure, I understand. Have the police been to see you about this as well Martha?'

'No not yet but I expect they will.'

'I imagine they might. Will you be OK?'

'Yes, I'll be fine. I don't believe Joe had anything to do with any of this Ray. He has his faults God knows but he isn't a killer, I'm sure of that. I'm also going to tell them about what I suspect Kate was up to that week-end. '

'And what was that?'

'Oh I think we both know the answer to that Ray'

I wasn't sure if Martha knew of Joe's violent past and saw no point in bringing it up now. I also sensed a kind of family dignity in her tone, protecting her own in times of crises. I was impressed, humbled even.

'I don't know what to think Martha.'

'Will you go and see him Ray? As a friend if not a lawyer.'

'Well I'm pretty busy at work just now Martha, working from home to-day though, and Joe will probably get out on bail tomorrow. Then again with him resident in Spain I don't know. Christ what a mess.'

'I know Ray I know, all so very sad. I'll tell the police when I speak to them that Joe can stay with me, if they're prepared to release him that is.'

'Yeah, that's good of you Martha, are you sure you want to do that, given the circumstances?'

'I told you Ray, I don't believe for a moment, not a moment, that Joe hurt anyone, especially Kate and what possible reason would he have for killing Julie Connor, the whole thing is totally absurd."

'I'm sure, you're right. Martha, do me a favour and keep me informed about what's happening, especially if the police are coming to speak to you. They might say something I can pass on to help Joe.'

'Oh I will Ray, don't worry. If Joe could rely on anyone it was always you. I'll phone you as soon as I know anything.'

After Martha rang off I sat deep in thought. Unlike her, I was sure Joe had killed Kate and Julie and I knew I should really speak to the police but still my sense of loyalty to a friend was an issue and if I was honest with myself I didn't really want to become too involved in the whole thing. I reasoned that if Joe got out on bail he was bound to phone me and I would take things from there. I sat staring at the phone for a long time. I thought of Kate and Julie, thought of Joe, thought about Martha's call and knew what had to be done.

***

'Becoming quite a regular Joe.' Matt Healy was sitting opposite a rather bedraggled Joe Turner. Susan Dornan was the only other person in the room. Joe Turner "didn't need a lawyer."

'OK, I shouldn't have done it. But that cow Connor has never liked me. Didn't think I was good enough for Kate. Snobby cow. Don't think I don't know she was the bitch who told you about my ancient history.'

'Not that ancient Joe, Kate's body had a number of older bruises remember?'

'Yeah well.'

'Well what? She deserved them did she?'

'It was nothing, the odd push more than anything.'

'And what about Julie Connor, she need a push did she?'

Healy and Dornan were positive Joe Turner had killed Julie Connor, and probably Kate as well. But they were a little put off by the lack of blood on his clothes.

'Look I admit it. I hit her, I shouldn't have, I'm sorry. Charge me and let's get this over with. I've got a flight to catch.'

'Bit more to it than that Joe.'

'Yeah, what?'

Matt Healy kept his anger in check. He wasn't going to blow this. He knew Joe Turner was now a double killer and he wasn't going to let any stupid moves on his part stop putting him away for a long time.

'Julie Connor's dead Joe. That's what.'

Joe Turner looked from Healy to Susan Dornan and back again, trying to suss out the bluff.

'What of, Mad Cow Disease.'

Matt Healy had had enough. He rose slowly and lent over the table to within a couple of inches of Joe Turner's face.

'No, Joe. Knifed to death, just like Kate Joe, just like Kate, and I'm going to put you away for a long time for both of them.'

Matt Healy sat back down, never taking his eyes from Turner.

'Anything you want to say Joe?' Susan Dornan asked.

'Yeah.'

'What?'

'I want a lawyer.'

Joe Turner was given a plastic jump suit to wear while his clothes were taken to forensics. He sat in his cold, whitewashed cell picking a hole in one of the sleeves. He knew he hadn't killed Kate, he knew; but Julie, the red mist, he had kept it in check so long, but....

*Help me Kate, help me.*

Kate Turner didn't respond.

The next day Joe Turner was granted bail for the murder of Julie Connor. Martha Reid didn't attend but had made sure that the provisionally appointed defence lawyer made the court aware that he was welcome, as a valued member of the family, to stay at her address and that she, as a respected pillar of the West End community, would vouch for his appearance at any future court hearing. Joe Turner was given bail and left the court at 4.00pm in theory a free man, but one without a passport. Matt Healy had pressed the PF to strenuously oppose bail pointing out that Turner had actually been arrested at Glasgow Airport attempting to "flee the country" but he knew that bail was likely to be granted as Turner had only been charged with one murder at that point; not a major thing in modern Scotland apparently.

On being released some twenty minutes later Joe phoned Martha to thank her for everything she had done and told her that he was going to do some shopping for toiletries and things before heading out to her flat.

'That's fine Joe. I've had a set of keys made for you and you can come and go as you please once you have them.' Martha said.

'Thanks again Martha, I don't know what I would have done without you. I didn't kill Kate Martha, or Julie.'

'I know that Joe. Oh by the way I phoned Ray yesterday, I thought you'd want him to know. He was very concerned and upset as you can imagine. He would have come to court but he's very busy at work just now but he wants you to phone him when you can. He was confident you would be let out.'

'That's great Martha, I'll do that.'

## Chapter 8

*But what can I do*

*I can't control my mood*

*It feels like you mean so much*

*But you'll forget me soon enough*

I knew Joe would phone me. I sat compiling all my thoughts and fears surrounding his past, his fraught relationship with Kate, his intention "to kill" Julie Connor and my knowledge of the "smoking gun", the return ticket from Edinburgh's Waverly Station to Glasgow's Queen Street station for the Saturday that Kate Turner died. The one that Joe had discarded on the bedside table of his bedsit, the one the police would find in the inside lining of his brown leather jacket; if told them to look there. I knew that because I had placed it there. I felt like a Judas but I wasn't motivated by greed, there were no 30 pieces of silver for me. I just wanted the nightmare to end. I started to cry and didn't stop even though my ribs started to ache. I went to the fridge, poured a glass of wine and sat gingerly down in front of the TV. "Coronation Street" was on. A soap about an ordinary Manchester street that was nothing like any street I had ever come across. What was "ordinary" anyway? Up until a few weeks ago I thought Joe Turner and Julie Connor were ordinary, not to mention poor Kate.

*I'm just about to betray my friend. I don't know for a fact that he has done anything and I'm condemning him out of hand. Why would he kill Kate anyway? He's always been a good friend to me. What the fuck have I done?*

I needed to get out. Have a few drinks, relax. Think. I didn't have a circle of friends as such, more a few acquaintances that I occasionally teamed up with. Tonight I was going to try something different. Something that perhaps it was best your friends didn't know about.

\*\*\*

Although he had never asked Susan outright if she dated men, Healy suspected that perhaps she did occasionally. He felt that they were in some form of relationship but wanted to know where he stood. On the way back from the court hearing he had asked her if she fancied a movie. She had said sorry but she had something planned.

'No sweat, I'll see you Friday night anyway. Remember? Squad bonding night?' he casually responded

'Yes. Of course. Looking forward to it.' I'll see you then' she replied over her shoulder as she sauntered off, not wanting to admit that she had forgotten all about the night out with the squad. Healy sat in the squad room. He was looking over some case notes, pondering whether to go home or to the pub to watch a Scotland World Cup qualifying match that was on Sky, a form of self-flagellation that would maybe suit his mood.

*She'd better not sleep with this bastard whoever he is. Bet he's an arse hole anyway.*

\*\*\*

Susan Dornan couldn't believe she had actually been persuaded to try speed dating by her friend Myra. She had had a couple of dates with Tom Barbour but didn't see that going anywhere so had just thought *why not*. Myra had insisted that "it would be a great laugh" and certainly some of the guys, and to be fair some of the woman who had turned up, to Dornan's mind had to be having a laugh but on her second trip around the tables she had found herself sitting opposite a familiar face.

'Ray Ford. God, what are you doing here?'

'Same thing as you I'm guessing. Unless you're working of course' I replied.

'No. God this is embarrassing.'

'Why? I don't think so. In fact I'm quite surprised not to mention pleased you're here.'

Dornan was flattered, pleased and excited. Over a coffee later in the evening I explained that I didn't socialise much with work colleagues or others in the legal profession; that I preferred to separate my work and my private life. We had our first official "date" the following evening with comedy to the fore as l had suggested a visit to Jongleurs Comedy Club in Glasgow's city centre. Susan obviously knew of comedy clubs but had never actually been in one and had seemed to thoroughly enjoy the evening especially, like most Glaswegians, when there was a touch of cruelty in the rapid routines.

'Dyslexia, yeah, can be a bit of a problem. Like the agnostic one who didn't believe in dogs, or the pimp one who bought a warehouse or the Devil Worshiper one who sold his soul to Santa.'

'Hear those Glaswegian Siamese twins have written a biography.....Oor Wullie.'

'Thought I'd made love for an hour and 5 minutes last night until I realised the clocks had gone forward and hour.'

'Don't worry about Colon Cancer......it will get you in the end.'

Susan especially laughed at barbs aimed at certain women. I briefly wondered why, then realised all women seemed to think the same.

'Most of us have a skeleton in the cupboard but that David Beckham takes his out in public.'

'Grandchildren can be fucking annoying. How many times can you go and the cow goes moo and the pig goes oink? It's like talking to a supermodel.'

It was obvious from the outset that we liked each other but we both saw a problem given the situation with the Turner investigation. We agreed however that as long as we didn't discuss the case then there shouldn't really be an issue. We also agreed to keep the relationship quite for now. At least till the Turner case was resolved one way or the other.

***

Peter Harris sat in his Uddingston home wondering about the meaning of besotted.

*Was that what had driven him, a man who had never even had a parking ticket, to do the things he had done. Besotted? Was Kate Turner his Lolitta?*

He had no idea where his wife Sally was, or the kids. He couldn't deny that he loved his children but somehow, strangely, they didn't exert the hold over him that his first family did. He wished he could turn back the clock but when Ann died he couldn't cope with two babies on his own. Over the years he had tried to seek out his son and daughter but when, out of the blue, his daughter had gotten in touch it was more to punish him than any notion of reconciliation. He was upset when she told him that although she and her brother were close; he didn't want anything to do with his father. Indirectly Kate Turner had cost him two families but it made no difference to his feelings; she was his one true love and that night on the river bank was love no matter what that bitch Dornan said. He also knew that no matter what happened over the following weeks, his life was over.

***

As the only married member of the murder squad DC Rab Brown took plenty of stick.

'Hey Rab do you know scientists have discovered a food that diminishes a woman's sex drive by 90%?'

'Yeah it's called wedding cake.'

'Why do men die before their wives?'

'They want to.'

The squad's bonding night in the Bay Horse around the corner from their offices was in full swing. Dornan wasn't against these nights, but she did have her concerns for the younger members of the squad. If they couldn't handle the slating endemic in these gatherings they may become defensive, insular; and not contribute fully to the squad for fear of ridicule. She needn't have worried about Jill French. DC Jack T'Baht had pointed out to her that;

'Women will never be equal to men.'

Jill had agreed.

'Until they walk down the street with bald heads and beer guts and still think they're sexy that is.'

Dornan smiled, her fears dissipated.

'You were married once weren't you John?' Dornan asked John Frame

'Sure was. Thought she was Miss Right. Didn't realise her first name was "Always."'

Everyone was aware that they still had plenty to sort out with the two murders so the night didn't last as long as it otherwise might have, much to Matt Healy's pleasure. He had hoped that he and Susan Dornan might end up on their own.

'You didn't say too much on the man woman thing Matt. Surprisingly! What are your hopes in that department then?'

Susan Dornan wasn't quite sure why she had asked Matt Healy what she just had. Maybe the few glasses of wine had clouded her judgement, on the other hand she was curious. She wanted to know.

'Not sure really, never given it much thought' he replied.

'Come on then. That girl up at the bar, the one in the red dress, how would you rate her?'

'Out of two……. I'd give her one!'

They both laughed out loud.

'What about you. You ever had a boyfriend or are you too hard work?' Healy asked.

'No I'm bloody well not you cheeky bastard. I'll let you know that some of my many boyfriends took to drink after we split up and haven't been sober since'

'Really, celebrating that long'

Dornan gave Matt Healy a playful punch.

'One for the road?'

'Why not?'

Two hours later Susan Dornan and Matt Healy walked arm in arm through the city's St Enoch Square in their search for a cab. A pigeon shat on Healy's jacket.

'Typical, shat on from a great height, story of my life.'

'Just pretend it was a bird of peace.'

'What, Mother Teresa?'

Their laughter embraced them and they embraced each other. The Ingram Hotel was the closest. In room 212 Matt Healy was loving and attentive even though passion was their shared motivation. Susan Dornan lay in his arms. The effect of the alcohol was wearing off, replaced by doubt and bewilderment. She looked over at Healy.

'Matt why do you come over so rough so, well, uncouth? It's not you, I know that now.'

She could hardly make out his reply. Whispered, guarded perhaps, even pleading.

'I don't know. I can't help it. The force may be changing Susan, Culture Change, Paradigm Shift or whatever the "In" term is this week, but the sewer dwellers aren't changing; you have to live in their world Susan to catch them, they won't live in ours, operate in our "new, customer friendly" world. I know I don't really fit-in anymore but I'm good at what I do, I want to contribute but I can only do it my way, on my terms.'

Susan Dornan was more confused than ever. Her feelings for Matt were strong, very strong but Ray Ford was something different altogether, something special even. Something Healy could never be. She was sure of that.

*Jesus in 24 hours I might be in his arms, his bed, what the hell am I doing?*

## Chapter 9

The next morning Susan Dornan sat in her office uncertain whether to laugh or cry.

*What had she been thinking? She hadn't had that much to drink, had she, that she could blame that. Had she just made a serious career mistake, did she even care about that aspect of it? How could she face Matt Healy this morning, what would she say? How could she face Ray tonight? He had been the perfect gentleman up to this point but at their intimate meal the other evening "knowing" glances and smiles had definitely passed between them, all that was missing was Rod Stewart's throaty tones in the background musing that "Tonight's the Night.'*

All the squad were assembled this morning as she had ordered a case review for 10.00am. Matt Healy was on time and seemed especially jovial and animated.

'Morning everyone, feeling good, I am' he had declared rather too loudly to no-one in particular.

Susan had seen him coming in and going over to the coffee stand that was, mercifully, situated well away from her part of the room. She could detect the skip in his step even from her quick glances in his direction. She prayed he wouldn't make any sort of comment about last night's goings on. The morning's activities would have allowed Susan Dornan to avoid Matt Healy and the inevitable awkwardness that was bound to be there if her phone hadn't rung. She now had to get it over with and get on with the job at the same time.

'Matt, get your jacket an area car has reported movement in Harris's house.

Dornan decided to drive, it would keep her occupied.

'Susan about last night.'

'Yes, I know.'

'Know what?'

'It was a bit crazy, a bit stupid.'

'Oh.'

'Don't you agree?'

'Maybe to a certain extent but I want you to know I care for you, I want there to be something between us. Something worthwhile. I think it's possible. I'll move squad if I have to.'

'The thing is Matt, and this will make me sound like a right cow in more ways than one, but I have someone in my life at the moment. Someone I think I might be able to make a go of things with.'

'Oh.'

'Don't get me wrong Matt, I like you, really like you actually or I wouldn't have done what I did, it's just that, well, I like someone else as well. Shit Matt, I'm sorry.'

'No sweat, it's, I'm fine. Just friends and colleagues OK?'

'Deal. Great.'

They arrived at Peter Harris's house and immediately concentrated on the job in hand but Susan could detect that things wouldn't be the same between her and Healy from now on. Healy and Dornan could see Peter Harris sitting on his couch watching the T.V. Despite ringing the doorbell three times Peter Harris didn't respond. Healy rapped the window. Harris turned and stared at him with a blank expression, eventually rising slowly to his feet and going to the door.

'Peter Harris you are under arrest for the murder of.........' the rest tapering away from Peter Harris' consciousness.

'Where are Sally and the kids Peter?'

'She's left me, took the kids, "for the best".'

Back at the station Peter Harris refused both a doctor and a lawyer.

'What for?' being all he said in reply to being asked.

Harris explained that Sally Harris had hadn't paid much attention to the news stories on the TV about yet another murder in Glasgow and the pictures meant nothing to her. But when she did catch the name and then the connection with Spain from the papers, she knew. She had confronted him, said she would go to the police, had remembered the night he had come in late after he called from a call box saying he had run off the road, was a bit dirty but would be home once he changed a tyre.

"It was you, you killed her" she had screamed over and over.

He laughed at her.

'Killed her, why would I do that? I loved her.'

'Did you kill Kate, Peter?' asked Dornan.

'I have a tendency to be judgemental Inspector and as a result I get angry but I swear I did not kill Kate Turner.'

'Were you angry with her though?'

'Yes. How could she just sit there and tell me she was in love with someone else?'

'In love with who, Peter?'

'I don't know she never said. She just left when she saw my reaction.'

'But it wasn't her husband Joe?'
'Christ no.'
'Did she say if this guy was in Glasgow with her Peter?'
'No, but I don't think he was. He's in Spain I think. Probably a deigo bastard.'
'So you resented this guy in her life?'
'Of course, but what is it they say, resentment is like taking poison and hoping the other guy dies. I prefer anger.'
Dornan and Healy exchanged glances.
'Does the name Tunstall mean anything to you Peter?'
'No. Should it?'
'Explain how your semen got on Kate Peter.'
'We made love by the riverbank.'
'Really, before or after the row.'
'After. Anyway it wasn't a row more a tiff.'
'So you followed her out, made up and had sex. Is that what you're telling us Peter?'
'She wanted to. It's not our first time together. We slept together when we were dating.'
'That was an eternity ago Peter, when Kate was in her teens. A teenage infatuation on her part. Not sure how to describe your role. We know now that Kate was raped.'
Peter Harris looked around the room. He appeared to be going to another place.
'Not by me. Her blouse ripped open by mistake when I caught up to try to apologise. Black bra, beautiful breasts. Her panties didn't match her bra, I was surprised at that really. We made love, beautiful love. She was crying, I don't know why.'
'What happened after "you made love" Peter?' the words almost chocking Susan Dornan.

'I had to get home.'

'So you left her there. No lift back to Glasgow, the train station even. You just left her.'

'I felt she wanted to be on her own. She didn't say anything. I left'

'Couldn't say anything more like' said Healy.

Peter Harris looked straight at Susan Dornan.

'I didn't kill her though, I didn't.'

***

That evening two men sat on their beds. Both men had in their lives had sex with the same woman, both had in their lives loved the same woman, both had in their lives assaulted, to a greater or lesser extent, the same woman and both were now suspects in the murder of the same woman. One of the men, Peter Harris, was now charged with the murder of that woman. They both sat alone, a few miles separating them, each man oblivious to the thoughts of the other. Joe Turner had been informed of Peter Harris' arrest. He had always been a bit jealous of Kate and Harris' relationship but believed Kate when she said it was platonic and for old time's sake although he had never understood how she had become involved with someone older than her. He was going to go back to Spain. He'd been told that the trial and release of Kate's body was still some way off and;

*God knows what those pricks back at the bars would have been up to while he was away.*

He had decided to phone me.

'Ray?'

'Who's that?' I didn't recognise his voice at first.

'Fuck's sake Ray it's me, Joe.'

'Oh hi, Joe. Yeah. Sorry. Lots on, heads all over the place. Plus the reception on this mobile isn't great at times.'

'They got the bastard.'

'Who?'

'That killed Kate. It was that cunt Peter Harris.'

'Who?'

'An ex she used to meet up with when she was back in Glasgow.'

'Shit.'

'Yeah, shit.'

'So the story about an affair was bullshit? I told you Joe I told you.' I think I was more relieved than him.

'I know, I know. Thanks for everything Ray.

'Sure Joe. What are you going to do now?'

'Don't know really. I want to go back to Spain. God knows what's been happening over there. Any way you could appeal the release of my passport?'

'I'll try Joe but it will take a while and to be honest I don't think there's much chance.'

'Right. Well try anyway. I'll call you and maybe we can meet up for a couple of beers.'

'Yeah do that.'

I sat down on a bench in the park I was walking through at the time, green slats covered in a variety of gang – land names. I was glad that Kate's murderer had been caught so quickly but deep in my mind there was a nagging doubt.

*Why would someone who Kate had been friends with for years suddenly kill her? Why had Joe initially lied about being in Spain the night Kate died? Was this guy Harris the only guy Kate was in touch with? What about the "smoking gun", train ticket, only I knew of?*

When I learnt that my friend, the one I was about to betray, had been charged with Julie Connor's murder , a murder I was sure he had committed, I had no over-riding feelings or thoughts on the matter. Not because I was ambivalent to the situation, more because I was completely numbed by the whole sequence of events and my role in them. I was still convinced that Joe had indeed killed his wife Kate. The arrest of Harris hadn't changed that. He had actually told me he was going to kill Julie. Was his temper that out of control? And, if it was, what more was he capable of? Should I cut him off completely? Tell Susan Dornan my thoughts? Was I being selfish? Despite everything Joe had been a friend, a good friend, should I support him no matter what? He would never need to know that it was me who had supplied such damming evidence to the police; I could just "be there" for him as the day-time telly gurus are constantly telling us. On the other hand, I am a principled person, I don't want to be seen as somehow approving what Joe had done. I wandered home. The dilemmas in my personal life seeming to drain me more than my case load at work. I lay on the bed. Sleep didn't come, I lay and for some reason thought over my life and why I had become the man I had.

I'm not sure what age I was exactly when my Mum left my father for another man. I hadn't been aware of any tension or particularly bad arguments even. She was just there one day and not there the next. My father had just gently sat me down and explained that my mother had gone away;

'No, not to heaven son'.

But that everything would be OK and is was him and me against the world from now on. I can't say I missed my mother that much. I was aware occasionally of ripples of disapproval in the Catholic "community" but my father continued to take me to mass on Sundays; and every other day possible. His way of coping I suppose. She sent me a birthday card once, my dad recognised the writing on the envelope, but I never opened it. It lay on the worktop beside the fridge for a few days and then was gone. I never asked my dad where it went. My dad was a teacher and so could drop me at school in the mornings and was home by the time I got back in. He took me to see Celtic every other Saturday and to Ayr for our summer holidays. We were happy. Occasionally he had a lady friend around for tea but they were never around for too long. He never mentioned my mother and there were no pictures of her in the house. He brought me up to be compassionate and caring but not to allow yourself to be used and to be careful who you cared for. It also came back to me that there was practically always music playing in the house; either from the radio or one of those record players where you piled the 45's up on a spindle in the middle and they fell down on top of each other to be played. Perry Como, Andy Williams, Deano, Dad loved them all. I think that is why I now love the quiet. Dad died when I was 30. He was diagnosed with cancer and, thankfully, didn't suffer a protracted death. He knew he was dying but didn't seem too bothered.

'You've turned out to be a fine young man son. No father can ask for more than that.'

'Do you want me to contact Mum?' I said. I realised then that I had no idea where she was or if my father had ever spoken to her since the day she left.

'No.'

Several months after my dad died I got a phone call from his sister, Ann, my Auntie Annie, to tell me 'just so's you know' that she had known all the time where my mother was, and would have told me if I'd ever asked, but that she hadn't been going to instigate the conversation. She added that it was now all irrelevant anyway as my mother had been killed, apparently in a domestic dispute with husband number three or four a few months previously, although the husband a chronic alcoholic was vehemently denying any involvement. I remember feeling nothing at the news other than that I was now truly alone.

I thought briefly of my Dad's funeral. Joe Turner had come over from Spain to support me.

*Shit.*

My phone rang and dragged me back into the present. It was Susan.

'Hi.'

'Hi. How's your day been then?'

'Lousy. Well that's not entirely true. We've arrested a guy called Peter Harris for the Kate Turner murder.'

'I know. Joe called me.'

'Right.'

'Susan, I know we said we wouldn't discuss cases but one thing, off the record?'

'What?'

'Any chance Joe didn't kill Julie Connor? He swears he never, just like he swore he didn't kill his wife.'

'Sorry Ray but he did it alright. I need to leave it at that now OK.'

'Sure. How are you, apart from work?'

'That's why I'm calling. Fancy meeting up for a drink tonight?'

'Susan I'd love to but I'm out tonight, committed to an office leaving do. The powers that be frown upon it if you don't go. How about tomorrow night?'

'OK great. Tomorrow night it is. But Ray, no work - talk OK?'

'What kind of talk would you like then Ms Dornan?'

'I'll leave that up to you. Surprise me.'

***

'Fancy another? While I've got the barman pinned down....so to speak.' Paul Allan had seen his potential host in the club before. He thought the guy looked interesting and obviously the feeling was mutual.

'JD and cranberry thanks, the name's Paul.'

'I know. Max.' said Max Kendrick, offering a handshake, a faint smile creasing his left cheek.

A few minutes later Allan and his benefactor were sitting in a darkened booth to the left of the tiny dance floor.

'So how do you know?' asked Paul.

'I make it my business to know interesting guys' replied Max, the smile more pronounced now.

'Right, and why's that then Max?'

'Don't want to fall in with the wrong type.'

'Very wise. So what do you do for a living Max?'

'Estate agent, bloody great at the moment, building societies throwing money at anyone with a pulse, can't see how it can go on but make hay as they say.'

'Great.'

'What about you?'

This was dilemma time for Paul Allan. Experience had taught him that whatever he said now would dictate if this was to be the shortest romance in history.

'I work in an office.'

'Right, doing what?'

'Oh, you know, shuffling paper mostly.' which wasn't entirely untrue.

'Listen I have to shoot off, early start tomorrow, but how about giving me your mobile number and maybe we can meet up for a drink or whatever next week?'

Paul Allan sat in the back of the taxi taking him back to his flat in the east end of the city, a mixture of pleasure at what might be to come and distaste at what his job had shown him human beings were capable of, swirling around in his befuddled head.

Max Kendrick was already at home reading up on some house schedules, that he would be showing to young couples who couldn't afford them, the next day. He thought it was interesting that Paul Allan hadn't admitted to being a policeman.

*** 

*Azrael was standing in another club from Paul Allan. The woman had smiled at him earlier. Made it obvious she was interested. He noted her wedding rings. He bought her a drink.*

*'Jean. Nice name. What's your surname?'*

*'King' Jean replied 'my dad liked tennis.'*

*'Ah, JK. I'll call you Rowling, it's a quirk of mine.'*

*'What's yours?'*

*'Azrael.'*

*'Right. Where's it come from?'*

*'It's of Hebrew derivation.'*

*'Oh right. You Jewish then?'*

*'No.'*

*Jean King sensed that he was rather touchy on the subject of his name; 'probably married, who cares', so decided not to pursue it, besides she was rather taken by her admirer's quirky sense of humour, having fun not being one of her husband's strong points. Jean King's husband was away often on business. Always away on business. She was lonely.*

*'Would you like to go for something to eat?' Azrael asked.*

*'I could rustle you something up at my place if you like. I'm a good cook actually.'*

*'That would be great.'*

*Azrael was impressed by Jean King's home. Her husband was obviously a good provider. He also saw that Jean King was keen for him to know her husband was away on business for a few days, but he already had his sign.*

*Rowling, another whore, pedlar of heresy.*

*He lay on the bed in her room turning over the various possibilities in his mind.*

*The following morning Azrael made his own breakfast, his favourite, scrambled egg on toast with a pot of sweet tea, shortly after writing the single word Rowling in Jean King's blood on the living room wall. He thought over the previous evening's events. The evening meal prepared by Jean King had seemed a lot more elaborate than a quickly prepared snack. An effort to impress? Seduce? He had made no assumption though:*

*'There was always time to repent.'*

*But as they sat in the large lounge Jean King had lent over and caressed his neck.*

*He never got any enjoyment from his sexual encounters and it troubled him that he actually felt some sort of compulsion to even perform the deed.*

*Maybe it was the final confirmation of the harlot's downfall, justification for her punishment.*

*He collected his bag, placed a card amongst some magazines on the lounge coffee table, and left. Jean King lay on the floor of the shower cubicle, her blood swirling gently towards the drain.*

## Chapter 10

Susan Dornan looked out from her office at the unusually sparse squad room. She was a happy woman. The first two murder enquiries under her watch had been concluded successfully. And she had finally met a man who she truly felt connected to. She glanced at Matt Healy. He seemed fine, and focused on some notes that were scattered across his desk. The Incident Board still had pictures of Kate Turner and Julie Connor on them along with photos of Joe Turner, Peter Harris and Colin Boom Boom Banks along with various post - it notes placed throughout and coloured lines meandering over the whole surface area. The squad had worked long and hard to get the two results and she was pleased with their effort and commitment. She looked around the room. Despite her best efforts, she couldn't quite take to Jack T'Baht. She couldn't quite put her finger on what it was but whenever he was around her she felt uneasy. In her school days, "creep" was the word that would have sprung to mind. She wondered briefly if Matt Healy was still committed to doing his best but dismissed the idea almost immediately as she felt Healy was loyal to her even if disappointed in the lack of a romance. Jill French too looked focused and even Rab Brown looked awake. Paul Allan was keen, if a little green, but Dornan saw potential there.

The phone rang on Dornan's desk.

'Where?' She scribbled on a note pad.

'OK we're on our way.' She went through to the squad room.

'There's been another murder. Matt, Jill, Jack let's go. Rest of you stand by for me calling in.'

The drive way to the semi - detached red sand stone bungalow in Bearsden, an affluent suburb of Glasgow, was already cordoned off with blue and white tape. A constable stood at the entrance to the drive and another at the door to the house.

'Who discovered the body constable?' asked Dornan.

'Cleaner, ma'am. Comes in every morning at eleven. Called it in straight away. She's in the kitchen.'

'Right.'

French, Healy and Dornan scanned the house. No sign of a break in or disturbance. They looked at the writing on the living room wall.

'Jesus Christ' said Healy. French took the scene in and wondered.

Dornan went through and spoke to Mrs Jones, the cleaner, in the kitchen.

'What is the victim's name Mrs Jones?'

'Mrs King. Jean King.'

'Where's her husband?' asked Healy.

'Away on business. England I think. He's away a lot.'

'Who does he work for?'

'He's got something to do with satellite television. Sky. Not sure what he does.'

Dornan nodded to French to get on to tracing the husband. Healy went upstairs to the bathroom. A pool of blood encased the body, a shallow moat between Ikea and eternity. A blood stained knife sat neatly on top of the toilet lid. Dornan decided to leave French at the scene and go back to HQ to set up the Incident Room.

'Do you think there could be a connection to our other two cases Matt?'

'No chance. Not unless some connection comes up between Jean King and Joe Turner.'

Over the course of the next few hours Dornan's team and forensics officers went about their searches of the crime scene. At one o'clock Dornan decided to go back to the station to keep McFarlane up to speed but just as she was about to leave Jack T'Baht called her over and pointed down to something on the carpet that had fallen out of a magazine he had flicked through. It was a white business card: Azrael.

Dornan sat in Chief Superintendent McFarlane's office and laid out the new scenario facing the squad and the possible impact it had on their previous two cases. The link to Kate Turner's murder obvious. The link to Julie Connor's killing more tenuous but had to be considered.

'So what are you saying Susan? We're dealing with a serial killer?'

'Possibly.'

'Could Turner or Harris have done the three of them?'

'Possibly. Sorry Sir but I just don't know. We'll check their whereabouts for last night.'

'What about bringing in a profiler?'

'If you think so Sir, then yes.'

'Right, leave it with me. I know someone. Good bloke.'

Dornan returned to the squad room. Healy told her that the husband had been traced and was definitely in Manchester for the last couple of days. He was on his way back. Had no idea what Rowling meant.

'McFarlane asked if it could have been Harris or Turner?'

'It's a thought.'

'He's bringing in a profiler.'

'Jesus wept.'

'You not keen then?'

'Sorry Susan. Yeah. I suppose any help is welcome. What a fuck up. Harris will get off now you know. Certainty.'

'Let's just wait and see Matt.'

Five minutes later McFarlane phoned Dornan to say the profiler would be in the next morning at 10.00am.

***

Joe Turner hadn't called me and, in truth, I was glad of that. I knew I couldn't look him in the eye and there was nothing practical I could do for him anyway. I sat in my office and thought about Susan Dornan. I liked her, really liked her, but was concerned about getting too close to her in case it all ended, like most of my previous romances, in disappointment. The recent events had highlighted to me how brief life could be and how you could never be sure about just who other people truly were. That evening I sat with Susan Dornan in my flat. She was pleased I had called but seemed slightly detached as we sat watching nothing in particular on the box.

'Everything OK Susan?'

'Yeah fine. Sorry. Another woman was killed today. I can't say much Ray but there may be a link to the Turner killing.'

'Really? I thought Harris was the man.'

'Yeah so did we. He may still be but it's more complicated now.'

'What about Joe?'

'Ray.'

'OK but think about it. He's asked me to be his lawyer. You have to disclose everything to me eventually anyway.'

'Do something for me will you?'

'Sure. What?'

'Find out where he was last night.'

'I can't say anything to you that could harm my client Susan. Why can't you just ask him yourself?'

'We can. It's just.....well, will you just ask him?'

The rest of the evening passed in a rather subdued manner with Susan eventually saying that she'd better go home and get some sleep as she had to be on the ball in the morning. We hadn't slept together yet. I didn't want to waste things by pushing the physical side of things and maybe giving Susan the wrong impression of me.

\*\*\*

*Azrael lay on his bed listening to one of his favourite singers, Mary McGregor:*

*"Torn between two lovers."*

*'But repentant.'*

*Other people merely heard the lyrics of her songs but she was singing them only for him.*

*'Mary, beautiful name, mother of Jesus, Madonna......... but not that American slut calling herself Madonna and selling herself to Mammon.*

*His body hovered between the past, and the person he really was, and what he had become in order to function and be able to do His work. He didn't pretend that he always understood his calling and the tasks he was set, he only knew that he was privileged by being called.*

*He hovered in his world. He thought of a barmaid, Janet, that he had met that afternoon. He would take her to lunch one day....hoped she would pass the test, that she could honour her calling.*

*His path had already been clearly shown to him and the words of the repentant sisters, passed to him in the music, would always guide him. Initials were always the key.*

*He thought of Kate Turner, he thought of Jean King, he thought of his mother, he thought of the other sinners; he thought of many others and he moaned quietly as his seed stained the blue quilt beneath him.*

***

The following morning, McFarlane brought the Profiler, Alec Caldow in and introduced him to Dornan. He now sat alone in front of the board, rather surprisingly, to Dornan at least, apparently studying the people in the room as opposed to the pictures on the board. Robson Green he most certainly wasn't . Bald with some wisps' of greyish hair at the sides, John Lennon type glasses and a totally dishevelled look about him he reminded Dornan of the eccentric professor in Back to the Future. Dornan straightened her jacket, stroked the lines out of her skirt and walked out into the Incident Room. She introduced Caldow to the group and suggested that he start proceedings with a brief word on just what defines a serial killer before they looked at the specific cases. Caldow nodded, remained seated and surveyed the room as he spoke.

'A serial killer is the most mysterious and devious of criminals because he has no apparent motive in committing his crimes. There are some who say that all serial killers, deep down, want to be caught, they are engaged in an intellectual battle with their pursuers but I don't agree. If a serial killer gets caught it is because he has made mistakes and it is my belief that if a serial killer is indeed responsible for these atrocities then he too will have made mistakes, he too can be caught. I've looked over these cases and in my opinion the presence of a serial killer is not definite but nor can it be discounted. Perhaps the best way forward now is to hear a rundown on the cases and take it from there.'

Dornan had felt that this would be the way things would go and nodded to Matt Healy that he should take over.

'Mr Caldow is right. Serial killers kill strangers. That is why these murders are not the work of one. A good murder detective does not wait for a pattern to emerge that proves that separate murders are the work of the same killer, but looks for signs that any murder is the work of someone who will do it again. As most of you know I still think that Joe Turner killed his wife Kate. He did it with such ferocity that it is obvious that he would be capable of doing it again and we know that he began his tendencies to violence, including a stabbing, as long as 30 years ago. He then, for whatever reason, definitely confronted and killed Julie Connor.

Once again, someone he knew. I repeat neither of them strangers. I know Harris has been charged with the Kate Turner killing, and he may well have done it, but even if he did my theory still stands. He knew his victim and Turner knew his. We are also looking into the circumstances surrounding the death of Harris's first wife Ann. Again the possibility of a propensity to kill a person they know present. I've read over the Jean King killing and can see absolutely no connection to either of the other two killings, other than she was stabbed. I know that the presence of the same, rather strange, business card at two of the scenes might be viewed as something more than coincidence but I think they're just some kind of marketing gimmick and there are probably loads of then floating around Glasgow. It's Glasgow for Christ's sake. Stab Central. If she was the victim of a serial killer then fine but there is no connection to our other two cases in my opinion.' Healy sat down. The rest of the officers looked from Healy to Dornan to Caldow not quite sure of what Healy's speech had done to the idea of a serial killer. Caldow stood.

'Thanks for that Matt but can I just say that it's a rule of thumb that serial killers don't just stop so it would be remise of us would it not if we didn't at least examine all the possibilities if, in your opinion at least, they are not probabilities.'

Susan Dornan could see that Matt Healy was getting agitated, she didn't want him exploding into one of his expletive strewn outbursts and putting her and the squad, not to mention himself, into a box marked "closed minds."

'I'm sure we all agree with that Alec, anything else to add?' Dornan quickly said.

'Yes. In my opinion the person who committed these murders is someone who didn't finish school, probably doesn't have a regular job, and is probably not married or in a stable relationship; possibly with a mother fixation. This, as I understand it, does not fit with either of the two suspects in the initial killings.'

Jill French and Jack T'Baht were both deep in thought. French appeared to be doodling but her thoughts were anything but wandered. She was focused on her own theory and what she had just heard galvanised her thoughts.

'Ma'am could I put forward something?'

'Yes Jill, what's on your mind?'

'Well to be honest it's just a theory, probably nothing, bit off the wall maybe.'

Healy groaned. French remained unaffected, even drew some spirit from Healy's disdain.

'Well, it's just that I've always wondered about the Tunstall necklace found on Kate Turner. What did it mean? Where did it come from? None of her friends or family could throw any light on it yet she was clearly happy to wear it. What if it was the killer who gave her it?'

'What if it was? What would that mean or prove?' Matt Healy asked.

'Tunstall is clearly a name. Google it and KT Tunstall, the singer comes up. KT......Kate Turner.'

'And?' it was Caldow, the Profiler, he was clearly interested.

'Well I just thought it was a coincidence but not now.'

'Why not?'

'The writing on Jean King's living room wall.'
'Rowling,' said Healy.
'JK,' said Dornan.
'Exactly ma'am' said French.
'Shit' said Healy.

DC Paul Allan's concentration was interrupted by the phone ringing on his desk. He left the main group and went over to answer.

'DC Allan speaking.'

'Hi. This is Yvonne Chambers. I'm the Receptionist at The Cathedral House Hotel. I'm sure it's nothing but we have an unclaimed suitcase that we have just uncovered and I'm pretty sure it dates back to the time that Spanish women went missing and the police were checking all the hotels.'

'Did you say Cathedral House Hotel?'

'Yes.'

'I'll be right over.'

Allan catches Dornan's attention.

'Yes Paul.'

'Ma'am, when I was going around trying to find out where Kate Turner and perhaps a man friend might have been staying the girl on reception at the Cathedral House Hotel told me it wasn't as unusual as you might think that people booked into hotels and just didn't come back in. Leave clothes behind and everything.'

'And?'

'Well she's just called me to say they just found a suitcase that they think was left from the weekend Kate Turner went missing.'

'OK Paul, well done. Go back to the hotel and get the suitcase & check out the hotel's register for the week-end of Kate's murder.'

'Yes ma'am.'

Allan parked in a side street opposite Glasgow's Museum of Religion. Every time he saw the museum he reminded himself of two things, firstly, that he must visit the museum some time and secondly, that the museum was built of the wrong stone. He knew he was no designer or architect but he knew when something just didn't look right and this was certainly one of those times.

*We always seem to cock things up. Christ knows what kind of mess we'll make of the Commonwealth Games. Discus in Dalmarnock, fuck me.*

'Hi Yvonne, DC Allan, we spoke before.'

'Yeah, hi.'

'You've got a suitcase? Have you opened it, tried to trace the owner?'

'I haven't, can't speak for anyone else but I wouldn't imagine so. It's just not something we do.'

'Can you get me it?'

'Sure.'

Paul Allan put the case into the boot of his Mondeo and decided he'd grab a sandwich before going back to HQ, hopefully with Max if he was free. 'Hi Max, its Paul Allan. You free for a coffee in the city centre by any chance? I've a free half hour.'

'Yeah great. Meet you in Dino's in ten minutes or so?'

'Sounds good. See you then.' Paul Allan was a very happy man.

Max Kermack was a happy man as well. He was happy to mix business with pleasure and in actual fact felt that he might quite like Paul

Allan but he had to remember his primary goal in cultivating the friendship.

'Come on Paul, I can't believe you're just an office worker, too sharp' said Max.

Paul Allan liked a compliment.

'Well, you might not like the truth!'

'Oh I don't think you could put me off dear.' Max replied, his best, exaggerated camp mode to the fore.

Allan laughed, he really liked this guy.

'I'm a copper.'

'How fantastic, a police woman!' Max shouted.

Allan laughed again, despite himself.

'Watch it or you're nicked.' he replied.

'You know something Paul, this is really great. In my spare time I'm trying to write a detective story, a murder, you could be a great help.'

'No problem Agatha, no problem at all.'

They both laughed. They were both happy. For now.

## Chapter 11

Joe Turner was sitting having a meal. He couldn't taste the food. He had gotten drunk the night before. Couldn't even remember where he had ended up. He had a vague memory of the red mist descending, walking down a gravel drive way. The surroundings being unfamiliar. Paying thirty pounds for a taxi to take him back to Partick.

*Christ, must have been well out in the sticks.*

Peter Harris was also having a meal. Both men were oblivious to each other and the strands that connected their past, and their futures. Both were, however, having similar thoughts about themselves. Joe Turner knew that, given the right set of circumstances, the boxes that triggered his anger duly ticked, he acted as though out - with his own body, almost able to look on as "another" person acted out his thoughts. He thought of Julie Connor. He thought of the possibility of his guilt.

Peter Harris on the other hand had always felt a bit of an outsider, someone who needed to be part of something but who never quite managed to be appreciated for what he was. He did not have a group of friends or, in fact, any friends. People had tried to form friendships with him but he always felt that as they didn't know the real him, the person inside. It was best to keep them at arm's length. He had however always found it easy to get girlfriends. He now had had two wives but neither of his marriages had fulfilled him. Neither had been to Kate. He too pondered his guilt.

***

That evening Healy and Dornan sat in Cafe India. They had both ordered chicken korma with chapattis, mango chutney and poppadoms. Neither of them liked wine with Indian food, "just not right" and had elected for a pitcher of lager. They had gone over both of the day's events but still couldn't agree. To Dornan's mind everything had changed. The Azrael cards, French's initials theory, what the profiler had said. They were looking at a serial killer. Healy pointed out that there was no card or "initials thing" connected to the Julie Connor killing. Turner was a definite for that and if he could kill with such impunity once he could do it twice. Maybe even three times if they could link him to Jean King.

'Sorry Matt, it's too much of a long shot.'
'Fine but let's get him in anyway. Rattle him.'
'OK.'
'Oh and remember we still have that week-end in Marbella riding on this.'

They left the restaurant and wandered up past the city's Mitchell Library that, when illuminated at night, would not look out of place in Florence or Rome. They were headed back towards Headquarters to collect their cars but decided to pop into one of the budget hotels that had sprung up around the area for a night cap. They sat in a darkened booth in the corner watching the other patrons, silently guessing about their reasons for being there, their true relationships. They watched a young man's lumbering attempts at courtship towards an older woman who may or may not have been his boss; a squeeze of her hand, a stroke of her arm, the exaggerated laugh at her, to them, unheard comments. Healy looked at Susan Dornan.

'I'm going to book a room.'

Susan Dornan looked down at her glass, swirled the golden liquid around, looked back at Healy, said nothing. Matt Healy got up and walked over to the reception desk.

***

Jack T'Baht and Paul Allan were in the squad room early the next morning. Neither Healy nor Dornan were in yet but that made no odds to either of them. They were both driven by their own thoughts of how to move the investigation on. Allan glanced across at T'Baht. He couldn't quite fathom him out, what drove him and, if truth be told, he didn't like him. T'Baht on the other hand neither thought nor cared what Allan or anyone else in this Godless country thought of him. He only knew it had lost its way with women openly flaunting themselves on a daily basis, established churches allowing them to be priests and whatever and, now, his own boss was a woman. However, he was confident that he would soon move up from this squad. He wasn't talking about that idiot Jill French's theory about the victim's initials. He alone knew what was driving the killer. He alone realised the significance of Azrael. He couldn't go as far as saying he agreed with what the killer had done but he could sympathise. What did this country expect, could it not see the ruinous road it was taking despite the warnings. Like everyone else he had had watched with a kind of sick fascination when two brave doctors had driven a bomb laden Range Rover into Terminal One at

Glasgow's International Airport the year before. But unlike everyone else he could not condemn them, he understood what they were doing, their righteous motivation.

*Doctors, not terrorists or gangsters, doctors. Instead of killing and imprisoning them would it not be better to sit with them and learn from them. Learn the only true path?*

He had pulled the file on the death of Colin Bank's mother which he had found out had been classified as suspicious at the time but no further action had been taken. He knew that only a well read, educated man would know of Azrael's righteousness and Professor Colin Banks was that if nothing else. The so called Profiler was wrong on that aspect at least.

Jill French had also come into work early and was sitting staring at a piece of paper with various sets of initials written on it. Even using Google she couldn't come up with anything that would help her pinpoint who the perpetrator was.

Frame and Brown slumped into the room and headed for the coffee machine. John Frame was asking Rab Brown why the space between a woman's breasts and her hips was called a waist.

'Don't know' said Brown rather reluctantly.

'Because you could easily fit another pair of tits in there Rab, that's why.'

Paul Allan was on the phone to the lab people in what he knew was a futile attempt at getting them to speed up the DNA results from the Jean King killing.

'Do you know how many crimes are committed in Glasgow detective constable?' the distant but cultured voice at the other end of the line asked.

'Crime is dropping according to the latest Government figures,' Allan ventured tongue in cheek.

'Less of them are fiddling their expenses perhaps but that's about it. Look we'll be as quick as we can.'

Allan hung up. He wasn't too bothered if truth be told as he was so happy with his life since Max came into it that nothing seemed to faze him anymore. Max still pestered him for access to the "criminal world" and Allan did think every day about how he was going to manipulate an opportunity but he was also aware of the repercussions if he got caught so he was making sure that the circumstances were just right before he organised anything.

Susan Dornan and Matt Healy hadn't said much that morning. Neither knew what to say really. They weren't kids, weren't going to come out with any "love" rubbish and weren't sure anyway what word could be used to describe their relationship. They had ordered up room service for breakfast, exchanged some small talk and even smaller glances. Since the hotel was so close to the police station they made sure they left separately, each as confused as the other.

Despite his conviction that Joe Turner had killed both his wife and Julie Connor Healy didn't really feel that the Jean King killing could be attributed to him. He also knew that he had far too easily dismissed the Azrael card at two different crime scenes. He could at least be honest with himself and stick to his own belief that coincidences in different murders didn't exist. He arrived at his desk and started reading a book he had bought the day before about the investigation into a serial killer of women. He hoped to get some insight into the mind of a man who killed women. Women he didn't know. He was reading a passage where the killer is quoted as saying "Woman are like a soufflé; when they are fresh from the oven they are crisp and fresh outside but the filling isn't yet mature and is hard to digest. When they become older, the crust may not be so pretty, but then the filling develops. There is an age at which a woman must be beautiful in order to be loved, and there is an age at which a woman must be loved in order to be beautiful." Healy would not have been able to put it so eloquently and, although he slightly despised himself for admitting it, he tended to agree. Did Dornan need to be loved he wondered.

\*\*\*

I had taken a day off work, "working from home"; and sat trying to comprehend day-time TV. Lorraine Kelly was commiserating with, and appeared to be in tears over, a guy who had been kicked out of X Factor the previous weekend despite the fact that his wife had died six months earlier giving birth; this tragedy apparently qualifying him as a great singer. She then quickly ran through an appeal for the thousands who had lost their lives that same week-end in the floods that were decimating the Far East. No tears necessary here apparently. I wandered through to the kitchen where coffee was brewing and thought over how well things with Susan had gone up to now despite the strain of the other night. She had made it obvious she liked me and I was definitely going to call her for another date but I'd leave it for a few days.

*No point in scaring her off.* My phone rang. *Maybe she didn't believe in waiting.*

'Ray, it's me, Joe.' My heart sank.

'Joe. How are you? Everything OK?' *Jesus, what a stupid question Ray.*

'Cops want to see me again. Will you meet me there?'

'OK. But put it off till tomorrow. Tell them you want your lawyer present but that I can't make it today. Ten tomorrow morning, tell them.'

'OK.'

'OK. See you tomorrow.'

'Right. Ray?'

'Yeah?'

'When we were in the bedsit in Partick did you see a train ticket?'

The phone pips went. I laid the phone on the kitchen counter and held my head in my hands. I eventually pulled myself together. I needed to get some fresh air, maybe a pub lunch, then phone Susan Dornan. My dilemma was beginning to crush my spirit.

\*\*\*

*Azrael liked Glasgow. He walked around the city centre admiring the architecture and browsing in the shops. He always felt a slight sense of wonder that a city that was built on heavy industry, and that had such a reputation for crime and "hardness" could produce such beauty. He thought of his calling. He remembered he had promised a barmaid, Janet, a meal a while back, and he always kept his promises. Lunch would be nice.*

'Hi Janet, remember me?'

*Janet was surprised but really pleased he had come back into her bar.*

'No.' *she said making sure she put just enough of a smile on to let him know she was teasing.*

'Oh well in that case I'll go. It's just that I was hungry and thought of you.'

'You saying I'm fat Azrael.'

'Thought you didn't remember me?'

'It came quickly. Hope you don't. What's your full name anyway?'

'Azrael, just Azrael. Yours?'

'Janet Rice, Janet Rose Rice to be precise but I keep that to myself obviously.' *Janet laughed.*

'Ah' *exhaled Azrael,* 'what time do you finish?'

\*\*\*

Dornan was headed for the exit. She had managed to avoid Healy all day and was hoping to get away for the evening without having to deal directly with the previous night's events. Healy too had been happy to stay well clear of Dornan during the day. *Get his head together,* but followed Dornan out, hoping to catch up with her in the Car Park. Maybe go for a drink. He was only a few feet behind her when her mobile rang.

'Hi handsome.'

Healy could see an unmistakable look of pleasure cross her face.

'Yeah. Tonight? That would be lovely. I'm on my way home know. Yes, eight o'clock would be fine. See you then. Looking forward to it too.'

Mercifully, as far as Healy was concerned, Dornan hadn't realised he was behind her. He let her walk on to her car and drive off before he went to his own car. He drove home. His anger and resentment growing all the way there.

\*\*\*

*Azrael looked around Janet's flat. He hadn't been expecting luxury but he was pleased to see it was at least clean and tidy. He was especially pleased to see a hi fi system sitting in the corner. 'Not surround sound but adequate.' He didn't see any reading materials. Mindless magazines detailing imaginary truths about the lives of Z list, so called celebrities, but no books.*

*'Do you like to read Janet?' he asked.*

*'I've not really got time to be honest. Why, do you?'*

*'Oh yes, as much as I can. I like to read in bed. Have you ever heard of Tolkien Janet, JRR Tolkien?'*

*'Can't say I have, and you won't have any time for reading this afternoon,' Janet giggled from the bedroom.*

*'He was a heretic Janet, a heretic.'*

## Chapter 12

*Azrael arrived back home a few minutes before six. The milk was nearly empty but there was just enough for a cup of tea. He loved these moments. A special time. He had switched on his stereo and the music had enveloped him. He was completely content. Satisfied that he had once again been able to achieve what he had been instructed to do. He spread himself out on the couch. He liked Nina Simone. He always felt black singers had more spirituality about them, more true understanding. He noticed a couple of spots of discolouration on his shoes. He knew it was blood, sinner's blood, but he was safe here no reason to disturb the mood. He made a mental note that he would need to buy milk on the way out later. He would maybe get some shoe polish as well.*

\*\*\*

Later that evening two men again sat in their own worlds, deep in their own thoughts. But there was no contentment in their lives. They sat miles, and worlds, apart but unknown to them their torments were similar and irrevocably entwined. Matt Healy was sitting in his living room. No lights, no music, no sound but he was engulfed never the less. His eyes were closed, his fists clenched. The whisky had numbed his mouth but his mind was agonisingly clear, his own voice lucid in his head, talking only to him. He had watched earlier as Susan Dornan, beautiful Susan, had met Ray Ford. He had watched them enter a restaurant and watched them leave. He had followed them back to Dornan's flat. He had then bought a bottle of Glenfiddich and gone home. He knew what they were doing now.

*Would Ford have gently slipped off Susan's blouse as he had done or would he have been more assured, forceful? Would Susan want that, like that? Would Susan have pushed his head down onto her neck, willing him to run his tongue along and down onto her breasts, willing him to torment the hardness into her nipples? Would Ford right now be tasting that mix of heat and perfume, running his hands over her moist skin, down, down until his fingers found her pantie line, pushing on to their ultimate goal. Would Susan be running her tongue around the tip of his cock, letting out that small groan of pleasure she always did with him, would she already be mounting him, gently guiding him inside her, arching back, her hands on his knees, her movements getting faster, more urgent, till she felt Ford explode inside her.*

*They would be lying spent now. Her head would be on his chest. Ford would have the smell of her hair, the feel of her breasts on his side, the taste of her on his tongue. Would Susan think of him? Compare them?*

Healy poured the last dram from the bottle. It had been 20 years since he had felt so strongly about a woman, he pondered, looked back, tormented by thoughts of what would have happened to him had Pamela gone to his bosses, even back then. Since then he had never really trusted woman who showed any affection for him. He knew that what they saw in him was a mirage. In reality he was closer to being the kind of man he tracked down than the people he purported to protect. At one time he'd blamed his mother, and the fact that he felt duty bound to look after her after his father upped and left, especially since she never once acknowledged his sacrifice. He had learned though that that explanation was too easy a get-out. He was responsible for his own short comings with women and only he could do anything about it. His thoughts returned to Susan Dornan.

Bitch.......*just like all the rest.*

Peter Harris was also sitting in the dark, his despair even worse than Healy's as there could be no redemption for him. Not ever. He was glad he had been able to make love to Kate one last time, show her his devotion, but was tormented by why, how, she had found someone else? He sat on the kitchen floor staring at the door of the washing machine his own distorted image staring back. He was glad that Kate was now dead, grateful that no other man would ever have her. He had been her first love and now he was her last. His wife had never been to see him and he'd heard that she had taken the kids out of school and moved down to her mother's in England. Harris never thought of them but did think of his first family. He thought about his son, wished they could meet up, talk but he wept for his daughter and what he had done to her.

***

I hadn't stayed over at Susan Dornan's flat the night before. We were both tired. Both of us needed to be fresh in the morning. Be prepared to be evasive with each other as we fenced over Joe Turner's future. I had felt that the Azrael link to two murders, including Kate Turner's, which had been leaked to the press by a civilian police clerk named Jim Rodgers, eliminated him from Kate's murder and my relief was palpable. Although we had agreed not to talk about the specifics of the case, I had reiterated to Susan over dinner that Joe was more than just a client. He was a friend. I recounted some boyhood tales, some glorious victories with the local football team, if not the local girls. I told her of my alarm at the time at seeing the train ticket on Joe's bedside cabinet and how glad I was to know I could discount it now. I laughed nervously as I told her of "planting" the ticket through a tear in the lining of Joe's jacket. Later, back at her flat we sat watching a DVD picked by Susan; Tom Cruise being "lush" apparently. Susan had suddenly sat up on the couch and shouted, "of course." I asked what she was on about but Susan had just said it was a work thing.

I sat in my car in the office car park and thought over my relationship with Susan. She had been the only woman at the "horrendous experience" of the speed dating evening that I had been interested in and I was glad and relieved that she had taken up my offer of going on a date. The fact of the matter was that I really liked Susan, was fascinated rather than put off by the fact she was a detective, and hoped Susan was keen to keep the relationship going. Past disappointments had shown me that you couldn't assume anything when it came to relationships and I had a habit of always looking for signs of what way a relationship would probably go. I had always been right in the past and this one felt so right.

*Yes Susan, you could well be The One. I hope so.*

I would have been even happier had I known that Susan Dornan was thinking exactly the same. Especially when events over the next few hours would show me that Susan was a police officer first; and a potential partner second.

Susan Dornan had called Matt Healy into her office. Awkwardness ignored.

'You were right all along Matt.' she said to him.

'What, you ditched the bent shot?'

'Very funny. No, about Joe Turner. I think he did kill Kate.'

'Why, what brought this on?'

'My boyfriend and I were watching a movie last night'.

'How nice for you.'

'Shut up and listen. The film was Jerry Maguire, not bad as it happens. Anyway, the point is that the tag line for the movie is "Show me the money." Tom Cruise plays a sports agent.'

'So?'

'So it got me thinking. Julie Connor told us that Joe Turner's businesses were shit so he obviously had money problems. I'm not sure of the laws in Spain but it's a safe bet to think he'll get everything including any insurance money.'

'Shit. We'll at least he won't get to enjoy it. He's a cert to get found guilty of Julie's killing alone so he'll get life for that.'

'How do people end up so evil Matt?'

'That's not the main point though Susan.'

'No? What is then?'

'When we going to Marbella?' A note of bitterness in his voice not going undetected by Dornan.

Joe Turner and I walked into the Interview Room. He looked a whole lot the worse for wear since the last time we had all seen him. The look of a haunted man. Susan looked radiant. Healy his usual self.

'How you getting on Joe?' asked Dornan. Healy sat to the side and slightly behind her. His role was to observe, come in as the bad cop when the time was right.

'How do you think?' replied Joe.

'Been drinking a lot?'

'Depends what you mean by a lot, doesn't it?'

'Suppose.'

'Where were you on Saturday night Joe?'

I was taken by surprise. I had assumed the interview was to tell Joe he had been eliminated for enquiries surrounding his wife's murder. Maybe to ask him some more about the Julie Connor case.

'Why are you asking Superintendent?' I asked. Talking to Susan in this way feeling bizarre after the intimacy of just a few hours previously. The look of disdain on Healy's face even more pronounced than usual when I glanced over to see him staring at me.

'A woman was killed on Saturday night in much the same way as Julie Connor was. Much the same way as Kate Turner was actually. So where were you Joe?'

'Wait a minute. It's common knowledge that a link between Saturday night's killing and Kate

Turner's death has been established. A link that eliminates my client,' I said.

'No it doesn't. It could in fact link your client to all three murders.' said Susan.

'Don't be absurd. Say nothing Joe.'

'What were you doing in Glasgow the night your wife was raped and murdered Joe.' shouted Healy.

Healy was studying Turner carefully. He could see the panic in his eyes. I prayed he could not see the same in mine.

'I wasn't,' said Joe.

'You were Joe, we have your train ticket, found it in the inside pocket of your jacket. Bit careless that Joe.'

My mind was racing, in turmoil. I couldn't understand it. Neither could Joe. He was positive he had tossed that ticket, positive. I knew he hadn't.

'No you haven't.'

'Yes we have. It's at the lab now and when it comes back with your finger prints on it Joe then you are in big soapy bubble Joe. Very big soapy bubble indeed.'

'Well, what's it going to be then Joe?' Healy's gruff tone interrupting my train of thought. I repeated to Joe to say nothing. He ignored me.

'OK I'll tell you about that week-end but let's get one thing straight from the beginning, I did not kill Kate. I loved her.'

Over the next twenty minutes Joe Turner explained that he suspected his wife was having an affair and that he had decided to follow her to Glasgow to try and find out and "sort out the git" if it was true. He had decided to kill two birds with one stone by taking his own girlfriend along for a romantic break in Edinburgh at the same time and nipping through to Glasgow on the Saturday while she met up with some distant family relatives, the hypocrisy of his own affair not seeming to register. He said that he had been in Glasgow on the fateful day but that he hadn't been able to find Kate, as he had planned on following her when she left her mother's house unaware that she had never actually been there. He claimed he spent a bit of time wandering around Glasgow in the off chance he might see her but that he had returned to Edinburgh well before the time his wife was apparently killed, and that he had definitely never been out to the Clyde Valley. Healy and Dornan asked a couple of questions but basically just took the story in to ponder over later.

'And what about Saturday night just gone Joe. Where were you then?'

'I can't remember. Pissed.'

'Need to do better than that Joe. But in the meantime tell us about how many people you've stabbed, oh let's say, since you were a teenager.' Dornan said quietly.

'Right. That's it. We're leaving now. If you have anything more to ask you can ask once you get the results from the so called train ticket.' I said staring at Susan Dornan. I hoped to appear calm on the outside but inside I was all over the place. I wasn't even sure if I had been guilty of a dereliction of my duties to my client as his lawyer. 'You can call me Superintendent. You have my number I believe.'

A few minutes later Joe and I found ourselves in a coffee bar around the corner from the police station.

'You've not been sticking me in it have you Ray?'

'Don't be daft, what are you talking about?'

'It's just that I've been thinking Ray, a lot. Especially during that last interview.'

'What's that supposed to fucking mean?' I tried to sound offended, hurt even, but my eyes betrayed me.

'Well I'll tell you Ray will I? The cops seem to know a lot of detail about things and in fucking sharpish time too if you ask me. Conveniently finding things now too it seems. Makes you wonder. If she wasn't dead I'd be thinking that bitch Connor was blabbing. I didn't kill her by the way, I know that now.'

'You told me you didn't know what you'd done at that time Joe, totally lost it you said. For Christ's sake you even told me you were going to kill Julie and you obviously don't know what you did with the train ticket. Now you're using "I can't remember" as your defence for this latest murder. You'd better get a grip Joe.'

'Yeah, I told you Ray, only you. Don't think I'll be using you as my lawyer any more Ray.'

I didn't see the blow coming. Joe's punch knocked me off my seat. He wasn't able to land any more blows as two waiters had rushed over and stood between me and a man I no longer recognised as my boyhood friend. I scrambled to my feet and tried to preserve some form of dignity but Joe had already left. Ten minutes later I was still sitting staring at my coffee. My heart had stopped racing but my mind had not.

A lump had formed on the side of my eye. A young waitress approached the table.

'Are you OK, I bet you didn't deserve that' she said.

'No, I did actually, I truly did.'

**Chapter 13**

Joe and I's relationship had reached what was surely a point of no return. The irony of a situation where one person who was clearly in the wrong, possibly border line mad, appeared to have no regrets or feelings of guilt over what they had done and another person, namely me, who had only tried to save a friend from himself yet was riddled with guilt, even shame, was not lost on me. I had tried in vain to put the whole series of tragedies to the back of my mind and move on as best I could but the enormity of what Joe had possibly done kept dragging me back. I started spending time reading about serial killers. Was that what Joe was, a serial killer? I didn't know but nobody seemed to write stories about people who only killed once. The one thing that did seem to apply to all the murderer was that an early, perhaps traumatic, experience could be the trigger for actions that unfold decades later. What could drive a man to brutally kill a person he loved? I didn't know every detail of Joe's early life but could there be an explanation lying there, waiting to make sense of the madness? And even if there was, what of poor Julie? I looked back on my own upbringing. If that sort of early experience had not soured me against women then what did it take? What the hell could have happened to Joe and why did I not know about it? I was sitting in my office quite dispirited. I would have been even more so had I known about my erstwhile friend Joe Turner's activities in recent days. I still thought of Joe every day. The Glasgow papers had quickly moved on from the insignificance of some mere murders and were fretting over how many kids Brad and Angelina were going to adopt this week. I wondered if I should get back in touch with Joe, try and bury the hatchet. Speak to Susan. Let her know that Joe was not all bad, that he had been a loyal friend, a good father of sorts, that he just had a bit of a temper that was all.

***

*That evening Azrael sat in his apartment listening to his music. He felt the stirrings coming on but couldn't quite pick up the signs. He needed His guidance, to be pointed in the right direction, to be shown who had to die. It was true that sometimes His guidance had troubled him but even then The Lord had sent him a message. "Collateral damage" the American President had called it. It was just the way things had to be sometimes. Innocent people have to die so that what is right can be done.*

*He was happy, had a sense that he was loved and capable of loving, not at all devoured by hate for all women, merely distracted by the evil in some.*

***

The next morning Susan Dornan sat in her office going over the previous day's revelations. Like Healy she couldn't really accept that there was no connection between at least some of the victims. Could it possibly be true that it was just all some huge coincidence? Or could it be that there was a serial killer preying on women and that his activities had somehow over-lapped

Turner's. Or was Turner Azrael? Or Harris? Either way her instinct was to concentrate on the King killing now and that was what she was going to do. She called Healy into her office.

'Matt you and I will go back over everything in the Turner and Connor killings starting back at her hotel, then try to link them to the Jean King killing.'

Dornan and Healy walked into the foyer of The Marriott in Argyle Street. They identified themselves at the reception desk and asked to speak to whoever was on reception duties the day Julie Connor was murdered. By chance the girl they spoke to was the one who was on duty.

'Can we have a quick word then please?' asked Dornan.

'Yes of course. Take a seat over there and I'll get some cover for the desk and be right over.' replied the girl who's name badge read Helen. Five minutes later she came over and sat down beside Healy.

'The man who has been charged with Julie's murder is a guy called Joe Turner. Did he come to the desk and ask for Julie?'

'Yes.'

'Did you know him from him being in the hotel at any other time?'

'No but I did get the impression he knew Julie and wasn't in to book in or anything like that, even though he had a suitcase with him.'

'When you called Julie to tell him Turner was here did she seemed concerned, worried, hesitant at all?'

'No quite the opposite in fact.'

'What do you mean?'

'Well she said "Oh good, tell him I'll be right there" then she appeared almost straight away and give him a kiss when they met.'

'Did you hear what they said?'

'Not really. Something about a drink and going across the road.'

'So she was happy to go with Turner?'

'Yeah I'd say so. Mind you, no surprise there.'

'Why?'

'She was always desperate to get away from the sado who kept coming in and asking for her. She was with him in her office when Turner came in. I think she was glad of the excuse to chase him.'

'Do you know who the guy was?'

'Not really he just called himself Mr Harris.'

Dornan and Healy sat having a coffee in the glass fronted lounge area of the city's Radisson hotel, a few hundred yards from the Marriott.

'What do you think Susan?'

'It could just be a co-incidence. There must be plenty of Harris's about.'

'I know but still we'd better look into it.'

'Say for a moment it is our Harris. What does it mean? Could he be Azrael do you think?'

'No but maybe we need to go and speak to some of Julie Connor's family, see if they know of any Harris connection.'

'Right, we'll do that but let's head back to the station first. See what's happening there.'

'You meeting The Special One tonight?'

'No.'

'Good, fancy dinner?'

'Maybe, we'll see.'

\*\*\*

Ryan Jones, the manager of the Counting House, was not happy with Janet Rice. She was normally reliable enough and a good bar maid, popular with the male customers especially, but she hadn't shown up for two shifts now and wasn't answering her mobile. Moira Semple wasn't happy with Janet Rice either. Janet was a good neighbour but music had been playing constantly now for two days. It wasn't particularly loud more just a constant thumping sound. She decided if things were still the same when she came back from work she was going to call the police.

\*\*\*

In the squad room the phone rang on John Frame's desk. It was John Forrest from the lab looking for Paul Allan. Forrest explained that Allan was out but he would take a message. Forrest let him know that DNA samples found on and in the suitcase found in the Cathedral House Hotel matched Kate Turner's. Frame had just finished making a note of what had been said when he saw Dornan and Healy coming in. He followed them into Dornan's office.

'Just to let you know, the DNA on the suitcase, remember, the one from the hotel.'

'Yeah.'

'It's Kate Turner's suitcase all right.'

'Good, we'll get a team round there right away to go over the room she stayed in. Bit of time has passed but you never know.'

'John, who's out in the squad room at the moment?'

'Jack and Jill ma'am.'

'Good we've got a few hills to climb' said Healy.

Frame winced, Dornan smiled despite herself 'Tell them to come in.'

'Right everyone let's go back to the beginning. Kate Turner books into the Cathedral House Hotel with a man. Maybe her husband, maybe Harris, maybe bloody Lord Lucan but sometime later Kate Turner is killed, most likely it now seems by Peter Harris but not definitely, or possibly by the mystery guy she was staying with or by her husband, or a local tramp Colin Banks. Harris's and Bank's DNA found at the scene. Some days later Kate Turner's friend, and alibi, Julie Connor is also killed. Joe Turner practically caught at the scene, and has admitted assaulting her, but denies murder. Matt and I have now found out that Julie Connor was being pestered by a Mr Harris minutes before she was killed. We don't know if it's our guy but John, I want you to go to the Marriott with a photo and ask if they are one and the same. A third victim's body was then discovered at the week-end; Jean King. No DNA at this scene. Anybody got anything to add?'

'The calling cards and "names" left at the murder scenes ma'am?' said Jill French.

'Keep going Jill. What are your thoughts on those?' said Dornan.

'Ma'am before Jill goes on may I just say something about the cards?' interrupted Jack T'Baht.

'OK Jack, what is it?'

Jack T'Baht was torn. He didn't want to reveal too much of what he knew, especially to a woman superior, but at the same time he wanted credit for an input to the case.

'Ma'am, Azrael cards have been found at two of the crime scenes. I have a little knowledge of scriptures and know that Azrael was, according to the Old Testaments, one of the Archangels. The one who delivered God's wrath and justice.'

'What do you get from that Jack?'

'I'm not sure but if we now accept the notion that there is a serial killer at work here then maybe some warped religious notion is driving him. His motive will not be love or jealousy, money or revenge, but the desire for power, God's power, and the ultimate power is the power over life and death. Each individual killing is like the link in a chain. The chain starts with the reasoning and ends with achievement. I'm not at all sure the profiler is right.'

'So are you saying this guy thinks he's an angel or what?' asked Healy

'Who knows?'

The room fell silent.

'Jack, that's excellent work. Well done. Jill, how are you getting on with your theory?'

'I think Jack is absolutely right and I think the "reasoning" Jack mentioned comes from a link to the victim's initials, but to be fair I'm struggling to tie everything in. But I do have a view.'

'Let's hear it.'

'OK. Kate Turner, KT, books into a hotel, possibly with Mr X. Her initials link her to the singer KT Tunstall in the killer's mind. He gives her the Tunstall necklace before killing her. I'm going to jump now to Jean King but I'll work back. What if the killer sees himself as some sort of avenging angel, put on earth to avenge the wrongs done to, who knows, Mary Magdalene or whatever.'

'But wouldn't he kill men or priests if that was the case?' asked Healy.

'Well maybe if you put rational thinking into the theory but can you do that? I don't think so.'

'OK. Go on Jill,' said Dornan.

'Right, so he gets talking to Jean King in a bar, restaurant, some place. Finds out her initials are JK. Something clicks in his mind. JK...... JK Rowling. Bam, he kills her.'

'But why? That's it, her initials,' asked Healy.

'Why not? There was a similar case a few years back in the States. I can't remember the exact details but yes, initials were his motivation. You've got to remember, this guy is a serial killer, his reasoning process is different to most peoples. You yourself Sir say that there are no coincidences in murder enquiries. Two murders, two calling cards. Two murders, two stabbings. Two murders, two sexual encounters. Two murders, two women. It's got to be the same guy.'

'What about Julie Connor?' Healy asked, but hesitantly.

'No card.'

'So not our guy? Definitely Turner?'

'Well I'm not sure you can rule him out or that it wasn't Turner who killed all three for that matter. '

'What? Why not?'

'The other murders took place when the victim and killer were alone. Maybe the killer in the Connor killing didn't have time to leave a card, or have sex. There's also something else.'

'What?' said Dornan.

'Her initials ma'am.'
'JC - Jesus Christ.'
'You said it,' added Healy.

***

Moira Semple got home around 6.00pm. The music was still playing in Janet Rice's flat and she was determined that she wasn't going to sit through another night of its deadening thud. She also thought she detected a strange smell coming from the flat's front door as she passed it on the stairs. She was going to phone the police as soon as she had her slippers on.

## Chapter 14

The phone rang on McFarlane's desk.

'Where?' he said in a whispered voice although he was alone in his office.

'Right. Don't let anyone else in. We'll be there in ten minutes.'

McFarlane hurried over to Dornan's room, glad to see a few of the squad were there.

'A woman's body has been found in a flat in Partick. Sounds like our guy.'

When Dornan and Healy got to the flat the smell had eased slightly with the door being left open. A young police woman was taking a statement from a woman and another constable was standing just outside the flat door. The body of Janet Rice was lying beside her bed. The name Tolkien had been cut into her forehead, probably by a bloodied pair of scissors lying on the floor not far from her sightless eyes. Healy walked into the small kitchen. Some dishes stood on the draining board, two empty wine glasses and an empty bottle of Rioja lying in the sink. Dornan had picked up a passport from a bedroom drawer. She called through to the kitchen.

'Matt.'

'What?'

'Jill French is right. Janet Rose Rice, JRR. Christ Almighty.'

Dornan had lost all faith in her ability to deal with what was going on all around her. She had begun to wonder if she wanted to carry on. After putting everything in motion at the murder scene she and Healy went to the tea room in Kelvingrove Art Gallery not far from the murder scene. Healy sat at a table while Dornan collected two coffees. He looked out at one of the exhibition halls. Dinosaurs. *Is that what I am, a dinosaur?*

Dornan sat down opposite him.

'I need your help Matt.'

'Of course. What is it?'

'I don't know what to do.'

'About what?'

'About anything to be honest. Work. I've completely messed up. Can't even think what we should be working on. And God knows what McFarlane thinks. As for my personal life.'

'That's rubbish Susan. No-one could possibly have foreseen this. There has been nothing like it in Glasgow since Bible John back in the '60's and he was never caught. Peter Tobin doesn't count. His victims were practically kids and the connection between them wasn't made for twenty-odd years. Our guy is showing us the connection as he goes along. Mind you, some people think Tobin is Bible John just like I think Turner is Azrael. All we can do is plod away and see what comes up. I still think there's something about the Julie Connor killing we're missing. And I know I sound like a broken record but if it's true about a serial killer only killing strangers then what are the odds of him picking on a victim and her friend at random. I just don't buy it.'

'OK but today seems to back up Jill French's theory. Bible Johnnie Mark 2 seems to choose his victims because of their initials.' They sat in silence for a few moments. Healy smiled.

'You like this mystery boyfriend then?'

'Yeah I do. So before you ask, I don't bloody know.'

'Thought there was a kind of glow about you recently.'

'A lady has to try Matt. Think the rest of the squad have noticed I've lost weight?'

'Yeah, only the other day I heard John Frame say: what an arse!'

'Ha bloody ha.' Dornan's phone rang. 'Jill.'

'We've found an Azrael card' was all that was said in reply.

***

Paul Allan had never been so happy. He felt he was more than holding his own in the squad despite being a rookie but, even more importantly, he felt he was in love. Most guys he'd met in the past weren't really into commitment and, if he was being honest, neither was he. Until now. Max Kermack was caring and considerate and seemed genuinely interested in Allan's work. It was his day off and Max had thrown a sickie so they could spend some time together. They were sitting in a bistro in The Merchant City.

'Paul, remember I said about my attempts at writing? I know you're working on some murder thing at the moment. Is there any way you could get me involved, you know as a kind of observer. Maybe let me see a line-up, sit-in on an interview, whatever.'

'Difficult Max, difficult. Wouldn't bother me but I'm pretty low in the pecking order.'

'The girl that got murdered out in the Clyde Valley, Kate, I knew her once you know.'

'How come?'

'She was friends with my sister when she was young and I tagged along a couple of times. Lost touch though.'

'Maybe a good thing Max. It's not nice to be too close to a murder victim, affects some people really badly.'

'Got anyone for it?'

'Yes and no. One of my bosses thinks it was her husband and one thinks it was a kind of boyfriend she had over here. There are also other possibilities though so I'm not sure how that will pan out in the end.'

'What about that girl that worked in a hotel or somewhere, what's happening there?'

'Same scenario. It seemed pretty straight forward at first but now we're not so sure. Could be any one of two or three possibilities that one. Some talk of a serial killer as well but keep that to yourself.'

'OK but when you're more certain could you maybe arrange for me to meet the guy, would be brilliant for background, research that kind of thing.'

'Don't know Max. Tell you what, if I can wangle the boss into sending me to see him for something I'll try and slip you in.'

'Well you're good at that Paul, I should know.'

***

Two days has passed since the Janet Rice killing and at McFarlane's insistence the DNA testing from the crime scene had been prioritised and John Forrest was giving the squad a brief run through of the results.

'As you are all aware DNA from two individuals was found on the body later identified as being that of Kate Turner. Both of the samples were eventually traced to two known individuals. Subsequently we have tested DNA from a further two murders, those of Jean King and Janet Rose Rice. All the samples unfortunately match the victim's only, or, in the King case, her husband, who has been eliminated from enquiries. Thankfully I am not the detective, merely the messenger, so I'll now leave the rest to you.'

Dornan and Healy exchanged stares.

'Shit,' said Healy

'Shit indeed,' replied Dornan.

'It's what we expected to be fair.'

'Suppose'.

Most of the squad and McFarlane sat in the Incident Room attempting to make sense of what they had just heard.

'Christ almighty Matt, how wrong can we be?' asked Dornan.

'Hang on a minute. You are not trying to tell me that a woman and her friend are both killed within days of each other and there's no connection are you. You heard yourself the profiler saying that serial killers kill strangers. OK King and Rice appear to fit into that but come on, I just don't buy it.'

'How do you explain no matching DNA being present in these latest two killings then?' asked McFarlane

'And the calling cards?' added Jill French.

Healy stared, lost in thought.

'At the moment, I can't but the calling cards could just be a red herring. Someone already in the picture trying to throw us of track with this serial killer angle.'

'What about Jill's initials theory? It stacks up Matt.'

'Same as the cards. Smokescreen.'

'Pretty clever ones then don't you think?'

'Right here's how we proceed from here.' said McFarlane. 'We treat the Connor killing as a separate issue but look at the possibility that it wasn't Turner. The other three killings; Kate Turner, Jean King, Janet Rice are treated as one investigation.'

'There is another possibility' said Healy.

'What's that?' asked Dornan.

'Turner is Azrael.'

'You're obsessed by Turner, Matt.'

'Why? Think about it. He kills his wife for obvious reasons. Then her pal for shielding her plus he's admitted he hated her. Then King and Rice because he's now off his head and on a mission against women. We don't know where he's been and what he's been doing recently do we. He's stuck here with no work, no passport, I'm telling you it's him.'

'You could use the exact same thinking for Harris then. And we've placed him at the scene of the first murder and possibly close to the scene of the second. Which reminds me, I want that photo into the Marriott pronto.' replied Dornan.

'Could I add something ma'am.' said Jack T'Baht.

'Of course, what is it Jack?'

'Didn't the profiler say that the killer possibly had a mother fixation?'

'Yes...and?'

'Well we don't know much about Colin Bank's movements recently either. He certainly ticks that particular box.'

'He does but I can't see Jean King or Janet Rice having much to do with a down and out. Certainly not inviting him into their home. Did you smell him? No we can forget him, too off the wall.'

T'Baht nodded and looked away *'More off the wall than a stranger killing serial killer who just happens to kill people who know each other? I'm right, and I'll prove it somehow.'*

Healy walked over to his desk, picked up his coat and shuffled out of the room. Dornan watched and wondered.

\*\*\*

Martha Reid was sitting in her favourite chair looking out of the bay window of her flat. People, cars and dogs came and went but Martha saw none of this activity. She was pondering the meaning of what had popularly become known as 'closure.' She had now outlived both her children and her husband and, she felt, the point of living at all.

She thought about Joe Turner and her grandchildren in Spain. Joe had called by a couple of times and phoned once or twice but without Kate there was no real bond. Her grandchildren never called. She wondered if Joe had killed Kate. She wondered if Joe had killed Julie. She wondered if she even cared now.

\*\*\*

The following morning Susan Dornan allocated tasks to the squad. John Frame was concentrating on trying to trace Ivana Jakanowski, the former receptionist from The Cathedral House Hotel. Since the DNA evidence from Kate Turner's suitcase had proved that she had stayed at the Cathedral House he had quickly established that the employee who would have been on duty when Kate Turner booked in, with her mystery, perhaps, killing partner was Ivana Jakanowski but that she had now left the hotel. No-one seemed to know where she had moved on to or where she lived, a sad reflection on modern life he felt, but it was paramount to trace her as she may well be the only person who had actually seen the possible killer. *Seen Azrael?*

It had been difficult getting any back ground on her. With Poland now being in the EEC and the "Open Borders" freedom that followed from that, he couldn't even be sure when she had come into the country, far less where she might be working after leaving the hotel. He made an enquiry with the tax office to see if he could trace her work history through a tax code if she had one and been in touch with the Polish police to see if they could trace a relative who might have a phone number or address for her.

By 10.00am Jill French was entering the Marriott Hotel with a photo of Peter Harris. She had phoned ahead to ensure the receptionist Helen was working that morning.

'Helen I'm going to show you a number of photos. If you recognise the man you know as Mr Harris, the man who asked for Julie Connor the day she was murdered, can you just point him out to me.'

By 10.10am Jill French was leaving the hotel and on her mobile phone to Susan Dornan.

'It's our Harris,' was all she said.

Jack T'Baht was angry. Angry that his suggestion that Boom Boom Colin Banks could be Azrael hadn't been given the credence he felt it deserved and angry that his *superior* and his *inferior* work colleagues, *both women*, had formed some sort of mutual admiration society when it came to theories on these cases. He intended putting a stop to that.

***

Matt Healy had not gone into work that morning. He was sitting in his living room fixating on Joe Turner and any mistakes he may have made. *You may think you're some sort of avenging angel you fuck but I'll be cutting your wings off very soon. You can be sure of that.* He also thought of Susan Dornan. Why had she slept with him if Ray Ford was so special? Why are women the way they are? *Fucking bitches.* He looked at the side board and the photograph taken many years before of his passing out of Police College. Him and his mother. No father present. He in his crisp uniform, her in the blue coat he had bought her. He had liked buying her things. Although she had never seemed to appreciate his efforts he was certain that she was grateful, and proud of him. What would she have done in her later years anyway had he not stayed on living at home? Yes, she had been grateful. It just wasn't in her nature to show it. He got up, picked up his car keys from the hall table and left.

## Chapter 15

It was a Friday night that Susan Dornan and I first made love. We had been to a movie and then gone back to her flat. We had chatted for a while and when I had hinted about making a move to leave she had quietly said: 'Why don't you just stay?' So I had.

We were lying in her bed when she told me of the developments in the murder cases that were beginning to draw the attention of the Glasgow media.

'Looks like we're facing a serial killer Ray.'

'Christ.'

'Azrael actually.'

'What?'

'Calls himself Azrael. After an Archangel who dishes out justice apparently.'

'Right. Does this mean Joe Turner is off the hook?'

'Not really. Matt Healy thinks Turner is Azrael. Besides there is no doubt Turner killed Julie Connor. Although....'

'Although what?'

'Sorry Matt I can't say. If anything changes I'll let you know I promise but we will need to talk to Turner again.'

'Make sure I'm present Susan. You know the rules and I don't like the sound of Healy's thinking.'

'I will. If it's any consolation I don't agree with the Turner as Azrael line either.'

'Any ideas who it could be?'

'One but even that's a very long shot indeed.'

'Bet I know who you're thinking of.'

'Who?'

'Tony the Tiger, he's a cereal killer.'
'Oh ha ha, everyone's a comedian these days.'

***

Joe Turner was lying in bed as well. Unaware of the scenario that was forming around him or, if truth be told, unaware of a lot of what had been happening over recent weeks. He would never admit he had a drink problem but he was now willing to admit that he couldn't handle the binges the way he used to be able to. He could remember leaving his bed-sit a couple of days ago and he was definitely back there now but what had happened in the intervening time was a haze. He had staggered to the bathroom that morning for a pee and an aspirin, seen the scratches on his cheek and decided to go back to bed. He knew he had told Martha he would pop in that afternoon but he wasn't going anywhere looking the way he did, far less Martha's. He would phone her when he got the chance. He remembered deciding to walk into the city centre and stopping at a couple of bars on the way. He didn't remember how many 'a couple' consisted off but could remember being 'well on' by the time he reached the Counting House. From there it was a pick- up, possibly a bar maid, something to eat and a carry out back at her place. Then nothing.

***

Colin Boom Boom Banks was lying down as well but he didn't have the luxury of a bed to lie on. He too was unaware of what was developing around him, or of where or what he had been doing over the last few days. His bed was made up of two discarded tarpaulin sheets with a folded cardboard box as a pillow. The scratches on his face as mysterious as the whereabouts of his knife that he had searched in vain for earlier.

*He couldn't let his mother know he had lost his knife. He would save his pocket money and go to the shops and buy one that looked just the same. Money? He peered into his personal mist. He remembered going to some doors offering to do some work. Two kind ladies offering him food. Had he eaten? He couldn't say.*

\*\*\*

Susan Dornan had decided not to call Matt Healy. She was sure he would check in once he had calmed down and looked rationally at the evidence. Besides after the previous night with Ray Ford she wasn't keen on reminders of her stupidity getting in the way of the feeling of contentment she was enjoying at that moment.

She and Jill French were on their way to Uddingston to question Peter Harris about what his business with Julie Connor was on the day she was murdered. Harris didn't seem fazed or upset at their arrival. He asked them in and showed them into the living room. He offered tea. Both women declined

'Mr Harris were you at The Marriott Hotel talking to Julie Connor shortly before she was murdered?'

'Yes.'

'What were you talking about?'

'I was asking her for a favour, some understanding.'

'About what?'

'I'm not prepared to say. It was a private conversation and has no bearing on what happened later.'

'How do you know Julie?'

Harris paused 'we're reconciled friends.'

'Was she an ex- girlfriend of yours? The age gap is about right for you.'

'Petty, detective, very petty indeed. And you couldn't be further from the truth.'

'Tell us the truth then.'

'I have. I went there to speak to her. Shortly after I arrived someone else called in to see her and she left with him. Then I left as well.'

'Did you see this other person?'

'No.'

'Where did you go?'

'Into the city centre. Some shopping.'

'What did you buy?'

'Some CD's, couple of books.'

French caught Dornan's understanding glance reflected from the glass coffee table.

'What kind of music do you like then Peter? Any favourite authors?'

'It varies. Why? You going to arrest me for bad taste now. Oh and by the way my lawyer says that there is no chance of this ridiculous rape/murder charge going to court.'

'Did he indeed?'

'Yes and he's a she actually.'

'So come on, what music do you like?'

'Leona Lewis, Amy MacDonald, Shania Twain...'

'All women. Interesting. KT Tunstall?'

'Maybe.'

'What about authors?'

'What about them?'

'Who do you like to read?'
'Terry Pratchett, that kind of thing.'
'Not real world stuff then. You like fantasy stuff?'
'Is there a point to this?'
'Ever read the Bible, Peter? Old Testament.'
'Yes.'
'What you think?'
'About what?'
'The Bible. Any hidden messages there do you think?'
'Wouldn't say they were hidden actually. But before you ask anything else, my taste in garden furniture or whatever, I'd like you to leave now.'

Harris escorted French and Dornan to the front door.

Dornan turned 'We'll speak again Azrael.' Harris paused, smiled, then gently closed the door.

French looked across at Dornan as she started up the car. 'What do you think?' she asked.

'I think it's him.'

\*\*\*

*That afternoon Azrael sat in his car. He watched the women walking through the city centre. Shopping, going to work, some with children, some with friends, all dressed like whores. His In Car I Pod connection allowed him to listen to his own choices and save him from the inane ramblings of local radio cretins. He sat, he watched, he could feel sweat on his forehead yet he was calm. He felt his work may soon be done. The Lord rewarding him for a life time of devotion. He focused again on the passing crowds. Perhaps one or two more, one or two.*

By the time Dornan and French had returned from speaking to Harris Matt Healy was at his desk. He had the file on the Kate Turner murder spread across his desk. Dornan gave him a quizzical look.

'Thought you were concentrating on the Connor killing Matt?' She said as she pulled up a chair to his desk.

'Oh you know what the song goes "Let's start at the very beginning, it's a very good place to start", Sound of Music I think, Julie Andrews,' Healy replied.

'Take your word on that one Matt. Before my time.'

'Aye right.' They both smiled.

'Susan, let's think, open minds, outside the box and all that shit. Who are the possibles for this?' he said pointing at the open file. 'Harris, Turner, Banks, Mr X. So it's fair to assume that one of these four is Azrael as well. Right?'

'OK.'

'OK so the guy has sometimes left us cards. The guy has sometimes left DNA. But we are the ones that have assumed that they are linked. Like Alex Caldow the profiler said; this guy is engaged in an intellectual game with us. T'Baht got me thinking. Banks used to be a doctor right? So he's intelligent right? He's a whacko right? Bodies and semen aren't exactly off limits for him right?'

'I get what you're saying and we've looked at all this before in relation to the Kate Turner killing but it's a stretch Matt to go from that to him definitely killing Kate and being Azrael. I don't buy it, sorry.'

'Let's go and see the work colleague of Banks, Mary Stringer her name was, based at the Nuffield. Can't do any harm. Meantime give Jack some credit and tell him to try and trace Banks and get him in here.'

'You're right. You phone the Nuffield and I'll speak to Jack T'Baht. I'll tell you on the way to speak to Stringer how French and I got on with Harris.'

On the way to the Nuffield Hospital that afternoon Dornan told Healy about the meeting with Harris and her view that he may well be Azrael.

'Well it's either him, Banks or who I told you all along it is, Turner. So let's get to the truth by elimination; starting with Banks if only to show up McFarlane's profiler.'

'What about Mr X?'

'Susan, we don't really know if there even is a Mr X or Harris could be Mr X and Azrael. Fuck, anything's possible the way this load of shit is going.'

Mary Stringer's office was larger and more homely than either Dornan or Healy expected. She saw the slight surprise in their faces and explained that this was also the room she saw her patients in so it needed to put them at ease.

'I suppose I don't need to ask what you are here about, or should I say who?'

'We know you spoke to DC Allan before but could you perhaps go over what you know of Colin Banks for us? We feel it may be important.'

'Of course but can I preface everything by saying that Colin Banks was a good, highly intelligent, kind man. He just fell to the demons that's all, it could happen to any of us.'

'We're not making any assumptions doctor I can assure you and Colin's, well proclivities shall we say, are not of immediate concern to us unless they impact on current enquiries.'

'Well as I said, Colin was a brilliant doctor but his childhood was troubled. His father abandoned him and left his mother to bring Colin up alone. Outwardly she did an excellent job, worked hard to send him to private school, catered for his every need if you like, except the emotional side that only a mother can give. Colin became what used to be called "A Mammy's Boy" and, I think, he ended up with a mother fixation in later life. Paradoxically he also seemed to have problems relating to other women probably because of the incessant hammering into his sub consciousness of the "other woman" who had ruined his father and mothers marriage. Anyway, as you know, Colin eventually turned to "other ways" to express himself and deal with his emotional issues.'

'How do you know these things doctor? Was he a patient as well as a colleague?'

'No but he did confide in me. You should be grateful because had he been a patient I couldn't have spoken to you about him.'

'To your knowledge did he ever actually assault a woman?'

'Not actually assault but we did receive a number of complaints from some female members of staff that he had flown off the handle with them and they feared he might hit them. We spoke to him obviously but he hadn't actually done anything wrong per se and he was shy and timid more than anything. But just before "the end" he was suspended for threatening a Ward Sister with a knife but before any formal action was taken his actions with dead bodies came to light and that was the end of Colin's career obviously, and his time inhabiting the world as we know it.'

'You didn't mention any of this to DC Allan.'

'He never asked the questions you're asking.'

Dornan and Healy both sat trying to react normally to what was not a conversation that most people would regard as normal; both with a feeling that the medical fraternity were closing ranks.

Dornan thanked Stringer for her help and she and Healy headed for their car but before they had reached it Dornan had phoned in to stress the importance of finding Colin Banks.

***

Max Kermack and Paul Allan were sitting in Jamie Oliver's recently opened Italian Restaurant in the city's George Square flicking through holiday brochures.

'I can't really take any leave at the moment Max. Too much going on.'

'Fair enough but no harm in looking. Honeymoon suites look nice. I'll be bringing my laptop by the way. I'm serious about the writing thing.'

'Good, I'd like to read some of your stuff.'

'Only if you contribute dear. Come on Paul what's the latest in poor Kate's murder?'

'Look I've told you I can't say much.'

'What about the hotel receptionist then. How did she actually die?'

'Throat cut.'
'Anything sexual?'
'No.'
'Was Kate's throat cut too?'
'No.'
'Could the same guy have killed them both?'
'Maybe. Look we just don't know Max and that's all I'm saying.'

They left the restaurant shortly after with Allan pondering where to go for a drink and Max Kermack pondering his next move.

## Chapter 16

Healy and Dornan were sitting in McFarlane's office early the next morning. McFarlane was in high spirits; convinced that now all the murders had been cleared up. Over the previous half hour Dornan and Healy had detailed their conversation with Mary Stringer.

'So what you're saying is that you think Banks killed the three victims, other than Connor, he is Azrael,' asked McFarlane.

'Well it's a possibility, yes.'

'Sick bastard.'

'We haven't proved it though Sir.'

'Oh you will Susan, I'm sure of that. Too early to call in the press boys do you think?'

'We haven't even arrested him yet.'

'Fair enough but let me know as soon as you do. And Matt, we've got Turner bang to rights for the Connor killing right?'

'Well...probably...yes.'

'Great.'

Dornan walked to her office and called the profiler. 'Alec, Susan Dornan here. We've got a strong suspect for the Azrael killings. You said the killer probably had a mother thing, can you tell us anything else?'

'Well he's probably killed before. You linked the Connor killing to any others?'

'No not really.'

'Your suspect, is his mother still alive?'

'Wouldn't think so.'

'Start there then.'

Dornan called Jack T'Baht in. 'Any luck finding Banks?'

'No ma'am. I called the solicitor who vouched for him but he hasn't seen him for a few weeks he says.'

'Some guarantor. OK phone his solicitor back and tell him we are going to apply to exhume Banks' mother's body. It's a long shot I know but it might get a reaction' instructed Dornan.

She would be right about that but it would not be the reaction she expected.

***

The day had worn on and spirits were beginning to sink in the squad. Boom Boom Banks was nowhere to be found and nor it seemed was Ivana Jakonowski. Dornan was meeting Ray Ford that evening and had hoped to at least have Banks in custody and have arranged for Ivan Jakonowski to have a look at him the next day. She had had to admit to herself that she found it unlikely that Banks would not have raised an eyebrow or two had he tried to book into a hotel so he obviously wasn't the man with Kate Turner in The Cathedral House so it looked as if the identity of her mystery lover, if he existed, would go to the grave with her.

Jill French also had unanswered questions over Banks as Azrael. *After such elaborate planning would he really have bothered with the initials clue? Would he even have heard of KT Tunstall? Where did the gold necklace come from? By all accounts Banks was a complete mess so could he even have managed to plan all this?*

Matt Healy had gone home. He had hinted to Dornan about a meal but she had pretended not to catch on and he had just left it. *Bitch.* He felt strangely detached over the Banks situation. He had made the running on it and had stormed ahead after speaking to Mary Stringer but now he had similar doubts to French. He sat in the near darkness, only a table lamp light in the corner illuminating the gloom. His stereo played quietly in the back ground. He stared out the window for a while seeing nothing. His eyes turned to the sideboard and the expensively framed photo perched there. *Think I may have made a mistake here Mum. Sorry.*

***

Boom Boom sat by the river. That afternoon he had been semi – coherent and had remembered to call his lawyer by reversing the charges from a call box. His friend told him of the police action over his mother's death. Now he neither knew nor cared what plain he was inhabiting at that moment. His mind was in a state of flux, somehow moving between catalogues of times and places past and present at a rapid rate. Yet moving slowly, drifting; able to drink in every detail.

The doll he adored but his father abhorred; the room where bad boys go; the priest who comforted him; the priest who discussed his wrongdoing well into the night with his mother; his success at exams but never "full marks"; his joy of medicine but hospitals "full of whores"; his realisation that Potter was right and that religion was "the wound, not the bandage"; his mother passing over and now, as he'd always feared, passing back.

Boom Boom stood, his stature unsteady.

He knew there were so many wrongs, so many things that only he could put right.

He walked to his favourite restaurant.

Boom Boom's favourite Italian eatery was busy. Not full, a handful of tables were available, but Boom Boom would only need one. He had been fortunate when he arrived at the front door. There were no members of staff near the entrance and Boom Boom had entered and was approaching a table fairly near the centre of the restaurant before he was really noticed. A few customers had noticed his distinctive odour as he passed their table but by the time a waiter had noticed him it was too late.

Boom Boom climbed on top of the table he had chosen and had let his stained, baggy trousers drop on to the pristine red and white checked table cloth before any member of staff had been able to intercept him. They were now in a state of complete apoplexy as to what to do about the unfolding events, especially when Boom Boom brandished a large knife from within the folds of his coat. There were no shouts or screams, more a case of groups of people sitting in mesmerised silence, some even laughing nervously.

'This has been my favourite restaurant for some time now, delightful cuisine. Mine hosts graciously phoned the police for me a couple of weeks ago and I am now allowing them to repeat their kindness' Boom Boom announced.

'I have done many wrongs in my time on this earth, some I am even unaware of I'm sure, including killing a woman I met by the river only a few weeks ago. What has driven me to this sorry excuse of a man you see before you today? This, always this.'

Boom Boom reached down, slipped his hand between his legs and pulled his withered and wrinkled penis from what appeared to be a pair of soiled football shorts.

'Well no more, the pain has to stop.'

Boom Boom took the knife and in one movement cut off his penis.

There were no more sniggers from the diners. Screams and shouts filled the space that once housed casual chat. Blood arced from between Boom Boom's legs but he remained standing, his eyes shut tight, his lips mumbling some long forgotten prayer. The inside of his head began to swirl, he shouted something about not wanting to go to his room.

\*\*\*

Ivana Jakanowski was pleased with her choice. Her new job, and no tax to worry about, had allowed her to save up enough to buy a mobile phone. The sales assistant in the Costco Store not far from her flat was taking her details. Ivana had known that she would have to give proof of address etc and had brought her rent book and passport with her as the utilities were not yet in her name.

Some phone companies are a bit difficult with handing out contracts to, eh, foreigners, no offence, but if I photocopy your passport and fax it over to them they're usually OK.'

Some 15 minutes later Ivana had her new phone. She was in the system.

\*\*\*

Susan Dornan had reluctantly cancelled her dinner date for that night and was now sitting beside Colin Bank's bed. When the call had come through about what had happened to Colin Banks, she couldn't quite take it in but the bizarre seemed the norm in this man's case. She had interviewed both staff and customers in the restaurant and all agreed that the tramp had admitted to killing a woman "by the river.' She had been informed by doctors when he arrived at the Victoria Infirmary that, under normal circumstances, the patient would live but that Colin Banks was in such a state of bodily decline that he wouldn't see out the night.

'Colin, Colin my name Susan, I'm from the police. How are you feeling?' Dornan knew the question was banal but just what do you ask a man who's just cut off his own penis.

'It all had to stop. No self-control. Make things happen don't let them happen eh constable.'

Dornan let the rank issue pass, she had to establish Banks' meaning.

'Did you kill Kate Turner Colin? The woman by the river, the woman you found, did you stab her with your knife?'

Colin Banks seemed to be examining something on the ceiling. Saliva seeped from the corners of his mouth, moving slowly across the grey stubble of his weathered face and staining the pillow.

'Colin listen to me. You are going to die. If you killed the girl tell me now, a death bed confession. It's the right thing to do. Are you Azrael?'

'Death? Mark Twain said he had been dead billions of years before he was born and not suffered the slightest inconvenience from it. But he spread joy, I spread misery, it's right that it stops now.'

'Do you like to read Colin?'

'No more reading for Colin I fear.'

'Are you guilty Colin, I must know. Did you kill those women? Are you Azrael?'

Colin Bank's brow furrowed.

'Do you believe in angels sergeant?'

'Yes, yes I do Colin. Are you an angel Colin? An angel of mercy maybe?'

Boom Boom's eyes closed.

'Colin, Colin. The women Colin, did you kill them?'

'An angel? Yes, it's true I'm an angel, I'm not innocent. So many bodies,' BB muttered

'Then you deserve to be punished Colin.' Dornan was surprised by the venom in his voice.

'Ha officer, I've had a life time of punishment, this isn't punishment, this is release' merely a whisper now.

'Did you kill your mother as well Colin?'

Boom Boom felt the tears forming in his eyes as he turned his face into the pillow.

*Even now she is here.*

A nod of confirmation seemed to follow as Colin Bank's head slumped onto his skeletal shoulders.

Susan Dornan left the room to phone McFarlane and Healy; Professor Colin Boom Boom Banks, Good Boy, left the room forever.

\*\*\*

It was a dank morning in the Incident Room. The atmosphere a strange mix of satisfaction, pleasure even, uncertainty and disbelief. No-one was quite sure how to react to the fact that the recent spate of murders had all apparently been solved. All the squad knew that normally people confessing to murders meant virtually nothing as every nutjob and zoomer in Glasgow usually held their hands up for any crime that appeared in the news, but this was different. Colin Banks was a front line suspect and, most importantly, his had been a death bed confession. Chief Superintendent McFarlane had called a case review meeting for that morning where all the details of the case were to be gone over with a member of The Procurator Fiscal's Office there to advise on the way forward. Followed by a press conference, that he would obviously chair. Susan Dornan was deep in thought.

'What do you really make of this confession Susan?' Healy's voice bringing her back into the present.

'Not sure really. You?' Dornan replied.

'Could be true but I'm not convinced. I know I started the ball rolling with Banks, well T'Baht did really but you know what I mean, Banks was a weirdo without question but I just don't see him for this.'

'I still think it was Harris that killed Kate Turner and him hanging around when Julie Connor was killed bothers me more than slightly. I saw his face when Jill and I questioned him Matt. There's something not right there.'

'That long week-end in Marbella still says it's Joe Turner for his wife and Julie. The other two

I can't quite work out. The cards are the flies in the ointment. But if either of us are right about the first two then the same guy did all four. I'm sure of it.'

Chief Inspector McFarlane was standing at the front of the room just to the right of the Incident Board where the photos of the four victims and three suspects were pinned. Colin Banks' face eerily appearing twice; one from when he was alive-ish and one from when he was most certainly dead. Strangely Banks looked more content in the mortuary photo.

'Well done Susan, another case wrapped up quickly. I've called a press conference for 1.00 p.m. if you want to sit in.'

'I'm not sure things are definitely resolved Sir. Still a lot of unanswered questions.'

'Yes, yes, but mostly side issues. The murders are the issue and we've got our men.'

'Well I'm just about to review the case with the squad Sir if you want to sit in, hear all these, eh, side issues.'

'Listen Susan I don't see your problem. We're under intense pressure internally and externally with the press etc. You've solved the murders in pretty record time, not to mention spectacular style as far as the press goes, and you seem to be looking for reasons to scupper the whole thing.'

'I just want to be sure sir.'

'Did you or did you not ask Banks if he was Azrael?'

'Yes.'

'Right. Did you or did you not ask him if he had killed three of our victims?'

'Yes.'

'Did he or did he not answer yes to those two questions?'

'Yes....kind of.'

'Right, cases closed, job well done. Speak to the PF agree what the final scenario is and move on. Matt organise a night in the pub tonight for the squad will you, first couple of rounds on me.'

The meeting with the PF was brief. She was happy with McFarlane's assessment of the situation and pointed out that the defence lawyer of any other suspect put on trial for the Kate Turner murder would only have to tell the jury of a death bed confession from someone that the police themselves had proved was at the initial scene to have the case blown out of the water; then the Azrael card would be introduced and everything would fall apart.

That evening's celebratory drink had started all fairly subdued. McFarlane excepted. He had been true to his word and had stood the first couple of rounds and left a further fifty pounds behind the bar before making his excuses and leaving. As time passed and McFarlane's generosity had started to kick in the atmosphere lightened.

'At least you've made a whirl wind start to your new post Susan' said Healy.

'Yeah, I suppose but....'

'Look, I know what you're thinking and I'm not entirely happy with all of it myself but you know yourself that's police work. You never get all the answers. Besides we've got Turner, we've got Harris and closed the files on the two others.'

'Well I wouldn't say closed. I'm still going to follow up on Harris being at The Marriott and we've never really pursued him over his first wife either. But not tonight. A few more drinks in here is my sole plan.'

The table John Frame was sitting at ended up being shared by a group of girls obviously intent on getting a head start on the alcohol front before heading off to a club to celebrate one of their numbers recent engagement. Much to Jack T'Baht's disgust. Frame had entered into the spirit of things and, at McFarlane's expense, was giving the girl's his lowdown on marriage.

'I blame my mum for my views. When I was a kid I asked her what a couple was and she said, oh two or three.'

One of the girls tried to bring T'Baht in to the conversation but he made it clear he wasn't interested. She stood 'I'm going out for a fag.'

'Smoking is bad for you' said T'Baht

'Yeah, well my dad lived till he was 86' she replied.

'Smoker?'

'Naw, he minded his own business,' she shouted as she headed for the door, convulsing her friends.

T'Baht turned to Dornan. 'Godless' he said.

'Oh I don't know Jack. Religion is not always the answer.'

'You don't believe?'

'Well I like Jesus but he loves me so it's awkward.'

*Just another harlot.*

Shortly afterwards Jack T'Baht made his excuses and left. Frame was in full flow with the future bride.

'So hen, how long should it take for your man to open a can of beer?'

'Dunno.'

'No time, it should be open when you bring him it. I'm only joking, marriage is actually a magic thing.'

'You think so?'

'Aye, it turns a fox into an elephant.'

'That's awful you.'

'I know. Actually I like fat girls.... and mopeds.'

'How's that?'

'Well they're both fun to ride until your pals find out.'

Healy and Dornan were enjoying the banter, the tension of recent weeks ebbing away. Dornan though slightly peeved that Ray Ford hadn't replied to her text saying she wouldn't be over later.

'Fancy catching something to eat Matt?' asked Dornan. 'I stay here much longer I'll be totally pissed and Frame will have me committing suicide for even thinking of marriage.'

'Sounds good to me.' They left the pub a few minutes later to cat calls and shouts of "Light weights." Healy practically oblivious to the ribbing, deep in thought.

\*\*\*

*Later that evening Azrael too was deep in thought. The Lord had called on him. His mission was not yet over. He listened to his music, searching for signs, but none came. He walked to the window. Looked out. Orange tinted darkness. Not tonight. Soon, but not tonight. He slipped into bed. He lay lost in his calling. He thought of the whores. His blood thundered through his brain and penis. He plunged the knife into Kate's breasts. His mind swirled. His body rigid. His torment spurting from his body. He slept.*

## Chapter 17

I could tell Susan Dornan was more than a little surprised to see me walking into the chapel. There were only half a dozen or so people there to attend Colin Banks' funeral. Susan came over to me after I had helped place the coffin in the back of the hearse and watched it make its final journey.

'I didn't know you knew Colin Banks.'

'We were at school together.'

'So you were the lawyer who vouched for him. Why?'

'Like I said we were boyhood friends. Kind of kindred spirits I suppose. Both from single parent homes; frowned upon in those days, especially in Jesuit Taliban land.'

'Why didn't you say you knew him when you knew his connection to the Kate Turner case? I would have thought you could have confided in me considering.'

'Like the train ticket you mean?'

Susan and I both looked at the retreating hearse.

'Susan it's done. I don't want to fall out over it. You mean too much to me.'

'Do I honestly?'

'Honestly....I think.'

'What?'

'Nothing. Let's go for a coffee or something. I'm not going to the crematorium, too depressing. Besides, Colin's body might go off like an atomic bomb.'

We walked down Garnethill and found a coffee shop close to the city's dental hospital.

'Sorry about last night Ray. McFarlane insisted on a celebration and I'm afraid I celebrated, if that's the right word, a bit too much. What did you get up to, once you found out the love of your life; that's me incidentally, wasn't coming over.'

'Stayed in Jezebel. No, I was fine. Read a little, had an early night. Thought about poor Colin.'

'What do you think?'

'About him being Azrael?'

'Yes.'

'It's possible I suppose but no, I just don't believe it. Colin was, well a zombie, for most of the time and for the rest of the time he was a sad, gentle soul.'

'Yeah a gentle soul who lost his job for threatening women, desecrating dead bodies and admitted to me that he was the killer.'

I looked down at my plate, fidgeted with my knife.

'It's true.'

'What is?'

I looked into Susan's eyes 'You are the love of my life.'

***

Matt Healy knew Dornan was going to the Banks funeral that morning so hadn't rushed into the station. He had made himself a cup of tea and was standing in his kitchen looking out at a squirrel stealing the nuts he had put out for the birds. Something his mother had done religiously. He had a good feeling about the previous night. He had gotten out of the pub with Susan before the alcohol consumption would have left him hung over that morning but, more importantly, Susan had asked him to leave with her. She had suggested the meal. *Maybe she's the kind of woman who likes to make the running, be in control. Fine by him.* He had made a point of not mentioning a boyfriend and hadn't attempted any parting kiss or romantic gesture of any kind. *Cool Matt, very cool.* He looked at his watch and decided to make a move. As soon as Susan came in he was going to suggest a run out to grill Harris again.

***

Paul Allan was standing in his own kitchen. Max Kermack wandered in wearing only his boxers. Allan had told him the whole story around Banks the previous night, adding in the suggestion that it had been his initial interview with Mary Stringer that had provided the vital clue. Max as usual showed great interest in what Allan had to say about his work; was eager for further details.

'So this tramp killed everyone but definitely not Julie Connor, is that what you're saying?'

'That's it in a nut shell. Things will slacken off a little now Max, want me to put in for some leave? Take that holiday we talked about?'

'So who's in the frame for that?'

'What?'

'Julie Connor.'

'Christ Max I've told you we're not sure. What is it with you?'

'OK sorry. It's just that I'm passionate about the writing, you know that. I want to get it as authentic as possible. Remember your promise that's all.'

'I didn't promise Max. I said I'd try. Now shut up and come here.'

\*\*\*

Dornan reached the squad room before Healy. Her joy was hidden but unbridled. She was uncertain whether to say anything to Healy but he had behaved impeccably the night before and seemed to have accepted that friends were all they could ever be now. She scanned the room. Only French and T'Baht were in. French seemed engrossed in some paper work but T'Baht seemed to be staring at her.

'Everything all right Jack? I'll remember to give special mention to the fact that you were the first to raise concerns over Banks. I've just left his funeral by the way. He should be well on his way to meet the other Archangels by now.'

'Thank you ma'am.' T'Baht looked down at his desk and opened some old case notes. *Heretic slut.* He glanced across at French. *JF...Jezebel Fuck.* He rubbed his eyes, rose slowly and walked out of the office. Controlled breathing containing his rage.

Healy entered the near deserted office shortly after T'Baht left.

'My God Susan, it Christmas today and nobody told me?'

'I know but I don't mind them having a bit of a lie in after last night. Can't see McFarlane making an appearance anyway, can you?'

'No chance. Anyway, how you feeling?'

'Absolutely great Matt. Honestly, life couldn't be better.'

Healy smiled, *he was right.*

'How you feel about tackling Harris this morning then?'

'Let's go.'

Susan Dornan and Matt Healy sat in Healy's car a few yards from Harris' front door. They would walk to the door giving Harris less time to see them and perhaps attempt to cover whether he was at home or not.

'Right, let's get in and have a word with this bastard.' Susan shook her head and suppressed a smile.

Peter Harris sat with his back to the patio doors studying Dornan and Healy.

'How's things with you Peter?' asked Dornan.

'Confused' replied Harris.

'Oh, what about?'

'As to why you are here.'

'Well we're confused as well as it happens.'

'Oh.'

'Yes, we can't work out what you were doing at The Marriott Hotel speaking to a young woman shortly before she was brutally murdered. Why you never came forward when you heard she'd been murdered. Small things like that.'

'I told you. We were catching up that's all.'

'Catching up on what?'

'Old times.'

'Need to do better than that Peter.'

'No I don't actually. I don't need to talk to you at all as it happens. As I'm sure you know.'

'Heard from Sally?'

'No.'

'The kids?'

Harris just stared with hollow eyes.

'Right Peter, tell you why else we're here. We think you killed your first wife Ann.'

Harris stared at Dornan for a moment. He appeared about to say something. Stopped. Wilted. Looked out into the garden.

'I did.'

'What?'

'You're right I did.'

Dornan looked at Healy, back at Harris, and back again at Healy.

'You're admitting to killing Ann Harris?'

'Yes.'

'Why did you kill her?'

'She'd just told me that our daughter wasn't mine.'

'What happened?'

'We were having a shouting match at the top of the stairs. I pushed her. Not hard but she went down the stairs and that was that.'

'Do you know who the real father was?'

'No. I never asked. Never got the chance really. It didn't make any difference to me. I still loved my kids. But I couldn't cope on my own. They went into foster care and were eventually adopted.'

'Nice.'

Harris stared. He looked from Healy to Dornan.

'Neither of you have kids do you?'

Neither Healy nor Dornan spoke.

'Thought not.'

\*\*\*

John Frame appeared at work around 2.00pm. The office was still empty apart from Jill French.

'Get me a cup of coffee will you?' he ventured.

'Bugger off.' French's considered reply.

'Charming. You'll go far.' He smiled, he knew he was "at it."

'Suppose a romantic evening at your place is out of the question then?'

French looked up and smiled 'Maybe twenty years ago John.'

'Ouch. Where is everybody anyway Jill?'

'Most are off skiving, Matt and the boss are off interviewing Harris again.'

Frame looked at a couple of messages on his desk. 'All right' he exclaimed.

'What?' asked French.

'A number for Ivana Jakonowski. You phone her Jill. She might panic if a guy calls. Let her know straight away you're not from immigration or tax or anything like that. Try to set up a meet. Get an address.'

Ivana had not seemed perturbed at all at receiving the call and had happily agreed to meet Frame and French later that afternoon.

***

*Azrael stood and watched a number of women "doing lunch" in the various eateries around Buchanan Galleries. Where were their children, their husbands? Who was taking care of the homes? Not one head covered. Not one attempt at even token modesty. Bare legs, bared breasts. Azrael chose a table. He would now let God choose.*

***

I got into my office after lunch without a care in the world. The sadness of the morning's funeral had passed and I felt relieved for Colin that his torturous life was finally at peace. My overwhelming feeling though was one of unbridled joy. I hadn't planned to tell Susan how I felt about her but when she made the flirtatious remark about being the love of my life I just felt I should. When she leaned across the table, took my hand, and told me she felt the same way then Luigi's Coffee House could have been in Paris or Rome; I was truly happy. We had decided to keep things to ourselves in the meantime; choose the right time to tell colleagues and friends. I felt nothing could spoil my day but I was wrong. I hadn't heard from Joe Turner for a while so when my phone rang I answered without checking the caller ID.

'Ray, it's me, Joe.'

'Hello Joe.'

'Look Ray I'm sorry about the last time but you've no idea what it's like to be in my shoes. Anyway, I've been reading about this fucking Banks bastard. It was him who killed Kate then, not Harris after all?'

'It appears so yes.' I didn't say that Colin Banks had also been a friend. A more deserving friend than Joe in many ways.

'Could he have killed Julie Connor as well then? I swear I didn't do it Ray, I swear.'

'Whether you did or whether you didn't Joe is not the issue. I'm still your lawyer despite what you want, I'll instruct the QC on your behalf and we will do everything we can to help you.'

'Ray I need my passport back. The season's over in Spain, if it ever fucking started that is and god knows what's happening with the takings and things. I've got to get back over there. What if I leave money, a bond or whatever, I swear I'll come back. Even if I didn't I can't hide over there, the deigos would just extradite me. What do you think?'

'Let me give it another go Joe. I'll let you know.'
'OK hear from you soon then.'

I sat and thought about Joe. Our childhoods, our different, perhaps preordained paths. I thought again about Colin Banks. Is it all just chance? Pre - destined, fate. I returned to the present. *Life is what you make it and mine was now complete.*

## Chapter 18

Matt Healy showed Peter Harris into an Interview Room while Susan Dornan went to organise three coffees. Harris hadn't said a word on the way to the station and Healy had sensed that Dornan's thoughts were elsewhere so he had kept small talk to a minimum.

'Just to let you know Peter we'll be seeking an exhumation order for Ann. Forensic science has moved on in the last decade, we'll be able to tell now if she fell down the stairs or was pushed' said Healy once they were all seated. Harris didn't respond. He appeared a defeated man.

'Did you rape Kate Turner Peter? I know you didn't look at it that way. You thought she wanted to make love but that night, by the river, the woman you loved, did you maybe go a bit too far?' asked Dornan.

'Maybe. What does it matter now? She's dead. My Kate is dead.'

'But she wasn't your Kate Peter, was she?'

Harris seemed to stir. 'Well she wasn't that arsehole Joe's either, I can tell you that. She told me that herself. She was in love with someone else; not that no mark.'

'Do you know who?'

'I told you before, no.'

'So you did rape her?'

Harris stared at his coffee and said nothing.

'Did you maybe stab her as well Peter? Anger, frustration just blinded you.'

'The tramp killed her.' Harris muttered. 'I loved her.' Tears started to form in the corners of his eyes.

'What were you talking to Julie Connor about Peter?'

'Life.'

'What about life?'

'It's so unfair.'

'Did you kill Julie Connor Peter?'

'No.'

'Was she your girlfriend Peter, your bit on the side?'

Harris wiped his eyes.

'Is that what you think? Everything has to be in the gutter for you people hasn't it? Sordid.'

'Was she? Were you sleeping with Julie Connor?' shouted Healy.

Harris calmly stared into Healy's eyes.

'Julie Connor was my daughter detective so no, I was not sleeping with her.'

Healy sat in Dornan's office after handing Harris over to be kept in the cells before appearing in court the next day for his arraignment over the killing of his first wife.

'What do you make of all that Susan?'

'I don't think he killed Kate Turner, I was just trying to pressure him before leading up to Julie Connor. Don't know what to make of it to be honest. Whether it's relevant or not.'

'I think you're right. He raped Kate Turner and Banks, or maybe Joe Turner, came along and finished her off. Joe Turner killed Julie in a rage. The Harris connection is a coincidental.' He held up his hand. 'Don't say it.'

John Frame appeared at the door of Dornan's office.

'Just to let you know ma'am, we've traced Ivana Jakanowski, the receptionist at the hotel when Kate Turner stayed there. She says she thinks she could ID the man she booked in with and who booked out on his own but we showed her photos of Turner and Harris and she said; "yes, not certain" whatever that means. Her English isn't great. She said she needs to see "whole of man." Not sure where that leaves us.'

'Good work John. It's something to work on at least.'

Jill French knocked on Dornan's door shortly after Frame had left.

'Sorry ma'am, I know the case is closed but I was reading up on the Internet about Colin Banks. You know just trying to get into his mind, find out what might have set him off, anything really.'

'And did you?'

'No not really but something did come up I thought was quite interesting. Maybe nothing, but interesting all the same.'

'Well go on don't keep us guessing.'

'The initials thing.'

'What about it?'

'Banks was dyslexic.'

Healy and Dornan attended court the next day to see what the outcome with Harris would be although they were certain he would be detained. His defence lawyer seemed resigned to the fact as well and did not raise much enthusiasm on behalf of his client's case. Harris himself appeared not to care, even when the Sheriff duly remanded him. Dornan watched Harris being led away; a slight touch of pity in her heart. Once outside she took Healy's arm.

'Matt, let's go for a coffee somewhere. I want to talk to you.'

'No problem. Sounds mysterious.' Healy smiled. *He had been right, stand back, let Susan do the running.*

They found a coffee shop in one of the new developments that had sprung up in the previously run down Glasgow Cross area of the city, not far from the court building. Dornan went to the counter to order for them both. Their table was at a window and Healy looked at the large stone tower that dominated the area. A Jesuit priest, John Ogilvie, had been hung there in the not too dim and distant past. Healy's reverie on his own religious views was brought to a halt by Dornan's arrival with the coffees.

'So Susan, what's happening?'

'Matt do you ever feel that perhaps you've missed out by being so devoted to the job?'

'In what way?' *Gently does it.*

'Relationships, kids that sort of way.'

'Yes, kids especially.'

'You're roughly ages with me, do you think it's too late?'

*God she's not messing about, but good, I'm ready.* 'No not at all.' Healy leaned over and put his hand on top of Dornan's.

'I felt you'd understand Matt.' Dornan smiled. Healy smiled back.

'Any particular reason you're saying this now Susan.'

'Yes. I'm in love. I think he's the one but I'm uncertain about bringing up the question of kids. Any views on how I can bring it up without scaring him to death.'

Healy slowly withdrew his hand. He found it difficult to continue looking at Dornan. His coffee spilled as he tried to lift the cup. He looked again at the tower outside.

'Matt, you OK?' said Dornan.

'Yeah, sorry. Just got distracted there for a moment. Don't know really. If the guy loves you then I suppose he'll be OK about kids. Who is the lucky guy then?'

'Sorry can't really say at the moment. We want everything low key.'

'Right. Suppose we'd better get back now.'

On the way back to the station Dornan felt she sensed Healy's disappointment, but she was wrong. Disappointment was not the emotion that was coursing through Matt Healy at that moment.

***

*Azrael chose the same restaurant in Buchanan Galleries as the day before. He had gotten a good feeling there. Felt the setting was right. When he had left the previous day he was neither glad nor sad. He waited for the Lord, the Lord showed the way. The restaurant was busy. Shoppers and workers......and whores. A woman entered. Looked around for a seat. Glanced at the empty one opposite Azrael.*

*'Please if you're alone be my guest. If you're expecting someone I'm afraid you'll have to probably try next door.'*

*'No, thank you I will. I just felt like a coffee.'*

*The woman sat, placed her expensive looking bag on the window ledge beside the table. Azrael listened as the next background song came on; a female voice singing of listening to the beat and freeing her soul.*

*Lori McTear, the young Glasgow singer who was just coming to public notice but who Azrael had followed since seeing her perform in a wine bar one evening, was singing a cover of a Dobie Gray song. Azreal pondered....LM....DG. He glanced at the women's bag, sitting prominently on the window sill, the large gold lettering serving their "look at me, look how wealthy and important I am" purpose well, Dolce and Gabbana, DG.*

*He leant over and offered his hand 'since we're breaking bread together; my name's Azrael, and I insist I pay for your coffee. Beautiful women don't pay in my company.'*

*'Well thank you very much. Sandra, Sandra Graham.'*

\*\*\*

Joe Turner had surprised himself. He liked women, loved them, but in recent years he knew himself that he loved drink even more. The afternoon had gone well and when an attractive woman had sat down opposite him at lunch time he had enjoyed "the view" but had thought that would be as far as it would go. He was delighted therefore when idle chat had ended up with a dinner date for that evening. He resolved to only have a few drinks; enough to ease his nerves but not enough to encourage "the mist." He wanted to enjoy the evening but, more importantly, to be able to remember it tomorrow. He put his expectations for the evening to the back of his mind. He had run out of business cards and needed to find a printers.

\*\*\*

As she sat at her desk looking over the group of detectives gathered there, it seemed to Dornan that everybody in the squad was as unhappy as she was with the "solved" tag on three of the recent murders. She obviously had had to take her lead from McFarlane and the P.F.'s office and close the investigations, acknowledging Colin Banks as the killer. Added to that Joe Turner was obviously Julie Connor's killer so she, and Matt Healy, should be satisfied enough with that. Her thoughts diverted to Healy. He had made a lame excuse about "wanting to look into something" when they arrived back at the station, and dropped her off. She felt sorry for him in a way and deeply regretted "getting involved" but she knew she had now found "the one" and she, and Matt Healy, would have to move on. Her thoughts returned to the murders. The issue of the Bank's semen not being present at the two "other" Azreal killings bothered her the most. She accepted that Banks was definitely a complete head case and she had read of people like Jeffrey Dahmer keeping body parts in their fridges, body parts being another Bank's speciality, but the notion that Banks had somehow gotten close enough to a variety of women looking, and smelling, as he did was a stretch too far for her. On the other hand she knew desecrating bodies was a Bank's speciality and the other clues also hinted of an educated man; including the Azrael calling cards. But they also created another problem. The squad had checked every printers in Glasgow and had even checked with churches to see if they had any parishioners who had displayed any sort of over the top religious fervour. Nothing. Why were the cards being left anyway? The Profiler, Alec Caldow, had said that it was a common trait of serial killers to taunt the police, to leave clues, daring to be caught. Dornan shook her head to try to clear it. *Move on Susan, move on in every way.*

\*\*\*

Matt Healy hadn't gone "to look into something" unless you want to call the bottom of a glass something. He sat in his favourite chair in his living room. He didn't care what his neighbour thought, his stereo blared. *Fucking bitch. Leading me on. Just like the rest. Well fuck her. If she thinks she's getting away with treating me like that she's got another think coming.* He raised his glass, *you were right mum. Whores the lot of them.*

Jon Bon Jovi screamed about sleeping when he was dead. Matt Healy smiled, poured another Scotch.

\*\*\*

I smiled when I saw Susan's name show up on my mobile.

I answered 'Perry Mason's office.'

'Don't know if even Perry Mason had a client like Colin Banks Ray.' Susan replied.

'What's up gorgeous?'

'Oh it's nothing. Everything is nice and tidily wrapped up here and I know I should be pleased with that. It's just….'

'I know but listen darling one thing I do know about people, crime and everything else is that you can never fathom it all out. Just put the facts together, present them and let someone else decide. You've done that, so end of.'

'Do you think Bank's is guilty Ray?'

'I don't know but I can say that he was a very troubled soul Susan, very troubled, and he was guilty of some horrendous stuff so...'

'Heard from Joe Turner recently?'

'Yes. I've applied to get his passport back as you no doubt know but other than that nothing. Don't really want to hear from him to be honest.'

'Why? You not friends as such anymore?'

'Well, let's just say it's awkward.'

'You know he's guilty don't you. Don't tell me you're a lawyer with a conscience?'

'Guilt or innocence is irrelevant to a lawyer. Representing your client is all that matters.'

'Ray you know what you call six dead lawyers at the bottom of a loch don't you?'

'No, what?'

'A good start.'

I heard Susan laugh as she hung up.

After we hung up I thought about how my life had changed so much in the last few months. Two people I knew had been murdered. My erstwhile friend was now my client accused of one of the murders, another friend now dead being blamed for the other killing and I had, for the first time in my life, found love. I thought about children. *Was it too late? Would I be being fair to them? Did Susan even want children?* I thought about how my dad maybe felt when I was born. Would he have been keen if he had known what lay ahead, what my mother would do to him? I rarely thought of my mother but, strangely, I thought now about what she would have made of me; how I had turned out. What she would have thought of Susan. I wasn't sure that I cared either way though.

## Chapter 19

Dornan, Healy and McFarlane stared at Sandra Graham. Each experiencing a range of emotions they prayed that would never have to deal with again. Sandra Graham was expressing no emotions at all. She was lying spread eagled on top of her king sized bed, the motif 'D & G' apparently branded into her cleavage. Both her nipples had been cut off. They were found a while later by Jack T'Baht during a search of the murder scene sitting in a jewellery box in Sandra Graham's bedroom, efficiently holding a business card, Azrael, upright.

Susan Dornan felt sick but was concentrating on the scene before her. Matt Healy was also taking in every detail of the scene but anger was his over-riding feeling. McFarlane was in near panic mode in anticipation of the reaction in the press when this latest murder was revealed.

Healy motioned Dornan downstairs. She followed him through to the conservatory. They had only had the most cursory of exchanges over the previous two days. Dornan knew Healy was hurting but there was nothing she could do about that. She wanted to remain friends, close working colleagues if possible, but the ball was in his court.

'And then there was one,' said Healy.

'What do you mean?'

'Look Susan, we always knew these murders weren't down to Banks. McFarlane's not a cop he's a stats keeper. Hundred crimes, hundred charged, no problem. But one thing this murder does show us is that Banks and Harris are both innocent of the Azrael killings. So that leaves one, Joe Turner. I've told you all along it's him. Jesus, I swear I'm going to nail the bastard.'

'We don't know that Matt.'

'I do. Get him in. Phone your boyfriend tell him we want to speak to Turner.'

Susan Dornan stared at Healy. 'How do you know who my boyfriend is?'

'You told me.'

'No I didn't. I specifically told you we were keeping it to ourselves for the moment. We wanted this case out of the way.'

'Well someone told me. Can't remember who. What's the big deal anyway?'

Dornan wasn't able to reply before Healy had turned and walked away.

\*\*\*

*Azrael was content. He was sure that he had met his obligations to the Lord. There was no shame now in asking to be relieved of his burden. Jesus himself had asked to be released of his. 'But thy will be done Lord, thy will be done.' He wondered what direction his life would take now. He turned his head, pushed further down into the softness of the pillow, closed his eyes and slept.*

\*\*\*

I was pleased but slightly surprised to be getting a call from Susan early in the morning.

'Good news and bad news Ray.' Susan said.

'OK, what's the good news?'

'Colin Banks isn't Azrael. There's been another murder. Harris is ruled out as well obviously.'

'Well I suppose that good news of a sort. What's the bad news?'

'We need to speak to Joe again Ray.'

'What for?'

'We'll talk about that when you come in. I'm assuming you'll want to be there, so can you organise his appearance?'

'I'll phone him and call you once I've arranged something.'

'OK. Ray have you told anyone about us. Anyone at all?'

'No, why?'

'Oh nothing. Just something someone said.'

Susan's call had worried me. I knew Healy had a thing about Joe Turner's guilt in the Kate Turner killing and had put together a pretty water tight case against him in the Julie Connor killing. Now that Banks and Harris were out of the picture for the Azrael killings at least, they were maybe taking another look at Joe for killing his wife. The trouble with that was that I had my doubts about Joe's innocence there myself and, by revealing that Joe was in Glasgow at the time of the murder, I hadn't helped my client's case at all.

My phone call had obviously woken Joe up.

'Joe, its Ray, how are you?'

'Yeah OK but bored out my tits. Any word about my passport?'

'Afraid not Joe. Listen the police have been in touch, they want to have a chat with you.'

'A chat? Yeah right. What about?'

'They wouldn't say. Listen Joe if you'd rather use another lawyer for this then that's OK.'

'Nah, better the devil you know Ray. How about meeting me at the police station tomorrow at, say, eleven o'clock? Couldn't face it today.'

'OK, see you then.'

Once he had hung up Joe Turner reached for the bottle of Irn Bru beside his bed. Despite his best intentions he had gotten completely legless on his date. She had liked a drink as well which hadn't exactly acted as a restraint on him and when, at the end of the night, she had let it be known she had plenty to drink back at her house, *Mount Florida, or something like that,* then the rest of the night had just seemed to merge into a fog of drunkenness and naked limbs. He put the bottle back down and noticed a fresh red burn mark on the side of his hand.

*Toasted cheese at five in the morning or whenever never a good idea when you're rat arsed.*

He lay back and smiled; he couldn't even remember making it.

\*\*\*

Susan Dornan was pensive as she sat in her office. Whilst fully focused on the cases in hand, her thoughts kept returning to Matt Healy. Her suspicions, *surely I'm being paranoid,* troubled her. She could accept his disappointment, his slight antagonism even, but she could not accept that a deeper, darker side to Healy was coming into play. She shook herself into refocusing on the job at hand and called Jill French into her office.

'Any thoughts Jill?'

'The initials you mean?'

'Yes.'

'Well they're obviously a factor but I can't see any connection between DG and the victim's name. She was a divorcee but her maiden name was Munro so.....'

'You felt before that the initials were a trigger didn't you. Could it be that the "inspiration" for Azrael was linking the initials of his inspiration to his victims own initials at first but that in fact the initials could link killer and victim in any number of ways.'

'How?'

'Oh God Jill I don't know, I'm just fishing. You know trying to come up with something that might help us, anything.'

'I took a note of the books in the victims house, the author's initials; and the CD's but couldn't see a link to DG.'

'Don't suppose there was anything to go on with the card?'

'No nothing. I can't figure out why he doesn't leave them in a more prominent place; easier to see if he's "boasting" about his latest move. Anyway, I spoke to the profiler this morning, asked about the apparent increase in violence, you know the nipples etc, and he said it's a sign he's getting more relaxed in his belief about not getting caught but at the same time the increase in the "frenzy" of the attack means he is getting more out of control, more dangerous. If that's possible, that is.'

'OK Jill thanks. Keep plugging away. Send Jack in will you.'

'Will do.'

Susan's dislike for Jack T'Baht had not lessened over the previous few weeks. She couldn't exactly pinpoint what it was she didn't like about him; just an uneasy feeling she had when around him.

'Jack what are you working on?'

'Trying to trace the victim's last known movements ma'am.'

'OK good. Jack don't be disheartened about Banks not proving to be the killer. It was good thinking on your part.'

'I'm not. Is that all ma'am.'

'Yes.' *That's what I mean right there, arrogant sod. He's off this team first chance I get.*

The only other officer present was Rab Brown. Brown had mostly been involved in the administration side of the investigations; the mountains of paperwork and computer data generated. Dornan considered calling him in but Brown was so reserved, introverted, that she sometimes avoided speaking to him because she felt that she spooked him when she did. *Maybe it's a "dealing with a woman superior thing."* However, as she was swithering whether to call him in, Brown pre-empted the invite by rising up and coming over to Dornan's office.

'Can I have a private word ma'am?'

'Of course Rab. Come in, sit down.'

Brown entered the room, turned and slowly and deliberately closed the door, double checking it was firmly shut. *Holiday request coming up, maybe even a transfer* thought Dornan.

'Ma'am it's about these killings. Something is bothering me.' Brown was so nervous Dornan thought he was going to have a seizure.

'Just one thing?' Dornan tried to lighten the atmosphere.

'It's about the cards.'

'What about them.'

'Well I think I'm right in saying that, despite a thorough search at the time, the Azrael card wasn't found at the Turner killing till a couple of days later when it was collected up with quite a load of other stuff.'

'Yes that's true but......'

'Then, no card was found at the second killing, Julie Connor, but we do think these two murders could be linked as both victims knew each other.'

'Right, but....'

'And at the next two, now three, killings the cards weren't found straight way; always at some point during the searching of the various locations.'

'Rab, what are you trying to get at here?'

'Well it's just that we're trying to find a link in all the killings, Joe Turner being favourite if we can establish his presence at them all somehow. But he's not the only potential link and we can verify a presence at all the scenes.'

'Who?' Dornan was staring at Brown now, desperately hoping he wasn't about to say what he suspected he was.

'The police. Only the killer, if he did deliberately leave it, and certain police officers knew about the Azrael card thing. If the card was not left by the killer though and it was just another piece of detritus then only a police officer could have seen the opportunity to throw everyone along the lines of thinking about a serial killer.'

'But why do that?'

'Taunting? Plus something else seems strange to me.'

'What?'

'No DNA at the scenes. No fingerprints. Whoever is doing this knows what they are doing, knows how to leave no trace.'

'Like a cop.'

'Jeffrey Dahmer was a cop mam.'

Susan Dornan knew that only a few seconds had passed but she felt as though she had travelled into some sort of parallel existence.

'Who have you spoken to about this Rab?'

'No-one mam. It took me a long time to even speak to you. Please don't think I'm suggesting that you are involved in any way, it's just not something you say lightly. I don't have any individual in mind you understand, it's just......'

'No, you're right to bring it up. Leave it with me. Don't mention this to anyone Rab, not even McFarlane, I'll accept responsibility for that. I need time to think.'

Dornan watched as Brown returned to his desk and slumped into his seat. She had attended every murder scene and so had Jill French but she knew she herself wasn't involved and as women serial killers were so rare as to be discounted she also dismissed French from her mind. She searched her memory. She was sure that no two police constables had been the first on the scenes. The SOCO's may have been but the cards had already been found at all but the first murder by the time they arrived. The guys that transported the bodies to the morgue weren't all the same either. She calmly took a sheet of fresh paper from her printer, lifted a pen and started to write.

Matt Healy, Jack T'Baht, John Frame, Paul Allan.

Dornan picked up her phone and made two calls. The first was to Alec Caldow, the profiler. She requested that he E mail over all his thoughts on what he felt the killer's background could possibly be. Her second call was to Personnel requesting four staff files. She then opened a drawer in her desk and took out the staff rota sheets for the last three months.

***

Paul Allan was confused. To a certain extent he was glad that it had now been shown that Colin Banks had not been the killer. He had felt slightly aggrieved originally that his contribution to the Banks aspect of the case had not been fully acknowledged but now he was glad that he had not made any sort of song and dance about it at the time. On the other hand Max Kermack seemed to be becoming remote, less interested in their relationship. He could accept that he was serious about his writing and his dream was to actually make a living doing it but all their conversations seemed to centre on him getting Max "involved" in cases and despite his protestations that he couldn't have Max tagging along "willy nilly" Max could not be appeased. Allan was actually beginning to worry about Max's health. He seemed drawn, gaunt, obsessed even. *Maybe he should just take some of the leave he was due and book that much talked about holiday?*

Max Kermack, on the other hand, was not confused. A holiday was never in his thoughts. He looked at the almost blank screen of his laptop. The words Chapter One stared back at him along with the rest of the blank page. He couldn't even think of anything to write as a cover in case Paul Allan ever asked to see a draft of his work. *Fuck him, if he didn't start making progress with Allan he would have to start thinking of another way, another cop. Recognising Allan from the gay club in a news report on the TV of the murders one night had been a stroke of luck but not if he couldn't serve a purpose. That was all he was needed for.*

## Chapter 20

I entered the police station with my client, and possible friend, ten minutes before our agreed meeting time. I had spoken to Susan the night before but she had seemed pre occupied. Not off hand, more distracted, her mind elsewhere. She had signed off by saying she loved me so all was well with the world. My world anyway, I wasn't sure about Joe Turner's. He had either been living in a barrel of beer or had consumed a few since the last time I had seen him and I was taken aback by his appearance.

'Are you feeling OK Joe? We can cancel this if you want. I'll go in and say you're unwell.'

Joe seemed surprised. 'No, I'm fine. Why are you saying that?'

He was obviously unaware of how he was looking these days or maybe it was just me; age catches up on us all.

A uniform sergeant showed us into an interview room and a few minutes later the lovely Susan came in accompanied by Matt Healy who sometimes gave me the impression it was me he was accusing and not my client; staring at me like some sort of Nemesis figure.

'Joe, you will be aware that we originally thought that Peter Harris was guilty of your wife's killing. We were then led to believe that a homeless man Colin Banks had committed the crime as he made a death bed confession...of sorts. That has subsequently proved to be untrue.' Susan had started the session in the manner she wished to go on; factual and to the point.

'Who else could it have been then?'

'You' said Matt Healy.

'Not this again. Look if you don't have any further evidence concerning this then we're leaving. I think you're forgetting that my client's wife has been murdered. He's exiled from his family in Spain and he cannot attend to serious outstanding business problems there. Do you have anything new to say officers?' I asked.

'His cheating wife has been murdered you mean, and stabbing women is not out of character for him as we well know.'

Before I could reply Joe turner was off his seat and lunging at Healy. I fleetingly hoped he landed a couple of blows before he was pulled off. Order was quickly restored but I could tell Joe was on the edge.

'Where were you two nights ago Turner?'

'Shagging your wife. Why, she asking for more.'

'I don't have a wife actually.'

'There's a surprise.'

'You get riled easily Joe?'

'Just by retards like you Healy.'

'Not just by women then? Once again, where were you two nights ago?'

'Out.'

'Out where?'

'Out out. I don't know. Blitzed wasn't I.'

'Anybody vouch for that?'

'Yes as it happens Sherlock. I was on a date. Some of us can still get one you know.'

'What was the name of the fortunate lady?'

'Can't remember. Sally, Susan something like that. Look we went out, we got pissed, bit of rumpy, I went home.'

'Where did the rumpy take place?'

'Her place I think. Could have been her mates. I think she might have been married. Who cares?'

'We do. Where did she live?'

'Who knows? Taxi there, taxi back. She paid as well. Touch of class she was.'

'Easy to see the attraction in you then. Slumming it was she?' I was surprised at the venom in Susan's eyes; her tone.

'Jealous are you?' replied Joe.

'Enough.' I realised I was beginning to feel resentment towards my own client. Healy smirked at me.

'What's that mark on your hand Joe?' asked Susan.

'Dunno, a burn I think.'

'How you get it?'

'Making a late night snack I think.'

'You think?'

'Like I said, totally pissed I was.'

It was obvious that nothing of any value was going to come of the interview and I was also scared Joe was going to lose his temper again. I called a halt after a couple of further brick bats between Healy and Joe. I tried to catch a private moment with Susan out in the station foyer but the look on her face signalled to me to leave it till later.

Outside I spoke to Joe. 'Are you serious about not remembering things Joe?'

'Yeah.'

'Don't you see that as a problem? Health wise if nothing else.'

'Maybe I don't want to remember Ray.'

'Fair enough, I know it must be hellish for you Joe but I have to tell you the police are obviously looking at you for these other murders and eventually "Can't remember" is just not going to wash with them.'

'If they had anything Ray they would go for it. That Healy seems to hate me.'

'I know what you mean.' I said sheepishly.

I declined Joe's offer to go for a drink and went to shake hands. I noticed a book in Joe's jacket pocket.

'Didn't have you down as a reader Joe,' I said pointing at his pocket.

Joe pulled the book out. I was even more surprised. It was a Bible.

'Yeah I sometimes read the good book in times of strain Ray. Throw back to my mother's influence I think.' He laughed and walked off.

\*\*\*

Other than a couple of swear words Healy hadn't said anything on the way back to the office from the interview room, and went straight to his own desk. Dornan took the opportunity to call Jill French into her room.

'What are you working on Jill?'

'Same as everyone else ma'am, trying to find out as much as possible about Sandra Graham, trace her last movements etc'

'Find anything of note?'

'Not really but I did speak to a friend who Sandra called about lunch time on the day she was killed, we got onto her from Sandra's mobile records, and she told me Sandra had told her she was on her way into Buchanan Galleries to do some shopping so I'm going there now with a photo.'

'OK good. Jill close the door.' French rose apprehensively and closed the door. Thoughts of what she may have done wrong circulating in her mind.

'I want you and I to work on an aspect of this case that requires secrecy and tact. Rab Brown will be the only other officer involved or to even know about it. Would you be OK with that or would you rather not?'

'Well I......what is it?'

'Once I tell you then you are "In" so I need your answer first Jill.'

French didn't ponder for long, she trusted Dornan's judgement. 'OK, I'm in.'

'There's a chance, a small chance which I don't believe for a minute, but a chance never the less that our killer may be a police officer.'

'What! Are you serious?' French caught herself. 'Sorry ma'am, it's just that......well you know.'

'Yes, I know. It's OK but I need to investigate the possibility.'

'Who are we talking about?'

'Well, and I'm stressing this Jill, I don't actually suspect anyone but I've narrowed the immediate possibilities, very remote possibilities that is, down to Matt Healy, John Frame, Paul Allan and Jack T'Baht. While you're absorbing that I'm going to call Rab in.'

Brown entered the room with his usual hang dog look, carefully closing the door behind him.

'Rab, you'll appreciate that the investigation that I'm going to conduct into your suspicions has to be done quietly and with a certain degree of secrecy. I've decided to include Jill in the team as I feel she doesn't fall into the category of even possible suspects. But that is the whole team; you, me and Jill. I will be getting Jill to look into the officers in question's backgrounds, use her background in psychology, trying to see any links to the profiler's views on the killer's characteristics. I want you to look at their shift patterns, expenses claims, anything on record that would show opportunity at the times of the killings. I'll authorise leave "for family reasons" if you would feel more comfortable not having anything on your desks. You only report back to me and don't say anything even to wives, boyfriends, parents. Nobody. Any questions?'

Both French and Brown shook their heads, glanced at each other, rose slowly and left. They walked past the desks of Healy, Frame, Allan and T'Baht but did not look over at any of them. Healy rose quickly and strode over to Dornan's office.

'Can I have a word?'

'Sure, come in.'

'What was all that about?'

Susan Dornan just looked at Healy and raised an eyebrow.

'OK, nothing to do with me. Seems to be a lot I don't know about these days.'

'Matt.....'

'Doesn't matter. Look, I want to go to Spain.'

'What? What for?'

'Susan, I just know it's Turner. Remember what the profiler said. Serial killers just don't start up suddenly, kill someone they know then go on a spree. There's a build-up, a pattern. I bet Turner's been killing people over there. I want to go over there, see if there's a pattern, some unsolved, he's been there 30 years. Don't forget he was already handy with a knife before he went.'

'I don't know Matt.'

'Susan I'll take annual leave if I have to but that would just make things more awkward for me. I need to be "official" to get much co-operation from the cops over there. And don't forget what else the profiler said, these guys just don't stop. They either die or get caught. Well Turner looks healthy enough to me so I want to nail the bastard as soon as possible.'

'I'll have to say to McFarlane, he'll have to OK it.'

'He will. He's up shit creek, he'll grasp at anything that looks like he's on the ball. What phrase would he use "being pro- active" or some shite like that.'

'OK, leave it with me. Matt, are things OK with us now. I'd like to remain friends. I didn't intend to hurt you.'

'We all have to do what we have to do Susan.'

'So.......?'

Healy turned and left the office. Dornan watched him go. She thought back to a previous conversation with him. Teasing him about never marrying. "The job, my mother" taking on a different hue to her now.

***

Joe Turner knew he had been "off" not getting in touch with Martha Reid so when he saw her name coming up on his mobile screen he winced.

'Hello Martha. Listen, I'm sorry I've not been in touch but I'm a bit all over the place.'

'Oh that's OK Joe, I can imagine. I've been a bit like that myself but I've pulled myself together now hopefully. I just thought I'd phone and see if you'd like to come round for your tea one evening.'

Yeah that would be nice Martha. When were you thinking of?'

'Well how about tonight? You never know what's around the corner do you. We should be well aware of that.'

'Suppose so. Tonight it is then. How about six o'clock?'

'Perfect. See you then Joe.'

Joe hung up. *Christ, better go to the pub about three then. Build up my resistance.*

At seven thirty, and with no sign of Joe, Martha cleared away the well laid out table. She scrapped the uneaten shepherd's pie into the kitchen bin then sat at her bay window and watched the people who still had purpose in their life go about their routines.

*\*\*\**

The following morning Jill French was sitting in Susan Dornan's office. French was explaining some possible progress she had made the previous day in Buchanan Galleries.

'I went round all the shops and restaurants and finally one guy said he did think he recognised the photo of Sandra Graham. He said he was pretty sure she was alone when she came in but seemed to meet up with someone. Not much to go on I know but as I was leaving I asked about the background music they played; you know for the Tunstall, music angle. He explained that they just played the same stuff on a loop system and he had the playlist; gave me a copy. It's not much to go on but there was a track by a guy called Dobie Gray. Never heard of him myself but so what.'

'Dobie Gray, DG.'

'Exactly.'

'Good work Jill but........well, does it help us? The victim's initials were SG.'

'Yeah but with DG branded on her. I know it's hard to say at the moment but once we catch this prick it's another tick in my world famous "Initials Theory". Dornan and French both laughed.

'Seriously though. I was thinking of taking photos of Turner, Healy, T'Baht, Allan and Frame in, see if the barman recognises anyone.'

'Do it Jill,' Dornan said, inwardly praying that the barman couldn't.

***

Peter Harris had never considered himself as either a hard or violent man. He lay on the top bunk of his cell contemplating what lay ahead in his life. Neither his wife nor any of his kids had been in touch. His birthday had passed without a single card. His one true love was dead. His eldest daughter was dead and his eldest son still refused to even acknowledge his existence. His lawyer had told him that he remained confident that he would be found innocent of the killing of his first wife Anne, "confession under duress." He admitted that the rape charge would be more problematic but not a certain conviction, especially when Kate Turner's tangled love life was highlighted. Pete Harris hadn't liked his true love spoken of that way but had had to accept his lawyer's stance in the meantime. He stared at the ceiling. "All screws are cunts" the words of wisdom imparted by a previous guest, stared back. Harris wondered if the police were on to the full truth of what he had done yet. He felt the hardness between his legs and wondered if he would miss women if he was found guilty.

## Chapter 21

Matt Healy had been right. McFarlane had been only too willing to appear to be pushing the investigation on and an "International" manhunt hint to the investigation would go down very well with the local press. He had cleared for Healy to fly over to the Costa Brava and had arranged for him to be met at Gerona Airport by Inspector A. Dorado of the Mossos D'Esquadra who McFarlane had been assured were the people to deal with rather than the Policia Local. Healy had gotten some teasing in the squad room the day before about taking a summer holiday in the middle of an investigation, all expenses paid as well, and the other detectives had taken guesses as to what the A in the Spanish policeman's name would stand for. Their lack of imagination resulting in "Athletico" being chosen as the likely answer.

John Frame had also noted that Angel was a common Spanish name 'might even know our angel Matt. Mind you ours is an Arch Angel.'

Healy sat in the Elvis bar in Prestwick airport with a double brandy and soda in his hand, wondering just what The King had made of Scotland on his only visit to UK shores. He looked around him at some of the people about to board the Ryanair flight; *no wonder he didnae come back.*

Three hours later Healy was waiting for his bag to come around on the luggage carousel at Gerona Airport and getting himself worked up about the probable communication problems he was about to encounter when he met up with

Dorado. He picked up his bag and went through the sliding glass doors. Almost immediately he saw his name written on a piece of cardboard being held up by a distinctly un-spanish looking guy; tall with fair hair and gold rimmed specs.

Healy walked over hesitantly, building himself up 'Buenos dias. Me llamo Matt Healy.'

'Bon Dia big man, and we speak catalan here by the way, no Spanish.' He held out his hand 'the name's Alistair, Alistair Dorado.'

Healy found himself temporarily speechless.

'Spanish father, Scottish mother. My mum was born in Glasgow as a matter of fact, will probably know your murder scenes as well as you Matt. Got the car outside, with driver, so we can go for a wee drink while we chat.'

The drive into Lloret de Mar only took about half an hour and Healy liked the look of the countryside that they drove through, not quite understanding the tacky image that the area had generated over the years. Until he arrived in Lloret itself and all became clear; tacky was a compliment.

'What kind of bar do you fancy Matt, Spanish or tourist?'

'Normally Spanish Alistair but can we go to one of Turner's bars, maybe help me get a feel for the guy?'

'Sure.'

A few minutes later Healy and Dorado entered the Star and Garter. A drunk sixteen year old girl from Newcastle was slumped over a karaoke machine in the corner trying to look sexy while getting the words to her chosen song all wrong, and a few groups of lads, all wearing football tops, were suggesting that she remove her clothes while singing; but their request not quite framed in those words. Dorado went to the bar and ordered two bottles of Estrella. Healy picked a table outside on the terrace in order to get away from the racket.

'We could arrest that lassie you know?' said Healy as Dorado joined him.

'What for?' replied Dorado.

'She's just murdered Celine Dion.'

Dorado sat down with the drinks. 'Spanish bars from now on Matt?'

'Definitely.' They both laughed.

Dorado explained that when he got the request to assist Healy he had set the police computer to list unsolved crimes of females dating back 30 years. He had been surprised when the print out had come back that there were fourteen. The first went back to twenty eight years previously and the last one had been about two years ago.

'Same killer?' asked Healy.

'Impossible to say. We didn't have DNA obviously back then for a start.'

'Was there anything to connect even some of the murders?'

'I can't say at the moment as I only have names, dates and minimum details. I've requested all the files but that will take a bit of time. Some of the files will be here, some in Girona and I'm afraid some will be missing.'

'Missing?'

'Spain was going through a lot of changes post Franco Matt. Added to that there is a lot of tension between authorities in Spain and Catalonia, co-operation is not high on the agenda. Unfortunately, as well as this, there is also the problem that a British tourist getting herself raped and killed is not exactly uncommon here. But I'll do everything I can to help you and see where it takes us.'

'Can't ask for more than that Alistair. Now what about that Spanish bar? There will be one more dead British tourist if I don't get away from this din shortly otherwise.'

***

I could tell Susan wasn't 'with me.' We were lying in bed after having made love and she was in my arms but she wasn't with me.

'Is everything all right Susan?'

'Yes. Sorry Ray. It's just work, lot on my mind.'

'Want to share it?'

'Love to but I can't, especially not to you.' She elbowed me in the ribs. 'You're the enemy.'

'Thought we were both on the side of justice?'

'You'd better grow up then. Justice? What the hell is justice Ray?'

'Well it's........' My sentence tailed off, I knew Susan was right. A couple of minutes of silence passed.

'Healy's in Spain.'

'What? On holiday do you mean?'

'No, researching your client.'

'Why, what's he hoping to find over there?'

'Christ what am I doing. Look Ray forget I said anything.'

I turned, lay on my side facing Susan.

'You're more important than anybody Susan. You're going to be my wife so if you need me to support you then that is what I'm going to do. I'm going to drop Joe Turner as a client. I've always felt uneasy about being his lawyer anyway for a variety of reasons and that issue of the train ticket was a classic example. Too near to a conflict of interests.'

'Ray, I'm sorry about that.'

'No, you were right to use it. It's your job.'

'What will Turner say?'

'He won't be a problem. I'll tell him that the Law Society told me to hand his case over to another firm, baffle him with science, he's thick anyway.'

'Not so sure about that.'

'What?'

'Him being thick. We think he might be very smart indeed. You promise we're talking in confidence now Ray?'

'Of course.'

'OK. You accept Turner killed Jill Connor don't you?'

I paused momentarily 'Yes.'

'Healy is convinced he killed his wife as well. Do you think that's possible?'

My hesitance didn't even last as long as the previous pause; 'Unfortunately, yes.'

'Healy also thinks he's the Azrael killer as well. It is possible. He had opportunity.'

'Bit of a stretch don't you think? Comes over here, kills his wife and then just goes on a rampage for no reason.'

'Well there might be two reasons actually. One, his wife's killing is not his first, and that's what Healy's looking into and two, he's a psychopath.'

'Of course the other scenario is that Turner killed Connor in a moment of rage and somebody else is the psycho.'

'Yes, there's always that.'

I looked at Susan; she still wasn't 'with me.'

***

John Frame sat pensively at his desk. He sensed that something had changed in the squad. He remembered back to a previous similar occasion; an occasion where he had heard a whisper that his role in some dubious convictions was being quietly investigated. He had that same feeling now. Brown and French were hardly ever in the station now and when they were they were ensconced in Dornan office most of the time, Healy was in Spain hoping to achieve God knew what and T'Baht and Allan seemed to be wrapped up in their own worlds. Frame blamed Dornan for the disintegration of the morale of the squad. He felt that she had lost their confidence after the Rice killing. *What's a fucking woman doing in charge anyway?* He had also made sure that his personal lap top and none of his "special" photos were still in his house.

***

Healy slept late the following morning. He hadn't heard from Dorado but wasn't concerned as he had expected that things would move slowly here; the "Mañana Effect." He left the Hotel Samba and walked down a steep slope that the receptionist had told him would lead him into the centre of the town. Healy passed an array of shops that all seemed to be selling the same tat as each other, with none of them appearing to be owned or run by any Spanish people. Healy couldn't help feeling that it was a shame that the former quaint fishing village had come to this state of existence but also inwardly acknowledged that it was predominately UK tourists that had started the cultural decline. He stepped out of a narrow alley way and suddenly found himself on the main causeway through the town. The streets seemed busy enough with people heading either to or from the beach a few yards down to Healy's right but the shops and bars appeared deserted for some reason. Healy took a seat in a pavement side cafe, Blanco y Negro, ordered a much rehearsed cafe con leche and watched the world go by. He thought of Dornan and her betrayal, wondered what was going on with her and French and Brown. He looked around, tried to get a feel of Turner's home territory. Across the road he watched a tall guy with tousled hair and round shoulders offloading some boxes from a van into The Londoner disco. A few minutes later the same guy sauntered over to the cafe and sat down at a table across from Healy. Healy thought the guy looked British but not somehow a tourist. He ordered a curtado, which Healy had never heard of, and pulled out a copy of the Daily Record.

'Scottish then?' asked Healy.

'Yeah.'

'Do you live here by any chance?'

'I do as it happens.'

'Do you happen to know Joe Turner? I told a mutual friend I was coming here and he advised me to look Joe up.'

The man opposite seemed to ponder what to say next but Healy had expected that.

'Nothing sinister honest, just grab a few beers, talk football, usual crap,' said Healy.

'Yeah it's just that Joe's not here right now. He's in Glasgow as a matter of fact. His wife was murdered over there a few weeks back. Joe's stayed over there.'

'Christ. Did you know his wife?'

'Yes we worked together as a matter of fact.'

Healy already knew from Dorado that Kate Turner had worked at The Londoner but knew he had to tread warily. Healy got up and took a chair at the other table.

'Look I'm not going to lie to you, I'm from the press, The Record, as a matter of fact. I'm trying to get some background info on Joe and Kate. Can you help me out? I can't pay for information but I could stand you dinner. What do you say?'

'Oh I don't know.'

'What's your name?'

'Robbie.'

'Well Robbie I'm not looking for dirt or sleaze. I just want to be able to get a feel of what Joe and Kate are, were, like.'

'I can't promise anything, and I've got to go now, but I'll meet you in a restaurant called the C'Al Avi if you like. Tonight at eight?'

'I'll be there.'

***

Jack T'Baht watched as Jill French walked into Buchanan Galleries. He knew French had photos with her, presumably of Joe Turner, and was showing it to let the barman who had ID'd Sandra Graham see if Turner was the man she had met up with. But T'Baht wasn't concerning himself with that. He watched French. Long black boots, short skirt. He had sat in Buchanan Galleries and many other places watching women just like French exhibiting themselves; encouraging men to lust over them.

He couldn't take the chance of following her into the arcade but he would wait near her car for her coming back.

As he waited in his own car for French's return he opened the glove compartment and took out his well-worn copy of the Koran. A business card fell out of the compartment onto the floor unnoticed. T'Baht felt only the words of the Koran coursing through his head, and the hardness between his legs.

## Chapter 22

Healy arrived dead on eight at the restaurant and was pleased at the look of it from the outside, but was disappointed once inside that he and Robbie were the only customers. Robbie was obviously a regular there and he introduced Healy to the owner Pepe as "a friend from Scotland" which Healy felt augured well for the rest of the evening. They ordered quickly and whilst waiting for their seafood starters Robbie explained that the restaurant at one time had had a Michelin star and that although it had obviously gone downhill since those heady days the food was still good. Healy felt that the Michelin star must have been for Pepe's spare tyre but said nothing. After the main course had arrived and a half hour of small talk had passed by Healy decided to move things on.

'So were Joe and Kate happy Robbie?'

'They were generally viewed as an odd match to be honest but yes, I think they were happy enough.'

'Any lovers on the scene ever?'

'Thought you said this wasn't about dirt raking.'

'So there were lovers?'

'Look Joe was a bar owner in a holiday town; what do you think?'

'And Kate?'

'Who knows?' Robbie seemed awkward in his reply.

'I hear Joe has a temper.'

'Yeah he could be a bit wild at times but we all mellow with age.'

'Do you think Joe would be capable of killing Kate if he found out she was cheating?'

'Is this what this is all about? You think Joe killed Kate?'

'No, I'm asking what you think.'

'Well then no I don't. If you saw how upset Joe was when one of his customers was murdered way back in the early years then you'd know he hasn't got that kind of thing in him.'

Healy was struggling to remain passive.

'What happened?'

'One of his customers, Sally I think her name was, was killed near here.'

'How was she killed?'

'Raped and murdered, stabbed I think. Police reckoned it was one of the Moroccans that were around a lot in those days.'

'But no-one was arrested right?'

'Not as far as I know.'

'How long have you lived here Robbie?'

'Thirty-odd years.'

'You know of any other unsolved murders around here in that time?'

'There's been a few now that you mention it but it just seemed to go with the sex and sangria nature of the place. Don't get me wrong it's not a weekly occurrence or anything like that, maybe ten in all the time I've been here. An Italian girl was murdered two or three years ago but that's the most recent as far as I know.'

'So you've been here 30 years or so and Joe Turner was here when you first came?'

'That's right.'

'And there has been a girl killed, that you know of, every two or three years since you arrived.'

'What are you suggesting?'

'No nothing, honest Robbie. It's just the reporter in me, trying to see a story where there isn't one.'

'Right. Anyway, how many unsolved killings in Glasgow in the last 30 years?'

'Not as many as you would think Robbie, not as many as you would think.'

***

Max Kermack was listless; things weren't moving fast enough for him. Paul Allan came into the room carrying two bottles of beer.

'Paul, why don't you contact this Joe Turner guy directly? Tell him you need to meet him. He doesn't need to know it's not exactly official police business. I'll come along, get some useful background for my story. No harm done.'

'No harm done? My balls over hot coals if I got caught. Why are you so taken with Turner anyway? I've told you I'll set up a meeting with some other low lives I know.'

'No. It's got to be current and it's got to be murder. To fit into my main character's back ground you see.'

Allan paused for a few moments. 'I don't know much of your back ground Max.'

'Not much to tell.'

'Still, I'd like to know.'

'All I can really tell you is that we were adopted after my mother died, my father didn't want us. It's strange how the mind works, for a long time I never forgave my mother for dying. My father I just put from my mind.'

'We?'

'My sister and I, although I didn't know I had a sister until I was in my twenties. She traced me through the adoption agency.'

'And your father?'

'Don't know, don't care. He didn't want to know me then, I don't want to know him now.'

'Does he want to get in touch with you?'

'My sister eventually traced him. He said he would like to meet me apparently but he can go to hell.'

'Would that be so bad? Maybe you'd like him once you heard his side of the story.'

'He has no side. No. Never. Not under any circumstances. I've never even known his name and don't want to know it. Change the subject now Paul if you don't mind.'

'Where does your sister live now?'

Max Kermack paused for a moment 'I've lost her as well.'

'Eh?'

'Australia'

'Right. Maybe we could fly out there for that holiday we're always promising ourselves?'

'Maybe Paul, maybe.'

***

Matt Healy lay on his hotel bed. He had made his excuses to get out of going on a pub crawl with Robbie and come back to the hotel. He had phoned Alistair Dorado but go no reply. He had thought of phoning Dornan but wanted to wait until he had more definite news about Turner. *Probably lying screwing that bastard Ford anyway. Fucking bitch.* A group of girls passed by on the street below his balcony, arms linked and in full voice:

"Young hearts run free
Don't ever get hung up
Hung up like my man and me."

Healy's mind travelled back to Monday nights in The Savoy in Glasgow *Candi Staton; she always filled the floor.* He knew he wouldn't sleep now. He splashed some water on his face, straightened his hair and walked out into the Spanish night.

***

As I suspected Joe was neither up nor down when I told him I was no longer on his case. In actual court he would have been represented by a Queen's Counsel anyway, with his lawyer, me, merely assisting but I told Joe that the Q.C. was uncomfortable with me being friends with the accused and had suggested another lawyer.

'No sweat Ray. I feel you kind of wanted off the case anyway.'

'It's not that Joe, it's just.......'

'You think I did it.'

'Did you?'

Joe looked into the distance 'Christ, Ray I just don't know.'

'And Kate?'

'No way. No. I don't care if she was shagging the Rangers team, I wouldn't have killed her.'

'What if it was the Celtic team?'

Joe stared at me for an instant 'That's different, got to draw the line somewhere.' The ice broken.

'Listen Ray I know you've been a good friend over the years but the truth is we're totally different kinds of people. I know you're finding the whole thing with Kate's death and your doubts over me hard to deal with.' He held out his hand. 'Be at the end of a phone for when I might need you Ray and we'll call it quits at that.'

I shook hands and Joe turned and walked away. I felt like the lowest of the low. Why? Because I was and I was about to go even lower.

'Hi darling it's me. Can we meet for a drink?'

'That would be great. Nothing seems to be happening with the investigation and Matt Healy seems to be un-contactable so meeting you sounds great, and, no offence, a drink sounds even better.'

We met in the Rogano bar which, although always busy, always seems to have enough space for intimate chats. I wasted no time in reverting to Judas.

'Well I told Joe I couldn't represent him.'

'And?'

'He was fine.'

Susan looked at me quizzically 'and?'

'I think he knows within himself he killed Julie.'

'We know that....and...?'

'I meet Joe a couple of days ago. Something odd happened.'

'What?'

'When we were going our own ways I noticed something in his pocket.'

'A blood stained knife I hope.'

'A bible. He says his mum influenced him to use it in times of need.'

Susan stared at me. 'Shit. Why didn't you say anything before now?'

'He was still my client, and my friend.'

'And now?'

'And now Susan? Now I'm a guy who has turned his back on his friend and kicked him in the balls while doing it.'

I didn't know at that point that I was about to be offered redemption from the most unlikely of sources.

\*\*\*

Pete Harris sat in solitary and contemplated his future. He hated Joe Turner but also knew that merely knowing Turner had been found guilty of a crime would not bring him satisfaction. He also had come to realise that there actually was truth in the notion of confessing; clearing your conscience. *But will anyone believe me? Confess to who?*

Harris called over a warder 'On my next telephone call time I want to phone someone but don't have the number. Could you get it for me?'

The warder looked at Harris; hesitated. 'What's the name?'

Harris handed him a slip of paper. 'Thank you.'

The warder looked at the name 'Change of tack eh Peter?'

'Something like that.'

\*\*\*

Only a few miles away from Harris, Joe Turner was sitting in his own personal prison. He too was contemplating what life had in store for him. The inevitability of a mandatory life sentence and the subsequent loss of contact with his children, financial ruin. But of more immediate concern to him were the frequent lost periods in his life. He remembered leaving Ray

Ford the previous day, having lunch, phoning round his bars in Spain to see how things were, *shit obviously,* deciding to go for a drink; and then nothing.

Joe Turner hadn't cried for many years but knew he was on the point of an emotional breakdown now. He took his wallet out of the inside pocket of his jacket. Opened it, saw the face of Kate smiling back from the photo of her he always carried. *You're the cause of all of this.* He closed the wallet and reached for the bible that sat on the bedside cabinet.

\*\*\*

Martha Reid was walking slowly but contentedly back along Hyndland Road from the Post Office. She had paid her latest gas, electricity and phone bills but had not needed to pay her Council Tax as she had set up a Direct Debit at the bank for that a few years before. The owner of the flower shop had been sad that Martha had decided that the job "was just too much" for her now but knew that the death of her daughter must have taken a heavy toll on her; especially it being a murder. She had insisted on not charging Martha for the arsenic tablets she bought for clearing the weeds on her back patio.

Martha got back home about fifteen minutes later, made a cup of tea and picked up the phone to Directory enquiries.

'Yes, I'd like the number of Buchanan Street Bus Station please.'

\*\*\*

The strong sun light piercing the gloom of his hotel room woke Matt Healy otherwise he would have slept on for hours. He went to sit up,

"Christ" he said to the empty room before half staggering into the tiny toilet. Healy stood relieving himself and caught a glimpse of himself in the mirror "Christ" again the only response forth coming.

He sat back down on the edge of the bed. Contemplated then dismissed the notion of breakfast and reached for his phone. Alistair Dorado answered on the first ring.

'Matt, bon dia. I've got a little stuff for you but not much and I'm afraid I'm not going to be able to spend much more time with you on it.'

'Oh, why's that?'

'We had a murder last night. Young British girl, over here with friends on, what do you call it, a chicken night?'

'Hen, hen night.'

'Well her friends say they somehow all got split up and this one, Claire Strong, didn't arrive back at the hotel.'

'Are you at the scene now?'

'Yes.'

'Can I meet you there? I might be able to add something, help in some way.'

'Matt you have no authority here and unless your friend, Turner is it, flew over here during the night then you have no interest in this case.'

'It's just.....'

'No Matt, sorry. My boss would not like it. When is your flight back?'

'Tomorrow. The budget only stretched to a couple of days. I could stay on I suppose, at my own expense.'

'No Matt, don't cancel your flight. I will meet you this afternoon once I'm finished here but like I said I don't have much for you.'

Healy walked back into the toilet, knelt down at the toilet bowl and vomited out the previous night's excesses.

## Chapter 23

On first seeing Alistair Dorado coming through the door of the small interview room in Lloret de Mar's Policia Local station Healy was disappointed that he was only carrying one file. But as Dorado soon explained 'What would be the point of bringing everything; they're in Spanish.' Healy had to admit he had a point.

'I've taken notes as best I could Matt but as I said some files are minimal or don't exist at all. We might not even have all the unsolved murders on computer. People did go missing in Spain during all the political upheavals I'm sorry to say. Anyway, the more recent murders are covered as well as you would do in Scotland I'm sure.'

'What is the oldest case you have?'

'Well I went back 30 years and we do have an unsolved murder from 1980. A British girl, stabbed. No mention of rape but back then.....who knows?'

'After that?'

'Like I said we have approximately fifteen or so but it's impossible to link them.'

'Approximately? Christ Alistair, don't you know?'

'Some of the bodies weren't found for a while. Two had been dumped in the sea and, again, like I said, Spain took a little while to catch up with modern policing techniques.'

'What about the unsolved murder was it Sally somebody?'

'Yes, I have her name here. Sally Johnstone from Coatbridge in Scotland.'

'Was Turner questioned?'

'No record of that. Why would he be?'

'Been in his pub maybe?'

'Matt, she had probably been in a lot of people's pubs. Along with a lot of other people as well. Should we have questioned them all?'

'Yes.'

'Matt maybe in Glasgow you have the man power for such things but here, in Lloret, we do not.'

'A girl is murdered Alistair then you should get them in. Anyway let's move on. How many of the victims were stabbed?'

'Six definitely.....'

'All British?'

'Yes.'

'All Scottish?'

'No....two from England and one from Ireland.'

'All raped?'

'Can't say...two were in the sea too long.'

'Were all the bodies found away from Lloret?'

'Yes.'

'So the killer had a car?'

'Possibly.'

'How else could he get the bodies to where they were found?'

'OK.....but he could borrow a car from a friend, or maybe he's a truck or tourist bus driver.'

'Does Turner have a car?'

'Two actually.'

'Did he have a car back in 1980?'

'We have no record of it but.....'

'Where was her body found?'

'Fenals beach. It's not far from here. Ten minute walk over the hill. Deserted in those days, built up now though. Nice little secluded bay there; popular with lovers.'

'So no car required to get there?'

'No.'

'Any note of where else she had been to that night, who she was with etc.'

'Funny enough there is. She was in the only disco that was there in those days and is still in business.'

'Where's that?'

'The Londoner.'

As Healy walked back along the sea front towards the town centre he phoned Robbie.

'Robbie, remember you said to me last night that when you came here at first Joe Turner was already here?'

'Yeah.'

'Did he have a car?'

'God, are you kidding? We were all broke even him. Lucky to have a bed never mind a car.'

'Do you remember where he worked then, what he did for a living?'

'That's easy. He gave me my first job. He worked here in The Londoner.'

Healy had decided he had garnered all the information he was going to get, or need, in Spain. He changed his flight to that day and had gotten Dorado to arrange for him to be taken to the airport by police car; just making the Ryanair check-in limit by a few minutes. He had phoned Dornan before boarding the plane and she was waiting for him at Prestwick Airport when he came through the Arrivals doors. *God she's looking good. Cow.*

They exchanged small talk about tans and stuffed donkeys while waiting to get out of the car park but Healy wasted no more time once they got on the motorway.

'It's Turner alright. Fifteen unsolved murders in the area since Turner turned up there. The first definitely linked to the place he worked in at the time. Almost all of them definitely stabbings. Common knowledge he, and probably her, shagging on the side. He well known for having a violent side. Whoever dumped bodies needed local knowledge; he fits the bill.'

'There's more.'

'What?'

'Ray Ford's not representing him anymore; he told me Turner's prone to reading a bible, on his mother's advice apparently.'

'Well that's that. Pity the Marbella things off; us being so near an airport and all.' Dornan did not miss the bitterness in Healy's tone but outwardly ignored it.

'Right tomorrow morning we put everything we have on Turner together. We then try as best we can to link him to the other murders, then we pick him up.'

'Should put him under surveillance as well. I'll do it.'

'You have to remain detached Matt.'

'I am detached. I'll do it.'

'I'll review things in the morning Matt, take it from there. Get some sleep. You don't look great to be honest.'

Neither Dornan nor Healy knew that the morning would change everything.

\*\*\*

Jack T'Baht was taken aback by what he had just seen. He sat in his car across and slightly down from Jill French's house in Bishopbriggs, a few miles outside Glasgow. He had been sitting for half an hour watching to see if French would go back out again or was in for the night when Rab Brown had driven up and gone into French's house. French had answered the door holding what looked like a glass of wine in her hand, wearing a short skirt and low cut blouse. T'Baht couldn't decide if she was wearing a bra or not. *So, I was right. A harlot. And Brown? His wife who has just given him the joy of children is betrayed in favour of a temptress at her husband's work. A she-devil. We'll this will not go unpunished.* He switched on his engine and drove off. Brown did the same some ten minutes later.

\*\*\*

My secretary buzzed through to tell me there was someone who was on the phone who insisted on speaking to me but who wasn't a client.

'Yes, Ray Ford speaking. Who is this?'

'Peter Harris.'

The name was familiar but I couldn't quite place it. 'Yes.'

'Peter Harris, phoning from Barlinnie Prison Mr Ford. I have some things to say that will help your client Joe Turner.'

The penny dropped. Harris. Charged with raping Kate Turner. I was just about to say that I no longer represented Joe Turner but my curiosity, and possibly my guilt, held me back.

'And what would that be Mr Harris?'

No. I want you, Dornan and Healy to come out here today.'

'You'll need to do better than that Mr Harris. We are all busy people.'

'I'll prove Turner didn't kill Julie Connor. Is that enticement enough Mr Ford?'

A few minutes later I was on the phone to Susan. She said she would get Healy and meet me at the prison in an hour. I sat waiting for Harris to be led into the room; hoping he brought my own as well as Joe's salvation with him. When he came in he looked drawn but not distressed. If anything, he looked content.

'So Peter, what is it you want to tell us?' It was Susan who started the conversation off. I interrupted.

'Can I just say for the record Peter that I am not here to represent you. You do understand that?'

'Perfectly. I don't need a lawyer.'

'Get on with it Harris.' Healy's annoyance about being there obvious.

'Joe Turner did not kill Julie Connor.'

'Right, and you know this how exactly?'

'Because I did.'

There were five people in the small interview room counting Harris and the warder but the silence was profound.

'You killed your own daughter?' It was Healy, but even he was thrown. 'I asked you about this before and you forcibly dismissed the notion as I recall.'

'No Healy. You asked if she was my girlfriend.'

'Why are you telling us this now?' said Dornan.

'I don't want an innocent man found guilty and you can only serve one life in prison. I want to clear my conscience.'

'You've found God?' Healy's annoyance obviously back.

'If you like.'

'Why did you kill her?'

'I went to her, my own daughter, to tell her I did not kill or rape Kate Turner; that I loved her. She had no time for me. Then Joe Turner turned up and I saw that she seemed pleased to see him. Him! That arsehole. She dismissed me. Told me to "Go away." Sad little man she called me.'

'What happened?'

'I followed the two of them to some shit hole of a pub. I went into the lounge. I could see them in the bar though. They argued, he hit her. She went into the toilets. When he left I followed her into the toilets. Tried to comfort her. She waved me away. I cut her throat.'

'What with?' asked Healy.

'A scalpel.'

'Where did you get a scalpel?' I asked.

'I'm a nurse Mr Ford, remember?'

Silence again filled the room. I looked at Susan for confirmation that the story fitted the evidence. She seemed to understand and nodded slowly. I looked at Healy but he was just staring at Harris. Deep in thought.

'But she wasn't your daughter at all was she Peter?' said Healy, dragging us all, confusedly, into the present.

'Ah.'

'That's why you killed your first wife. Your daughter wasn't your daughter after all. So you killed your wife and now you've killed her. Is that the truth of it Peter? You've killed your shame.'

Harris shrugged and turned to look at me.

'We'll Mr Ford are you pleased that your client is now in the clear?'

'Well, to be strictly correct he isn't........'

'Well don't be.'

'What do you mean?' interjected Healy.

'He killed his wife Kate.'

I was beginning to think I was in some kind of dream sequence, some parallel universe. I looked at Susan and Healy, their states of mind not apparent.

'How do you know?'

'He was there. He saw Kate and I together.'

A chill ran down my spine and seemed to shake my whole body. Again I looked over at Susan and Healy. They too were beginning to show signs that what was unfolding in front of them was impossible to take in. I looked back at Harris. He had kept looking at me, smiling. I somehow formed some words in my head.

'You saw him there? You saw him kill his wife?' My words somehow came out in a measured calm manner that belied my true mood. For me this was worse than Joe killing Julie.

'Yes, I organised it. After Kate and I made love I didn't leave, I waited. I knew Turner would show up. It was dark and misty but then he appeared, quite dramatic in a way. I thought he would just freak a bit, hit her maybe but when I saw him stab her I panicked and ran off.'

Healy leaned over the desk. His face inches from Harris's.

'Look you sniffling little fuck. Just stop talking in riddles and say what you've got to say in plain English.'

'I knew Kate had had enough of Turner, knew she just needed help getting out, so I put that help in place. I made the arrangements to meet her, romantic setting etc, and then I wrote to Turner with the details. He was always a jealous pig so I knew he would flip when he saw us, probably resort to violence but that would have been a small price to pay to win Kate.'

'But Kate wasted it by telling you she had met someone else and it was you who flipped.' Susan said.

'In a way, but I did not kill her. Look why would I lie. I've admitted to killing two people and if it was just hatred of Turner I would let him take the rap for Julie Connor as well. No, I want the truth out and punishment meted out to the right people for the right things; including me.'

'But Turner knew you and Kate met up when she was over here. You weren't telling him anything new.'

'I elaborated on the content of our liaisons. Included some fake hotel bookings in the names Harris/Turner.'

'What hotels?'

'Moat House; Lorne; Cathedral House; The Ingram Hotel.'

Susan and Healy glanced at each other. Susan looked flushed. I knew there must be a connection to the case.

'In all the times you met up with Kate Turner over the years did you ever sleep together?'

Harris seemed to lose his calm demeanour, his confidence.

'No.'

We left the prison and drove to Coia's Cafe in Duke Street on the way back to the centre; busy but with alcoves where you can talk privately and enjoy the best minestrone soup in Glasgow.

'You can't warn Turner' said Healy as I sat down.

'I didn't intend to,' I said.

'It's still not proof enough. Harris is a fucking nut job. I do believe him though' said Susan.

'How did you get on in Spain Matt?' I asked.

'Fine, it's him.' Healy didn't even look at me as he answered. I decided there and then that I was finished even trying to re-build bridges that I didn't even know I had damaged with Healy.

'Great you say it so it must be so.'

Healy looked ready to explode. Susan raised a hand.

'We're all thrown by this, let's just get on and do what we have to do.'

I didn't even bother ordering. I made an excuse about client's waiting, leaned over and kissed Susan and left. I could feel Healy's staring eyes in my back as I walked out the door. *Just what was his problem? What had I done to rile him so much?*

## Chapter 24

Susan Dornan was in the office early the next morning. All the squad had been informed the previous day about Harris's confession which, unlike Colin Banks' confession weeks previously, was being taken seriously. The focus now was on confirming that Joe Turner was present on the river bank at the time that Kate Turner was killed and to go from there to linking him to the other Azrael killings. The problem of timing she had now was that once Harris was charged with Julie Connor's killing she would have to inform Joe Turner that the charge against him was being dropped. This would inevitably mean he would get his passport back and head back to Spain before they had sufficient time to put a water tight case against him in place for killing his wife. She knew that whether she liked it or not she would have to seek advice from Matt Healy who she felt was becoming more distant by the day; and who still remained a possible, if somewhat uncomfortable, suspect in the killings himself. Her feelings of unease were about to be compounded by the ringing of the phone on her desk.

'DI Dornan.'

'Good morning Inspector. This is Alistair Dorado from the Spanish police here.'

Healy had told Dornan of Dorado's background so the distinctly un-spanish accent had not thrown her.

'Oh, good morning Alistair. Matt Healy isn't here at the moment, you have been put through directly to my number. How can I help you?'

'Yes, perhaps you could pass a message on to him for me. It's just to let him know that unfortunately there was no DNA found at the scene of the murder. It was a stabbing, quite frenzied in fact, but no DNA. Strange really, there weren't any tell tales signs of anything other than a small partial print, no good for full identification, on one of the girl's patent shoes. The killer was careful, yes.'

Dornan was temporarily thrown; her hand began to shake. She needed clarity, a dreaded doubt removed.

'OK Alistair I will. Just to be clear, which of the murders are you referring to?'

'Oh the one that happened while Matt was here. Nothing more on any of the other murders I'm afraid.'

Dornan was sure Dorado said more and she must have replied and brought the conversation to an end but no more had registered; she was drowning in a sea of panic and doubt. She rose slowly, closed her window blinds, returned to her desk and put her head in her hands. *It can't be true Susan. Think. Unbeckoned, the memory of a hotel room came to her. Drunken passion. Listless night. Healy mumbling in his sleep. Unintelligible. Think Susan think. No it couldn't be; "Sorry mum, sorry." Dear God.*

Her door opened, no knock, Healy entered and sat down uninvited. 'Susan we need to talk.'

***

Paul Allan was delighted with the developments in the Julie Connor killing. *Finally get Max off my back about Joe Turner.*

'You'll never guess what's happened?'

'What?'

'Joe Turner didn't kill Julie Connor. See, I told you, you should never jump to conclusions.'

'How do you know?'

'Another guy has confessed. Her step-father would you believe.'

The silence on the line was so palpable that Allan thought Kermack had hung up.

'You still there Max?'

'Yes. Her step father, are you sure? Can you get me to meet him?'

'Doubt it.'

'Is his name Russell?'

'No, Harris. Look I have to go. See you later.'

Kermack opened the office desk drawer he normally kept locked. He looked inside. The drawer only contained two items; a photo and a knife.

***

'I know how we can nail this Susan.' Healy sat looking at Dornan, unaware of Dornan's inner turmoil.

'Nail what?' Dornan said quietly.

'What do you think? This whole Turner, Harris, Azrael thing.'

'And how's that Matt?'

'We get Turner in for a chat, tell him he's off the hook for the Julie Connor killing. Get him to relax. But we get the Polish girl from the Cathedral House Hotel and the guy from the restaurant in Buchanan Galleries in. They ID Turner, even unofficially at first, we've got him.'

Dornan didn't react, hardly seemed to be listening.

'Susan?'

'What?'

'Well what do you think?'

'How did Spain go Matt?'

'What? What are you talking about? I told you. Nothing concrete but I know it's Turner.'

'Nothing else of note?'

'Look Susan, what is this? What are you on about?'

'Nothing, I've just got a lot on my mind.'

'Right. Well what do you think?'

'Fine. Do it. I'll phone Ray. He's not officially acting for Turner but I'm sure he'll be happy to support him when he hears the good news.'

'OK.'

'Oh and Matt. You'll be here for it as well?'

'Yes.'

'Right. Will you make sure Frame, Allan and T'Baht are here as well?'

Healy sat and stared. 'What's going on Susan?'

'Nothing is going on. I just want everyone up to scratch about where we are. Anyway Matt, just do it will you.'

Healy rose and left without uttering another word. Dornan remained at her desk till Healy closed the door and then picked up her phone.

***

Martha Reid was glad it was a sunny day. She sat on the bus at Buchanan Bus Station waiting as the driver whiled away the minutes until departure time fiddling with his mobile phone. She was looking forward to the drive out through the Clyde Valley and to her lunch in The 4 Pillars. She had checked that morning that her reservation had been noted and that she wished a table looking out onto the river.

She was also happy with the outfit she had finally chosen. Some people would probably describe it as "Sunday Best" but she had never quite followed that kind of reasoning. Would God be bothered about what you were wearing when you visited him? The noise of the doors swooshing closed brought Martha back from her debate with herself. The bus pulled out passed the back entrance to the John Lewis store. Martha considered it one of her favourite stores and watched with a smile as two other 'ladies of a certain age' negotiated the revolving doors. Martha sighed and turned her thoughts to the day ahead.

\*\*\*

*Azrael had never felt such contentment. He knew he had never complained about the demands placed upon him by the Lord; but he was glad his time of serving appeared now to be over. He watched impassively as the whores and harlots passed by the window; they would be dealt with by someone else blessed by His calling. Dionne Warwick asked if he knew the way to San Jose. He smiled, No, but he did know the way to redemption.*

\*\*\*

Susan Dornan had never moved from her office. She couldn't decide if she was being practical or cowardly but she felt she had to detach herself in a way from some in the squad. She picked up her phone, rang Paul Allan's extension, summoned him through and made the biggest mistake of her career.

'I want you to go up to Barlinnie Paul and speak to Harris? I've had enough of the place, and him, and it might give you some experience. Take a full statement from Peter Harris. Cover everything; Kate Turner, his confessions over killing his first wife and now Julie Connor. I'm not sure who's available to go with you but just go about and ask.'

'No problem ma'am.'

Paul Allan left Dornan's office, went back to his desk and picked up the phone.

'Max can you meet me in Riddrie in twenty minutes?'

'Not really I'm due to show someone a bungalow in Knightswood in an hour. Why?'

'Oh it's just that I'm on my way to Barlinnie to interview Pete Harris, alone, thought you might like to tag along.'

'I'll be there.' Max replied in a quieter tone than usual.

Allan got an old Warrant Card from his desk that a retired officer had left behind. He'd get Max just to flash it quickly and sign in on the same name. Nobody would take much notice anyway he was sure and Dornan would never get to find out.

\*\*\*

Martha Reid enjoyed her lunch immensely. She was sitting looking out at the river when the waitress approached.

'Can I get you anything else?'

'No thank you. Everything was just lovely.'

'It's a lovely view isn't it?'

'It is yes. Did I read somewhere though that there was a terrible tragedy here a while back?'

The waitress seemed to retreat within herself, unsure what to say.

'There was. I was working that day too. The couple were sitting right over there.'

'Please tell me, did the girl seem happy?'

'She did but then there seemed to be some sort of lover's tiff. She left. He sat for a while and then he left. We found out later about, well you know.'

'Quite. Did the police say where it actually happened?'

The waitress's feeling of unease over the conversation heightened.

'Just at that tree there apparently. Well, is that all? Can I phone you a taxi or anything?'

'No thank you, I'm going for a walk.'

Martha Reid rose and called into the ladies toilet before leaving The 4 Pillars. She checked her appearance in the mirror and tucked a stray wisp of grey hair back into place. She strolled over to the area around the tree the waitress had pointed out. She wasn't sure but thought she felt her daughter Kate's presence. *Hello darling, is your brother with you?* She allowed herself a smile as she looked at the refection of the branches on the water. She put her bag on the grass bank, opened it and removed a small bottle of water and a number of weed control tablets. She hoped no-one would see her drinking out of a bottle, *so un-ladylike.* The tablets did not stick in her throat at all and, as she lay back on the grass thinking of Kate, she felt only contentment. *I'm coming children, Mum's coming.*

## Chapter 25

Healy and Frame sat in a bar around the corner from the station. They had worked together for many years and trusted each other although neither would describe the other as a close friend. Healy knew that Frame would have no problem helping him out with what he was going to pull on Joe Turner *and that prick of a boyfriend of hers* but he wanted to speak to Frame about recent events.

'John have you noticed anything strange about things recently?'

'What, stranger than normal?'

'You know what I mean.'

Frame knew exactly what Healy meant but also knew to confide in no-one.

'Suppose, but can't quite put my finger on it. What do you thinks' going on?'

'It's got all the smell of an internal enquiry but I can't think what anyone would be enquiring about.'

Frame couldn't see any link between the cases and his own particular preferences either but even the rumour of an enquiry had him on edge.

'Who do you thinks' behind it Matt?'

'Got to be Dornan. She's keen to make a name for herself and McFarlane's too thick.'

'Jack T'Baht hates her you know?'

'What, why?'

'Think it's a cultural thing. Women should be subservient to men, that kind of thing.'

'How do you become a Muslim then John?'

Healy bought Frame another pint and outlined his plan before returning to the station. Before either had the chance to sit at their desks the doors at the end of the squad room burst open and McFarlane teetered into the room almost crashing into the first desk he passed. He was panting by the time he reached Dornan's room. Dornan stood up and asked while McFarlane caught his breadth.

'Sir, what's wrong?'

'Harris's been murdered in Barlinnie.'

'For fuck's sake' roared Healy 'what the fuck's going on up there.'

'It's worse than that. DC Allan and DS Provan are being held for it.'

Everyone in the room stood in stunned silence.

Dornan's mind was reeling. 'Who is DS Provan?' she eventually asked.

'I don't know, you sent him. Get up there now.'

When Dornan and Healy got to the prison, the prison Governor Vince Farrell, was waiting.

'What happened?' asked Dornan.

'We don't know the details but your guys Allan and Provan were booked in to question Harris. They were questioning him in an interview room. After a while when a prison officer at the door never heard anything he looked in and Harris was on the floor in a pool of blood with a sharpened, plastic letter opener sticking out of him and your two guys were sitting staring at the wall.'

'I don't know anybody called Provan, he's not one of mine.'

'Superintendent, it gets worse. They were sitting holding hands.'

'Can I speak to Allan?'

Paul Allan was sitting in the prison's medical room. Susan Dornan looked at him and saw a young man who had aged forty years in the few hours since she had last seen him. *"I should never have sent him here. Who the fuck is this Provan guy anyway?'*

'Paul are you OK?'

Allan looked at Dornan but she got the impression he was looking into another universe rather than at her.

'I loved him. How could he have done this to me?'

'Who Paul? What are you talking about?'

'Max. He told me he only wanted to watch. To see a killer in the flesh. Appraise him. For his book.'

None of it made any sense to Susan Dornan.

'Max? Max Provan?'

'What? No. Max Kermack, my boyfriend. I used an old warrant card to get him in. Somebody called Provan.'

Dornan shook her head. She looked at the withered figure sitting in front of her. His ruination complete. There was a quiet knock on the door. It was Matt Healy. He looked at Allan but his face didn't register any emotion.

'Farrell has agreed to let me speak to the guy who says his name is Provan. They've checked the warrant card. Guy retired five years ago. What sort of fucking security they got here.'

Susan left Allan sitting alone in the medical room.

'Has he been seen by a doctor yet?' she asked a warder.

'Not that I know of. You want me to get him one?'

'I'd appreciate it.'

She turned to Healy.

'Apparently he brought this other guy in as some sort of favour. His real name is Max Kermack; he's Allan's boyfriend.'

'Jesus wept Susan.'

'Along with me Matt, along with me.'

Max Kermack was sitting in an interview looking fully in control. There was blood on his clothes and some flecks on his face but he didn't seem to mind.

'Max, did you kill Peter Harris?' asked Dornan.

'Yes.' Max quietly replied.

'Did Paul Allan know your intentions when he brought you here?' asked Healy.

'No.'

'Why did you kill him?'

'He killed my sister.'

Healy and Dornan quickly glanced at each other and then back at Max.

'Who's your sister?'

'Julie Connor.'

'But your name's Kermack.'

'Julie and I were separated as kids, adopted by different families. I went to the Kermacks; good people. Julie went to another family; the Russells. We never saw each other again for over twenty years, when Julie tracked me down. When Julie got married she changed her name to Connor but didn't change it back when she divorced.

'How did you know Harris killed Julie? There are other suspects, he hasn't been convicted.'

'Paul told me.'

'Paul being?'

'Paul Allan, your fellow officer.'

'What else did he tell you about Harris?'

'Something about him claiming to be her step father but that's shit.'

Dornan and Healy silently agreed to leave that point.

'Are you and Allan lovers?' asked Dornan. Healy inwardly winced.

'Yes.'

'You used him.'

'I saw an opportunity and I took it.'

'He's finished in the force you know. He'll probably go to prison along with you. Do you know what happens to ex-police in prison Kermack?' said Healy.

Max Kermack merely shrugged. 'He'll survive. Harris didn't, that's the main thing.'

'You ever killed anyone else Max?'

'No.'

'We'll need a DNA sample anyway.'

'Feel free. I don't imagine I'll be going far.'

'Are you religious Max?' Healy asked.

'Strict atheist. No God to deal with Harris so I did. Why?'

'Do you want to see Paul?' Dornan asked, taking Healy by surprise. They both looked at Kermack.

'No. Why would I?'

By the time they left the interview room Paul Allan had been seen by a doctor and had been taken to London Road Police Station to wait for his court appearance the next morning. Healy and Dornan sat back in their car trying to make sense of everything that had happened. The carnage of their investigations.

The next day, as expected, Max Kermack was remanded in custody. Paul Allan was given bail but suspended from duty and warned not to go near any police station unless requested to do so for questioning. Healy and Dornan both felt that they had failed in every way. Dornan had failed in leading her team and had at least played a bit part in allowing a young officer to completely ruin his life never mind his career. Healy's guilt stemmed from his closed mind on the original investigations with even a rookie like Jill French showing more insight than him. *"Maybe it's time for me to move on after all."* He looked over to Susan Dornan's office. He knew she was hurting and he wanted to help but knew he was history as far as she was concerned. He just wasn't quite sure why; what she really knew of him.

***

It always made me smile when I saw Susan's number come up on my mobile.

'Is that the most beautiful policewoman in Scotland calling?'

'Most stressed possibly but thanks for the thought.'

'Why stressed?'

Susan quickly told me of the sequence of events surrounding Peter Harris and Paul Allan.

'My God' my singularly insignificant response.

'Can you get a hold of Joe Turner Ray and bring him in to Police HQ tomorrow? Matt Healy will handle things our end, I'm going to see if I can salvage anything of Paul Allan's life.'

'Yes of course.'

We exchanged some small talk and then hung up. I called Joe and arranged to meet him outside Pitt Street at two the next day.

'All good news Joe, all good.'

I'd live to regret saying that.

***

A few minutes after calling me, the phone rang on Dornan's desk.

'Afternoon ma'am, it's a DS Blake from Hamilton here.'

'Yes.'

'It's more of a courtesy call than anything ma'am. We have a suicide out this way and we believe there's a connection to a case you are working on. The deceased is a Mrs Martha Reid.'

The name didn't register with Dornan at first but all too soon the drawn features of a grieving but composed older lady came into sharp focus in Dornan's mind.

'What are the circumstances?'

'It appears she's taken some sort of pills. Pretty painful death I hear but the poor old soul looks content somehow.'

'Near a pub called The 4 Pillars?'

'Yes that's right.'

'Poor woman. Thank you for calling, let me know if anything suspicious turns up but I wouldn't imagine it will.'

Dornan studied the back of her hand as it sat on the replaced phone. *Such a waste. So many lives ruined.* She called through to Healy.

'I've just heard; Martha Reid, Kate Turner's mum, has committed suicide.'

A few moments passed in silence. 'I'll be glad when this is all over' said Healy.

'I phoned Ray Ford, Turner will be in at two tomorrow.'

'Right.'

'You deal with it Matt, I'm going to go to speak to Kermack and Allan. Try to do what I can for Allan. I'll take French with me.'

'OK, leave it to me, I'll deal with it.'

Susan Dornan then called Rab Brown into the office and told him what she wanted him to do the next day.

## Chapter 26

Susan Dornan looked directly into the eyes of Max Kermack. She looked for regret, sorrow, perhaps compassion for Paul Allan; she saw nothing.

'So Julie Connor was your sister Max?'

'Yes.'

'Who were your parents, your blood parents that is?'

'My mother was called Anne Chalmers, she died in a fall when Julie and I were babies. I don't know who my father was, nor do I care.'

'What was your mother's married name?'

'I just told you, I never asked nor cared.'

'Your DNA doesn't match Julie Connor's.'

'What?'

'Oh I think you heard Max.'

'Your test is wrong.'

'No, but then again I didn't expect a match.'

'What are you talking about?'

'Julie wasn't your sister Max, not your full sister at any rate. She was your half-sister.'

'Why are you coming out with this crap? I killed Harris, you've got me, end of.'

'Not quite Max. What do you know of your father?'

'I told you, nothing.'

'Shall I tell you then?' Dornan leaned over the desk, got as close to Kermack as she could. 'Well you fucking bastard, you have ruined one of my young officer's lives so now I'm going to ruin yours. Your mother's maiden name was Chalmers. Her married name? Harris. Yes that's right Max, Harris because she was married to Peter Harris; the Peter Harris you have just killed. You killed your own father you fuck. Yes he killed Julie but Julie wasn't related to him, not really. Not like he was to you. So think on that while you're lying in prison for the next twenty years.'

'I don't believe you. Why are you saying these things?'

'Because I want you to suffer Kermack. Not for killing Harris, for destroying Paul Allan.'

Dornan walked to the door. She hesitated, spoke over her shoulder.

'I'm on my way to see Paul now. Is there anything you want me to say to him for you?'

Kermack studied the floor, said nothing.

\*\*\*

Matt Healy, John Frame, Ivana Jakanowski and Gino Franchetti, the barman from Buchanan Galleries sat having a coffee in an interview room adjacent to the room Joe Turner and Ray Ford were sitting in. Healy explained that they were running a little behind but that they would get on with things and let them away as soon as possible. Healy and Frame then left the room, unaware of Rab Brown watching them from the observation room.

\*\*\*

Joe and I were relaxed as we sat in the room waiting to clear up the final issues surrounding his charges. I could tell he would be glad to be putting all of this nightmare behind him and getting back to Spain. I didn't think that we would be in contact much after everything that had happened but I had no regrets, and I wouldn't have met Susan were it not for Joe in a way, *every cloud....*

The door opened and Matt Healy and John Frame entered. They too seemed relaxed, although Healy avoided eye contact with me.

'Well Joe, a bit of a relief for you eh?'

'You could say that.'

'Well, just to confirm things. We have established that Peter Harris was in fact Julie Connor's father and he has confessed to her murder. Unfortunately, he too is now deceased but we have no reason to doubt his story and we have informed the PF's office. So you're in the clear.'

'Right, I can go then? I'll get my passport back?' Joe asked.

'Not quite.'

'What do you mean not quite?' I said.

'Mr Harris also told us some other things before his untimely demise Mr Ford. Joseph Turner I'm arresting you for the murder of Kate Turner and......' The rest of Healy words didn't register in my mind although I'd heard them often enough.

'What is this? You told me this was just a formality.' I managed to blurt out eventually.

'I didn't tell you anything Mr Ford. Your fiancé might have, I didn't.'

I shot a glance at Joe; his bewilderment complete.

'Your client here will be processed now, you can see him after that. Just wait here till I inform the duty sergeant.' Healy left the room and rushed to the other interview room. He ushered Jakanowski and Franchetti out into the corridor. 'We'll be passing three men out here in a minute. One will be the other police officer who was in here with me a few minutes ago. Just take a good look at the guy with the fair hair but don't say anything. OK? Just walk by them.'

Frame already had handcuffs on an increasingly frantic Joe Turner. He lead him out the door and along to the charge desk apparently oblivious to my vociferous complaints. I saw Healy, and two other people approaching, I was sweating, the confusion swirling around my anger at these obviously contrived events almost tempting me to hit Healy but I decided that calm and apparent indifference was the best course of action under the circumstances. Moments later Joe had been charged and was being lead to a holding cell; all the time just staring at me. After another few moments I found myself outside the station unable to process what had just happened. *How do I deal with this? Did Susan know what was being planned?* Inside the station the situation was moving from bad to worse - than - terrible.

***

Healy had led the witnesses into yet another interview room. He didn't invite them to sit or sit himself. Rab Brown's entering of the room at his back barely curtailing his excitement.

'Well Ivana, was that the man you saw at the hotel with the woman who was murdered?'

'Yes, I'm sure it is.'

'Gino, what about you, do you think that's who you saw having a coffee with Sandra Graham on the day she was murdered?'

'I no sure, maybe...'

'Come on Gino, either it is or it isn't?'

Franchetti looked from Healy to Frame to Ivana. He shrugged his shoulders.

'Sorry, I no sure. Sorry, I go home now.'

Healy told Brown to make sure Ivana and Franchetti got home OK. He phoned Dornan.

'Good news Susan. Positive ID on Turner for being at the hotel with Kate Turner. I've got him in custody.'

'Oh I know Matt. Ray just phoned me. I'm on my way in, we need to have a serious chat.'

***

Susan Dornan stormed into the squad room, the ear-ringing she had just had from Ray Ford still reverberating in her head. Healy was surprised when she walked straight passed his desk and summoned Rab Brown into her office.

Brown remained standing as Dornan slammed a file down onto the floor from her desk.

'Well?'

'An obvious stitch up but I was in the room when Healy questioned the witnesses. There was no collusion or intimidation ma'am, the girl picked Turner out OK, The barman wasn't sure but I think it's more a case with him not wanting involved than him not recognising Turner. Called back in and put under the slightest pressure then I think he would pick out Turner too.'

'You definitely don't think either Healy or Frame could have pressured them in any way?'

'To be honest, no. It's definitely Turner ma'am, at least for his wife's killing. He must have followed her out to the Clyde Valley, maybe saw her having sex with Harris maybe not, either way he losses it and tops her. The Azrael thing might be more difficult to prove but we can concentrate on placing him at each scene now.'

'OK Rab thanks. Send Healy in.'

Healy walked in, his hand raised in apology. He sat down uninvited.

'I know what you're going to say Susan and I'm sorry if you think I've side stepped your authority but you must admit we needed something to give these investigations impetus, and now we've got it.'

'You honestly think Ray Ford won't challenge the ID's?'

'He can't. There hasn't been a formal ID done, nothing to challenge. Of course, Turner's Q.C. might bring it up at the trial but it's a minor point.'

'You think he's Azrael?'

'You bet he is.'

'There's absolutely nothing to connect him to the Azrael crimes.'

'Maybe not yet but there will be and I'm going to find it.'

'No. I want you to concentrate solely on the Kate Turner killing. Go over everything and make the case there, you've seemed certain from day one so see it through. I want Browne, French and the others to concentrate on the other women. Eastern Division have been given the Harris killing under the circumstances so we can forget that for the moment.'

'But....'

'That's all Matt. Oh and by the way, bring up my relationship with Ray Ford again, especially in front of a suspect, and you are out of here for good.

Healy had barely left the room when the phone rang on Dornan's desk.

'Dornan.'

'Inspector, it's Alistair Dorado here, from Spain.'

Dornan's heart sank. 'Yes Alistair, what can I do for you?'

'Well it's a little awkward I'm afraid. The friends of the dead girl have told us of their movements on the night of the killing and it seems that they got talking to an older man in one of the bars, a Scottish man, that's how they got talking. It seems he was keen to take one of the girls for something to eat but she was not so keen to go. The man apparently got quite annoyed at this and stormed off.'

'I'm not sure I follow.'

'Well it's just that the man's description seemed familiar to me but I couldn't understand why. But now, as you say over there, the pound has dropped. I think the man may have been Matt.'

'Penny.'

'What?'

'The penny has dropped. So you want to speak to Matt Healy?'

'Yes but with your permission of course.'

'I'll get him to call you right away.'

Dornan took a note of the number, walked out to Healy's desk and told him to call Dorado. She went back to her room and pretended to do paperwork whilst never really taking her eyes off Healy.

\*\*\*

*That evening Azrael sat waiting for guidance from the Lord. He didn't like uncertainty and confusion. Didn't like when it was unclear what he had to do. Didn't like it when people plotted against him but he knew the Lord would not abandon him. He thought of his mother. He listened to the music; he read the holy book; he sought the light.*

## Chapter 27

Paul Allan stood looking at the ceiling of the kitchen of his Dennistoun tenement flat. His mind was focused as he stood there motionless. He was resolute but smiled inwardly to himself that even the smallest of things can come into your mind even in times of crises. *Just how old will this flat be? When would the hooks for the old washing pulley system have been put in? Max had told him that the cornicing was original "couldn't get anyone to do workmanship like that these days Paul, never in a million years mate."*

That morning two detectives from Eastern division had come to the flat and questioned him about Max and what had happened at the prison. Allan could tell that their hearts weren't really up for a determined grilling over his role in what had happened *slightly embarrassed if anything, probably because of the gay issue more than anything else.* They had treated him with respect and he was grateful for that. He looked through from the kitchen into the living room at the picture of him and Max on top of the TV; the photo, like the TV, a purveyor of illusion.

An hour after the detectives had left Susan Dornan had called. She too had been sympathetic and supportive but everyone involved knew Paul Allan was finished. His uncle the Chief Constable hadn't been in touch though; his position in the force outweighing his position in the family. *Of no consequence now Uncle.*

Allan's grip on a scarf that he had given Max Kermack for his birthday tightened. He raised the scarf to his lips; *I forgive you Max, my true love.* Allan stepped from the kitchen table. He need not have worried, the pulley hook held his weight effortlessly.

***

Susan Dornan and Matt Healy sat in the court waiting for Joe Turner's case to be called. The PF was opposing bail but everyone knew that it would be granted. Dornan turned to Healy.

'What did Dorado want by the way?'

'Oh nothing really. A bag had been left behind in the Hotel Samba, the hotel I stayed in, he just wanted to know if it was mine.'

'Right.'

Dornan looked across the court as Turner was lead into the dock. Five minutes later Turner was granted bail and disappeared from the court the same way he arrived.

'We need to have him watched 24/7 Susan,' Healy said.

'Yes, there's a lot to consider Matt. A lot.'

Healy appeared slightly confused by the response but said nothing. Dornan pushed past him murmuring that she would see him back at the station.

She caught up with me in the court corridor.

'Ray.'

I turned, inwardly delighted to see her.

'Susan.'

'Ray, I know Healy was out of order but I swear I didn't know anything about his plans. You have to belief that.'

'Fine. I have to go down to get Joe through the formalities. See you tonight?'

'I'd like that.......Ray, Joe was definitely the person with Kate at the hotel.'

'Doesn't mean he killed her.'

'Doesn't it?'

Joe Turner looked over at me as I entered the room as he awaited the formalities of his release. I couldn't tell what was going through his head but I knew what was going through mine; his lying about being in Scotland, the train ticket I saw with my own eyes, his temper and now the fact he had been identified as being with Kate in her hotel.

'Here we go again Ray,' Joe said.

'Looks like it Joe. Don't worry I'll get you the best QC available.'

'Ray, do me a favour. Phone Martha, tell her what's happened but let her know I'm innocent.'

My guilt at how my relationship with Joe had deteriorated so much that I hadn't even phoned him to tell him about Martha hit me harder than words could say. I looked at the floor.

'Joe, I've got something to tell you.'

'Best OK it with your girlfriend first then Ray.'

We stared at each other for what seemed an eternity. Joe turned to the security guard.

'Know any honest lawyers mate? I need a new brief.'

'Joe...,' I said

'Fuck off Ray. My new lawyer will be in touch for any paperwork you've not already handed over to your shag.'

I got up, the weight of my guilt almost buckling my knees, and headed for the door.

'By the way Ray, once I walk away from this charge, I'll be seeing you.'

I opened the door and left the room without looking back, or telling him of Martha's fate.

***

Jack T'Baht opened his desk drawer and slipped his Koran in. He had spent most of the previous night studying it and praying for guidance. Dornan and French entered the room together. French was showing Dornan some feature in a magazine on the latest A List celebrity hunk. As they passed his desk he heard Dornan say "I wouldn't say no Jill, would you?" The laughed together like naughty school girls. *Whores.* He continued to watch French as she reached her desk and sat down. Her hemline slipped half way up her thigh. She crossed her legs as she waited for her PC to boot up. She glanced over at T'Baht and smiled, 'Morning Jack.'

T'Baht's mouth was dry. He murmured a "Morning" in reply then busied himself with paperwork, the hardness between his legs preventing him from concentrating. He looked up as Healy and Frame entered the room. He studied their faces. *Did they even have any beliefs? How did they accept their subservience to a woman?* Healy motioned as if he were going to Dornan's office but hesitated when he saw her on the phone, turned and settled at his own desk.

The door to Dornan's office opened and Dornan came out. T'Baht noticed a difference in her demeanour.

'Paul Allan has been found dead. Suicide. I'm on my way to McFarlane.'

Jack T'Baht didn't know how to react to the news. Allan wasn't a friend as such but he had always been friendly enough. But the prophet was clear; *homosexuality means death and death had indeed come to Paul Allan. Allah be praised.*

***

My meal that evening with Susan was a subdued affair. Understandably Susan hadn't wanted to go out so we had just ordered a Chinese carry out and were picking at that while not really watching a film on Channel Four.

'Why did I send Allan to the prison Ray? What was I thinking?'

'Don't be silly. There was nothing wrong in what you did. How were you supposed to know what he was going to do? Silly lad.'

'He was the Chief Constable's nephew you know. McFarlane's in a sweat about that more than anything else, the arsehole.'

'And you?'

'Oh I don't care about any of that shit. To be honest I'm thinking of quitting after these investigations are wound up.'

'Really? What would you do?'

'Why live off you of course.'

I looked at Susan, despite the forced smile I could see the sadness in her eyes. I leaned over and kissed her forehead.

'Do you know what I think?'

'What?'

'We should set a date.'

Susan looked at me with those eyes that would melt my soul forever.

'I love you,' she said.

'Ditto, so what do you say we start the ball rolling on the wedding of the century?'

'Why not?'

Making love with Susan was like nothing I'd ever experienced before. I wasn't perhaps the most experienced of lovers but I always remembered a discussion I had had with my father back in my late teens when he had simply said: "Son, it's called making love for a reason. If love isn't involved it's merely rutting. Animals rut, a man makes love." The conversation was awkward at the time but I had never forgotten his words but since meeting Susan I now knew what they meant.

\*\*\*

*Azrael usually slept well but the night moon was still in the sky as he looked out at the empty street, only a lonesome fox disturbing the stillness. He turned over in his mind how best to complete the new task the Lord had given him. There was no doubt in his mind that he would obey His command but for the first time he could remember he had doubt in his mind. He was not questioning the burden the Lord had given him but the signs were vague, somehow disturbing. His attention turned to a stray kitten making its way along the edge of the pavement. A sudden blur of orange, a brief squeal and the fox had his meal. His family would live another day. The innocent kitten had served a purpose. Azrael had his sign; an innocent's death could serve the greater good. He returned to bed, embraced the warmth and fell asleep immediately.*

# Chapter 28

The morning sun shone through the windows of the squad room and enveloped the assembled officers there but no amount of sun could pierce the pervading darkness. Susan Dornan received a nod from McFarlane and slowly stood and addressed the group.

'One thing I've learned in this job is that there is never only one victim when someone is murdered. The ripples of despondency that fan out from the initial crime touch so many other lives and the consequences of that contact can never be fathomed. Tragically for us one of our own has now been drawn into this latest web of despair. Our moments of despair are no doubt still to come but not now people, not now. Now more than ever we have to conclude these investigations and at least make some sense of the madness. I'm not going to go over every point of every investigation but I'll outline our new position on things and we will follow an agreed strategy to the letter from now on.

Joe Turner, husband of Kate Turner our first victim, has now been charged for killing his wife. We are satisfied that, despite first appearances, he did not kill the second victim, Julie Connor. He may or may not be the serial killer calling himself Azrael who it would appear is responsible for several other murders since the Connor killing. He has, unorthodoxically, been positively identified as being with his wife at the Cathedral House Hotel although he himself flew in separately the day before, and to Edinburgh, for reasons we are assuming of trying to form some sort of alibi. He then flew back out, again from Edinburgh, after the murder. I have spoken to Chief Superintendent McFarlane about what I want to do about Turner and he has agreed overtime etc to have him put under surveillance. Matt, I want you and DC Parker to cover Turner. I also want surveillance on Ivana Jakanowski. Jack I want you and Golding on that. Her surveillance is for protection purposes, if Turner is Azrael then he won't think twice about going after her. Jill I want you acting as a co-ordinator and making sure you know what's going on at all times. Everybody else has to concentrate on the other killings especially on trying to link them to Turner. OK, any questions?'

'Any other suspects for Azrael if it's not Turner Susan?' asked McFarlane.

'Yes sir. We're working on that separately.'

'Right. Good. OK let's get on with it then.' McFarlane strode out of the office.

'Rab, Jill can you both come into my office please?'

Brown and French sat on the chairs offered to them but Dornan remained standing.

'Rab, Jill I want you to monitor Healy. I know it's a horrible assignment but women are dying and now, indirectly maybe, one of my officers is dead. If Healy is shown to be in the clear then no-one will be happier than me, please believe me on that, but this has all got to come to an end. Are you both OK with that?'

'Yes ma'am,' both replied in unison.

French seemed subdued. 'Everything all right Jill?'

'Yes, it's just....'

'Well, what, out with it.'

'It sounds silly but when I got home last night I could swear someone had been in my flat. No damage or anything like that....just a feeling.'

'Anything out of place, stolen?' asked Browne.

'No, that's the thing, nothing. Maybe....'

'What?' Dornan asked.

'Maybe my knicker drawer seemed slightly disturbed but that could just be my imagination. I was a bit on edge by bed time.'

'Anything else seem odd recently?'

'Nothing tangible but you know how you sometimes get the feeling someone's watching you. I've felt that a couple of times recently.'

'Right. Well if anything else spooks you then contact me right away. OK work out between yourselves how you want to work things and report back to me as often as necessary.'

Once Browne and French had left the office Matt Healy entered. 'A quick word Susan?'

'OK.'

'Why am I working with a rookie; why not John Frame?'

'I want Frame doing something else.'

'What?'

Dornan stared at Healy. 'Anything else?'

'Yeah there is as a matter of fact. Who are the other suspects in the Azrael killings? News to me that there are any.'

'Well there are. I've got other people working on that.'

'Two separate squads are we now?'

'No but some things are on a need to know basis Matt don't you agree. For example I'm sure there are things about your goings-on that I'm not aware of.'

Healy looked hard at Dornan. 'What happened to us Susan? We were good together, in every way, but now. It's that Ford isn't it? He's poisoned you against me hasn't he?'

'It's nothing to do with Ford. We should never have gotten together Matt. My fault, but it's in the past. I've moved on, you should do the same. Look, you've always had Turner down for killing his wife and you were right. Go out now and make the case water tight.'

Healy shook his head but didn't speak again before leaving the office. Dornan picked up her phone and dialled the long number she had made a copy of. The phone at the other end gave a shrill ring.

'Hola, Inspector Dorado por favor.'

***

Joe Turner sat in his Partick bedsit reading his bible. But he was distracted and put the leather bound book down on the cheap, pine coffee table. He took his wallet out and looked at the sepia photo of his mother.

'Well mum, not even the good book can get me out of this.'

He sat and thought over recent months. He knew within himself he hadn't killed Kate *probably*. Yes he had come over in the hope of catching her out as he knew she had distanced herself from him. Yes he had followed her from the store at Celtic Park as that was the only place he knew for definite she was going to be at some point. Yes he had followed her and Whistle Test out to the Clyde Valley but the pub was too remote to watch without being seen and it didn't have bedrooms so he didn't think any shagging would be going on there. So he had waited in the car park of a near – by garden centre, watching the road back into Glasgow but after a few hours realised they must have taken a different road back. The black outs were the issue. Once he realised he had lost track of Kate he had gone into a bar and that was the last he could remember. *That bastarding traitor Ford was right about one thing, neither the cops nor the courts would wear that explanation.* He went to put his wallet back in his pocket and felt something else in the pocket. He fished the business cards he had had printed out and smiled *wonder if they worked?*

\*\*\*

'Cyprus,' I said to Susan.

'Cyprus?'

'Yes.'

'What about it?'

'For the wedding. Looked up the net. Alesium Hotel, Paphos. Looks great and they do wedding packages. What do you say?'

'Well…I was thinking more of a Scottish wedding.'

'Wear tartan then.'

'Ha ha.'

'Think about it then. At least I'm on the case.'

'True, true. Ray can I ask you something? In confidence of course.'

'Of course.'

'What do you think of Matt Healy?'

'Dinosaur, work wise and human race wise. Why?'

'Nothing, just a problem at work.'

'He seems to hate me as well for some reason.'

'What makes you say that?'

'Well he doesn't speak to me, more growls at me. Seems to have gotten worse since you let it slip about us.'

'I didn't let it slip actually........ but you might be right.'

'He wasn't after you himself was he? Upset his macho image.'

'No no.'

'Anyway Susan I've got to go. Need to make lots of money to pay for this wedding.'

In some ways I felt sorry for Susan. Preparing and looking forward to her wedding should be a high point in her life but I knew that her work was getting her down and she was taking Allan's death really badly. Even before she mentioned it I had also noticed that things between her and Healy had deteriorated beyond repair. I toyed with the idea of phoning him, trying to calm the waters but decided to wait till the next time we actually met up. Maybe even invite him to the wedding.

***

Jill French contacted Healy first. 'Evening Matt, you in place OK for Turner?'

'Just drawing up now,' replied Healy.

'Jack you in place for Ivana?'

T'Baht's throat had contracted on him hearing French's voice. He began to stutter, a small bead of sweat appearing on his forehead. 'In place.' He opened his glove compartment, his Koran was there but he left it where it was and pulled out the pair of lace trimmed knickers he had taken from French's flat. He unzipped his trousers and pushed the knickers in beside his erection; his eyes closed.

French changed frequency and spoke to Rab Brown. 'You OK Rab?'

'Fine, bit of a break from the twins to be honest. One thing though. After he parked up Matt went into an Off Sales. I thought at first he was going for fags before I remembered he didn't smoke. I'm pretty sure he bought a bottle of something and he's had a swig of it already.'

'Could be coke, Irn Bru whatever.'

'Could be.'

After a few moments T'Baht opened his eyes. In the meantime Ivana Jakonowski had left work and was already on her bus home.

## Chapter 29

It took about half an hour for Jack T'Baht to realise that he had lost track of Ivana Jakanowski. And why. He thrust his car into gear and speed to Ivana's home address praying for the prophet's intervention in his time of need. He pulled into the car park outside the run down block of flats where Ivana stayed and stared at her windows. The curtains were open but no lights were showing. T'Baht was in near panic. He knew he would have to contact French to report what had happened but could think of nothing reasonable to say by way of an explanation. He reached for his Koran but stopped as he saw a familiar figure rounding the corner of the block. Ivana Jakanowski was carrying a Lidl carrier bag and talking on her mobile phone. She looked happy but her happiness was nothing compared to the relief Jack T'Baht felt. As if on cue T'Baht's radio sounded.

French's voice swept over T'Baht as if she were sitting beside him. 'All OK Jack?'

'Everything is fine. Ivana has arrived home safely and I am in the car park outside her flat.'

'That will probably be you for the night Jack. When Frame and I spoke to her before she said she didn't go out much.'

'That's OK. The down time lets me think. What about you, are you off home soon?'

'No I've got a couple of things to catch up on and then I'm meeting the boss for a drink.'

'Right. Well I'll be in touch if anything happens but otherwise I'll speak to you tomorrow.'

'OK.'

French turned her attentions to Healy. 'How's things your end Matt?'

'Even less exciting than Jack's, at least he's had some movement. Turner's still in his bedsit but I get the feeling he does go out at night so I'm expecting things to liven up later.'

French sensed some slurring in Healy's voice but wasn't sure if Rab Brown's comments about Healy buying a bottle weren't putting thoughts in her head.

'OK. Let me know if he does head out Matt.'

'Sure.'

Switching channels French spoke to Brown. 'Were you listening there Rab? What do you think?'

'Hard to say. He's had a few swigs of whatever it is but, as you said yourself, it could be lemonade for all we know.'

At 8.00pm the lights went out in both Turner's bedsit and Jakanowski's flat. Ivana went to bed to read and save on electricity and Turner headed to the close door to wait for his taxi drawing up. Brown recognised Turner straight away, glanced over at Healy; he appeared to be dozing. Turner's cab drew up, Turner got in and the taxi moved off. Still no movement from Healy. Brown was unsure whether to follow Turner or watch Healy. He suddenly realised that Healy would not recognise his car from that distance in the dark and that the taxi would have to do a U turn at the bottom of the road and pass Healy on the way out. He slunk down in his seat and blasted his car horn. Healy woke with a start. His eyes focused as a car approached. He recognised Turner in the passenger seat. He quickly covered his face with one hand while starting his car up with the other. Turner's taxi turned right at the end of the street, Healy screeched round mounting the kerb and swept around the corner after the taxi. Brown followed. Healy was somehow surprised that the taxi seemed to be heading into the city centre. He didn't see Turner as a Night Club type *but how else is he going to meet women Matt*. But at Charing Cross the taxi veered off to the left away from the city centre and headed towards the motorway. Brown who was keeping a discreet distance behind Healy was nearly left behind by the traffic light changes edged forward. He couldn't help but notice that Healy's driving was erratic and wondered if he would be able to track the taxi at all. It took only a couple of minutes for the taxi to reach the cut off for Springburn and Sighthill. Although in two different cars Turner and Brown both came to the same conclusion at the same time; Turner was heading to Ivana Jakanowski's flat.

Healy grabbed his radio and tried to contact T'Baht. By the third attempt he was in full anger mode. 'TBaht you fuck where the hell are you. Turner's on his way to Ivana's flat.' The radio then slipped out of his hand. He jerked down to retrieve it while trying to keep track of the taxi and didn't see the other taxi approaching from his left until it was too late. He managed to swerve and avoid the full force of the impact but a collision was inevitable and Healy's car was spun around in a full circle as the taxi ploughed into his back end. Healy's head smashed into the side window and all went black.

Brown raced up to the accident and flashed his warrant card to the taxi driver who, remarkably, seemed unhurt. 'I'll get an ambulance organised and don't worry this guy is a police officer too, there will be no problem with the insurance or anything.'

Joe Turner's taxi carried on.

\*\*\*

Ivana was happy. Her new job was better paid than the hotel, she was able to send money back to Poland and Artur, her boyfriend, was coming over to see her the following week. If he got a job he would maybe stay.

The knock on the door had surprised her, she didn't get many visitors, especially at this time of night, but when the voice said "Immigration Officer" she was slightly concerned. The door had had a peep hole at one time but lazy council painters, or vandals, had painted over it. She was shocked when the figure at the door pushed himself into the flat as soon as the door was even slightly open.

*Authority the same the world over.*

She thought, for a fleeting moment that she recognised him, she felt rather than saw the sudden movement of his hand, was stunned when she thought the official had punched her.

The single knife wound to her heart ended all her thoughts.

*Azrael had been going to remove a few items from the flat, a desperate junkie's search for funds, the shit hole she lived in and the trolls that inhabited that area of the "dear green place" assumed to be the true backdrop to her killing. Drugs and a complete absence of conscience or humanity had been Ivana's neighbours.*

*But the flat was so bare there was nothing to take.*

*Azrael shook his head; Ivana Jakonowski didn't even have a CD player.*

Jack T'Baht's mind seemed to focus on the present of its own volition as opposed to any conscious effort of T'Baht's. He picked up his phone and panic and confusion over-took him. Rab Brown had left three messages on his mobile asking where he was and to get up to Jakanowski's flat straight away.

Susan Dornan felt the most relaxed she had felt for weeks. She liked Jill French and thought she had the making of a good cop: *whatever that is.* She had asked French about the surveillances and was satisfied that everything was in hand. Neither she nor French realised that the wine bar they had picked was a dead zone as far as mobile phone reception went.

French came back from the bar with two soft drinks; their alcohol limit reached by the glass of wine they had both had when they first arrived.

'Any more bad vibes Jill?'

'Well it's hard to say. Even in the office I get a bit uneasy at times.'

'What do you mean?'

'Oh it's nothing.'

'No, tell me Jill.'

'Well it's nothing specific but I sometimes feel Jack T'Baht is staring at me, I've even caught him a couple of times. And if I speak to him he just mumbles something and looks away.'

'Oh I wouldn't bother about him Jill. I catch him looking at me sometimes as well and I get the feeling he wants to strangle me.' Both women laughed. 'Maybe he just doesn't like women.'

'Two lasagne, ladies.' The barman shouted over to their table.

'I'll get them Susan,' Jill said. French went to the bar, collected the two plates, turned and shouted.

'Jesus Christ.'

Dornan jumped up 'What is it?'

'Jack T'Baht'

'What about him?'

'I can't believe I didn't see it.'

'See what? What are you talking about?'

'Jack T'Baht, JTB, John the Baptist.'

Dornan's shock only paralysed her for a moment. 'Let's go.'

Rab Brown was torn. Stay with Healy or get to Jakanowski's flat. He had tried contacting T'Baht and French but neither had answered. His phone rang. *Thank God, T'Baht.*

'Where the fuck are you Jack?'

'The flat.'

'Everything OK?' The line went dead.

Brown turned and nearly bumped into an unsteady Healy.

'Not sure how're you're fucking here Brown but let's go.'

'Matt you're in no fit state.'

'Either you drive Brown or I'm taking your car.'

'Wait a minute what is this?' shouted the taxi driver.

'Fuck off' shouted Healy. 'Well Rab, what's it to be?'

'Come on then' said Brown.

Dornan, French, Healy and Brown all arrived at Ivana's flat at the same moment along with two squad cars that Dornan had ordered up on the way over. Dornan and French entered the flat together. Their eyes quickly moved from the blood soaked body of Ivana Jakanowski to a seemingly dazed Jack T'Baht his shirt soaked in blood, an Azrael business card in one hand and a hunting knife in the other.

**Chapter 30**

My heart was racing as I opened the door to my flat and took the ring from my coat pocket. I had thought through whether to let Susan pick the ring or surprise her by just presenting her with one. I had spent two hours that afternoon browsing through a variety of jewellers, listening intently to all the various pieces of information that I apparently had to take into account when buying a ring. On a couple of occasions I had regretted not having Susan with me but I had phoned her earlier to suggest dinner but she told me she was pretty much tied up with a surveillance operation and would be in the station till about midnight, So, on impulse, I had decided on the "Surprise Approach to Engagement" stripped off and headed for the shower : *tonight Susan and I will be the talk of the Pitt Street Steamie.*

\*\*\*

'Christ Susan, tell me it's not true. T'Baht could be Azrael?' McFarlane spoke in despair rather than anger or surprise.

'I'm afraid it looks like it sir. To be honest I've been running a slightly covert investigation as there has been a suspicion that Azrael may have been a cop. To be honest for a while Matt Healy was in the picture.'

'Jesus, what a mess. What happened with Turner? Where the fuck is he?'

'We don't know. Matt was following him in a taxi but was involved in an accident and lost him.'

'There's no chance......?'

'No. T'Baht would have seen him for a start and, well, he never even mentioned him as a defence. It's odd T'Baht seems to almost be in some sort of trance. He's acting very strangely. Completely detached from what has happened.'

'He's a fucking nut job Susan; killed four, five, a hundred women, who knows. Of course he's detached.'

'Where is he now? We can't question him obviously. It will need to be officers from elsewhere. You go and speak to Healy and the rest. I'll need to phone the Chief Constable. That will be good.'

As Dornan entered the squad room a subdued John Frame approached her. 'You're wanted at the front desk ma'am.'

'God John, what for? Can't you deal with it?'

'I think you should go Susan.'

Frame's tone and expression told Dornan she'd better take his advice. She arrived at the front desk where two traffic cops were waiting. She introduced herself.

'Sorry ma'am but we've received a complaint about one of your officers. A taxi driver phoned in to say he had been in an accident with a police car. The driver of the car had been aggressive towards him and left the scene.'

'I know about this. It was a surveillance operation. Tell the driver we'll take full responsibility and apologise on behalf of the driver.'

'Sorry ma'am but the taxi driver says the police driver smelt strongly of drink. We have to breathalyse him.'

'You can't be serious?'

'Sorry ma'am but we have no choice. We'll do it in your presence if you wish. Is Healy here?'

Dornan was tempted to say no but instinctively knew that was the wrong course of action; *this squad is ruined now anyway.*

'Wait in there and I'll bring Healy along.'

Dornan rushed back to the squad room and shouted Rab Brown into her room. 'Just answer yes or no Rab. Any chance Healy was drinking while on duty tonight?'

Brown appeared to study his shoes.

'Rab?' Dornan shouted.

'Yes.'

Dornan walked quickly back into the main room. 'Matt can you come with me please.'

Healy knew he was in for a bollocking for losing Turner but didn't think it would be in McFarlane's room. He was surprised as they headed for the front doors. 'Taking me to a hotel Susan?'

Dornan ignored him and ushered him into the side room. Healy saw the two traffic officers, he turned to Dornan. 'You fucking bitch.' Twenty minutes later Matt Healy was suspended from duty.

***

My heart was racing faster than ever before. *What if she says no?* I walked with what I felt was a confident swagger into the foyer of the station. Matt Healy was walking towards me carrying a plastic hold all. *No time like the present.* 'Hello Matt, is Susan about?'

'Well, well if it isn't lover boy. Yes your bitch of a girlfriend is here Ford. Just suspended me as a matter of fact. No odds, I'm packing all this in anyway. How you two getting on these days anyway? Enjoying the pillow talk are you? I did when I was banging her. She likes a good moan don't you find Ford?' Healy walked on and was gone before I could even get my legs to function. *What had just happened? What had he said? Is this actually real?*

I looked over at the desk sergeant; he looked away, the embarrassment etched on his face. I turned and walked out onto the dark street, my world collapsing all around me.

Dornan sat in her office looking out into the squad room. *Her first "command" and now one was dead, one suspended and one the killer they had supposedly been chasing.* The phone rang on her desk.

'Dornan.'

'Sorry to phone you so late but I thought you'd like to know' said Alistair Dorado.

'What?'

'The fingerprint sample you sent; it matches the one on the British girl. Matt Healy must have had some sort of contact with her when he was here but, as I said at the time, it is not conclusive proof. I'll need to speak to him of course but I wanted to let you know.'

'Thank you Alistair. Healy is on holiday at the moment. I'll get him to call you when he gets back if that is OK?'

'Yes, yes, as I said, no hurry.'

Dornan rubbed her eyes, a mix of confusion and despair over-powering her.

I felt I had walked for miles but when I focused on my surroundings and where I actually was I realised I was not that far from where I started.

*I must have been going round in circles.* I realised that sleep would be impossible and I needed to face up to this, that my life, my happiness depended on it. I pulled out my mobile, my hand brushing the back of the ring box.

'Hi darling, I was wondering if you wanted to meet up for a very late dinner'.

'That would be just wonderful Ray. I can't wait to get out of here.'

I'm not far from the station and it's getting a bit late so do you just want to meet in the Taj Mahal round in Sauchiehall Street?'

'Fine. Ten minutes.'

We both picked at our food, both of us seemed distracted. I decided to face the demons.

'I spoke to Matt Healy earlier.'

'What, where?'

'At the station's front desk.'

'What were you doing there?'

'I came to see you.'

We looked at each other, the silence screeching in both our heads.

'What? Did Healy say something?' asked Susan.

'You could say that. He said you and him were lovers. I guess that's something.'

I continued to look straight into Susan's eyes. *What could I see? Fear? Disgust? Doubt?*

'I've something to tell you Ray. Don't interrupt me. This is killing me but under the circumstances you need to know.'

My heart felt as if it had been ripped from my body and thrown into the fires of hell. I reached for a glass of water to stop my throat closing up forever.

'Matt Healy has a drink problem. I suspended him tonight for messing up a surveillance operation by crashing his car while drunk. On top of that he is now a suspect for a killing in Spain, remember when he was over there looking into Joe Turner's past. Yes, he has made a few passes at me but I have never had any sort of relationship with him. When he found out about us he changed. You commented on it yourself. The man has lost it Ray, please don't let him spoil it for us. We have a life time of happiness ahead of us.'

The relief I felt as Susan quietly spoke, and when she leant over and took my hand, would be impossible to describe. I felt as though I had been plucked from a raging sea of anguish and despondency and placed gently down on a sun kissed idyll.

'Cyprus?' I said.

'Anywhere and as soon as possible,' Susan replied.

'OK, next week, Glasgow Registry Office, who needs the sun anyway?'

Susan came round the table and sat on my knee. 'Deal.' We kissed as the waiters laughed either with or at us, we didn't care which.

'I'll phone them tomorrow for a date' I said 'no doubt they'll need papers and things, I'll find out.'

Susan laughed 'Oh God.'

'What?'

'Can't keep it from you now my love.'

'What?'

'My name is actually Karen Susan Elizabeth Dornan. I've always hated Karen so Susan Ford it is going to be mister, OK?'

'OK Mrs Ford.'

I fretted over whether to give Susan the ring then but felt I wanted a more romantic setting.

'What have you got on tomorrow?' I asked.

'Surprisingly little. Eastern Division have taken on a lot of the work load; long story.'

'Right, let's go up to Loch Lomond tomorrow. Long walk, lunch at Cameron House.' I felt again for the ring in my pocket. 'I've got something I want to give you.'

## Chapter 31

*Azrael didn't like moments of doubt but the music had shown him the truth. Unusually he had been listening to a male singer, Tony Bennett, but a duet had come on. Azrael looked at the C.D. cover: "You can't Lose a Broken Heart" a duet with K.D. Lang. Azrael consoled himself that even one of the disciples doubted and The Lord forgave him. He thought of his poor father, betrayed by a whore. But he had triumphed, brought up his son to know Christ; to know what Eve did to Adam and how man had had to pay a terrible price. But just as The Lord had struck down those who displeased him, he had struck her down and he would continue His work. He would sleep for a while before setting off.*

Joe Turner didn't recognise the number on his mobile screen but thought it might be his new lawyer.
'Hello.'
'Hello, is that Joseph Turner?'
'Yes it is.'
'Of Turner Spanish Property Consultants?'
Joe beamed, the business cards he had had printed were working. 'Yes it certainly is, how can I help you Mr...?'

It had been raining when Susan and I reached Loch Lomond so we had decided to go for lunch first in the hope the rain would be off by the time we finished. Susan looked as beautiful as ever. We left Cameron House and drove further up the loch side, parked up and walked along a trail that eventually led on to the West Highland Way. The loch was calm, the birds were chirping an early evensong in the mist and it felt at that moment that Susan and I were the only two people in the world. I reached into my pocket and took out the ring box. I opened it and gave Susan the ring.

'Oh Ray, it's perfect.'

'It's engraved.'

Susan looked puzzled at first.

'Lang?'

'Yes, get it? Karen Dornan....KD......KD Lang.......great song writer.'

She paused for only a moment.

'Just like Kate Turner......KT....KT Tunstall....right?'

'Right.' I smiled. Experience told me that one blow would be all I would need. She didn't even try to run. Detective Inspector Karen Susan Elizabeth Dornan knew her life was over.

A few minutes later I, Azrael, roamed calmly through the gloaming. The rain had started again and their pitter-patter seemed to form tears on the leaves but I only heard the heavens applaud.

I left the ring clutched in Susan's hand. Criminal profilers often say that serial killers want to be caught and I can't say if that is true of others or not but for me the truth was that my work was done then, my mission had come full circle. I knew the "Lang" ring would lead to the "Tunstall" necklace and from there it would only be a matter of time. Susan had offered hope but ultimately, Eve, the Devil's mistress, manifested herself in her too. The Azrael cards too were, perhaps subconsciously, the start of the end game for me as I had not used them before Kate despite the other killings. The first woman who should have loved me, my mother, betrayed me and now, many years later "The One", had also betrayed me. But both they, and many others, have been judged and will now suffer forever. I am content. I have no regrets other than Ivana Jakanowski. When our paths crossed at the staged meeting in the police station I panicked. When Susan told me Joe Turner had been identified as having been at the hotel with Kate I realised that Healy's deviousness had back-fired and that he had taken Ivana's "Yes" as referring to Joe when she meant me. I would have let her live but the Lord called for her and I did his bidding.

# Epilogue

It is now six months since Susan's betrayal. I've been told Matt Healy left the police and after being cleared of having any involvement with a killing in Spain decided to open a bar in Lloret de Mar and was last heard of drinking himself to death along with Joe Turner and the other no hope ex-pats that haunt the town.

Jack T'Baht was quietly forced out of the police after it came out that, on realising that Jill French's flat In Bishopbriggs was not far from his surveillance post, he had left his watch and gone to her flat. He went quietly on agreement that no mention be made of the semen stained knickers found in his pocket on his arrest.

I am tired now. A young man called Brian will be along to see me shortly. His uniform is always spotlessly white and well pressed; his badge reads: Psychiatric Nurse. He passes four tablets through to me every day along with my dinner. He will ask how my writing is going today and I will be pleased to tell him today that I am done; my story has been told.

*But she's not there no more*
*And my head replays that closing door*
*As we walk away*
*And I'm begging for me to stay*
*Take me home*
*Take her home*
*Take us home*
*Where we belong*

## Acknowledgements

On looking back and thinking about everyone who had an influence on getting me to this point in my life where I have actually written a book; I realized that there were just too many to mention......so I will just mention the main culprits.......and can I just say at this point that any mistakes in the book either factual or in prose are all mine.

So thanks to: my dad, gone over 30 years but in my thoughts every day; James "Grubby" Kelly, English teacher par excellence; a beacon of light in a sea of disillusion. You won't even remember me but you were the only person in the Garnethill Colditz who ever showed that they saw something worthwhile in me. Thanks for that; Strathclyde University's Creative Writing Department, especially Linda Jackson for describing my early, hopeless writing efforts as "terrific" & for being a good singer; Sinclair MacLeod, fellow author, IT wizard, font of all publishing wisdom and all round good guy; Virgin Publishing Ltd..............good people; Audrey URTO, who's life choices never cease to amaze and depress me in equal measure......but for never stopping believing in my quest anyway; K T Tunstall, for being a great song writer & having inspirational initials; all the singers and songs mentioned, I like your stuff..........Lori, you're going to make it.

Finally, but most importantly of all....to my two wonderful sons, Anthony and Paul, my reasons for keeping going and for making me proud of the way they have turned out despite my no doubt many failings as father; Ann Marie my fellow traveller in the most complex journey of all – life, especially when the darkness comes; to Lynsey & Emma for celebrity info and showing me what not to watch on TV......and to all of them for putting up with me telling them for five years that I was writing a book. I am indebted to you all.

Lightning Source UK Ltd.
Milton Keynes UK
UKOW051813011012

199916UK00009B/12/P